THE WANDERER REBORN

Praise for The Wanderer Scorned

'A beautifully written account of the world's first family seen sympathetically through the eyes of Kayin (Cain), the first murderer. A compelling read.'
Bobbie Ann Cole, Bestselling Christian Writer, Speaker and Writing teacher.

'Beautifully written, Woodcraft brings the story to life using every carefully crafted word to its best possible advantage…it was as if I could feel every heartbeat, thought and feeling of the characters.'
Wendy H. Jones, Award-Winning Scottish Crime Writer and Public Speaker.

'The life of Cain as it has never been told before, by the man himself.'
Ruth Leigh, Author of the *Isabella M. Smugge* series.

Praise for The Wanderer Reborn

'An imaginative and evocative retelling of a story that scripture only hints at, and yet is utterly believable and so hope-filled. This beautiful book explores the fallout from one of the most famous crimes in history and celebrates the far-reaching redemptive power of God. It drew me in from the very start and left my soul deeply encouraged.'
Joy Margetts, author of *The Healing* and *The Pilgrim*.

'Natasha Woodcraft has given us another beautiful what-might-have-been account. Awan's growth in grace deeply challenges our own faith as we are faced with her grief and love. How do you forgive the murderer of your twin brother?'
Maressa Mortimer, author of *The Elabi Chronicles*.

THE WANDERER
REBORN

Book 2 in *The Wanderer* Series

By **NATASHA WOODCRAFT**

BROAD PLACE
publishing
www.broadplacepublishing.co.uk

www.broadplacepublishing.co.uk

First published by WW&S Publishing in Great Britain, 2022.
Second edition published in Great Britain by Broad Place Publishing, 2024.

ISBN **978-1-915034-83-0**

A catalogue record for this book is available from the British Library.

Cover by getcovers.com
Model courtesy of Nesrin Danan at Pexels.com.

AUTHOR'S NOTE

Dear Reader,

This is a work of fiction. It is inspired by Genesis Chapter 4 in the Bible, but you don't need to be a Christian to read it. I hope you will enjoy it, whatever your beliefs.

If you are a Christian, it is worth noting that this work is the result of my imagination and is not intended to replace or add to the Bible. I approached this story with trepidation, aware that some of the content may raise eyebrows. If you have difficulty with anything in the text, please refer to the appendix at the back where I discuss the reasoning behind my decisions.

This story is the second in a series. I would encourage you to read *The Wanderer Scorned* first (details at the back). I have used British spelling and punctuation conventions throughout. Included at the start are maps and a cast of characters for ease of reference. Some study questions are after the appendix for those interested in reflecting further.

There are songs dotted throughout the book. If you want to know what they sound like then head to my YouTube channel youtube.com/@natashawoodcraft

As I have been writing, it has been my hope and prayer that this book will be used to bless you, the reader. Please read it with an open heart, safe in the knowledge that His love for you took Jesus Christ all the way to the cross.

N.W.

ALSO BY THE AUTHOR

The Wanderer Series:
The Wanderer Scorned
The Wanderer Reborn
The Wanderer's Sister

The Wanderer's Sister is a novelette exclusively for
subscribers to the author's newsletter.

You can subscribe at:
natashawoodcraft.com/subscribe

Hear songs from the series on YouTube:
youtube.com/@natashawoodcraft

CHARACTERS

Clarifications

Abba means Dad/Father. It applies most often to Adam, but also to Kayin in the prologue.

Ima means Mum/Mother. It applies most often to Chavah, but also to Kayin's wife in the prologue.

Elohim means God. **Yahweh** is commonly translated LORD, but is God's name. They refer to the same being, **Yahweh Elohim**.

Characters in age order

Adam (Ah-dom)	*1st man (aka Abba)*
Chavah (cHa-vah)	*1st woman (aka Ima)*
Kayin (Kay-in)	*1st child of Adam(aka The Wanderer)*
Havel (Ha-vel)	*2nd child of Adam (Twin to Awan)*
Awan (Ah-wan)	*3rd child of Adam (Twin to Havel)*
Chayim (cHigh-yim)	*4th child of Adam*
Avigail (Ah-vi-ga-yil)	*5th child of Adam*
Shimon (Shim-on)	*6th child of Adam (Twin to Channah)*
Channah (cHan-nah)	*7th child of Adam (Twin to Shimon)*
Dorit (Dor-it)	*1st child of Chayim*
Set (Shet)	*8th child of Adam*
Techiyah(Te-cHee-yah)	*2nd child of Chayim*
Liora (Lee-or-ah)	*9th child of Adam*
Nadav (Nah-dav)	*10th child of Adam (Triplet)*
Raham (Rah-ham)	*11th child of Adam (Triplet)*
Shalom (Shah-lom)	*12th child of Adam (Triplet)*
Yemima (Ye-mee-ma)	*13th child of Adam*
Ronel (Ron-el)	*14th child of Adam*
Chanoch (cHa-no-cH)	*1st child of Kayin (& The city name)*
Lamech (La-me-cH)	*5th generation descendant of Kayin*
Adah (Ah-dah)	*1st wife of Lamech*
Tzillah (Tz-il-lah)	*2nd wife of Lamech*

MAPS

Eden
Northern mountians
Realm of Leviathan
R. Euphrates
R. Tigris
Kayin's Hill country
Eastern Mountains
The Lake
Settlement
Marshland
THE EAST

Eastern mountains
Entwined trees
Hills
Caves
Tigris
Farming land
Forest
Huts
Cliffs
Washing point
THE SETTLEMENT

PROLOGUE

T he Wanderer was a man shrouded in legend – until now. It had taken most of the night to recount the tale of his descent into depravity – often the subject of rumour and whispers in the marketplace. Finally the people knew the truth regarding the murder, curse, mark and banishment that left this man a fugitive, never farming or settling, despite his family being numerous.

Yet to me, he is just Abba, Chanoch thought as his foot twitched. *And he is suffering.*

For The Wanderer was Chanoch's father, Kayin, and the common ancestor of those gathered. With pride, Chanoch had watched him standing firm across the hall the entire time he recounted his story. Not once had he taken a seat. He was strong and robust and hadn't needed one physically. Yet as he'd reached the final scenes, describing how he killed his own brother, the emotional weight had taken a toll on his centuries-old body, and Kayin had begun to stoop. Indeed, he looked like he might fall.

Chanoch surveyed the crowd, laid out thickly before him. Pushing through from his position to his abba's wouldn't be easy, yet his heart told him he must. Then Adah, the first wife of their host, Lamech, darted from the shadows carrying a stool and placed it behind Kayin. Kayin murmured a word of thanks and lowered himself onto it.

Relief escaped in a breath. *Bless you, Adah.* Chanoch had noticed her careful attention throughout the story and taken hope from it. Others had listened too, but not all.

Tzillah – Lamech's second wife – had welcomed 'The Wanderer' into the party, but had soon lost interest. Those who hadn't understood Tzillah's flippant welcome had realised quickly that the speaker was the legend who lived in the wilderness, mostly unmet and unknown by his kin. That had peaked their interest for a while. Several had turned to scrutinize Chanoch, seeming awed that he would bring his abba to this gathering.

Yet the story had gone on for a good deal of time, and now Kayin had finally stopped, the crowd grew agitated and impatient. Their wine had long since worn off. Some had fallen asleep on the floor; a few were even snoring loudly. *How can they, given what Abba just described?*

Chanoch's eyes flickered to Lamech. He knew his host never appreciated silence unless he was the centre of attention. Indeed, he was surprised Lamech had remained quiet throughout. Several times he'd seen Tzillah giving her husband a discreet nudge – when Lamech's chin had lowered to his chest in slumber. Now faced with lack of sleep, lack of attention and awkward silence, Lamech looked decidedly grumpy.

Yet Chanoch had little sympathy. After all, the interruption was Lamech's doing – it was he who had invoked Kayin's name when he placed a curse on any who might avenge his own murderous actions.

Chanoch had put up with Lamech until that point, but such brazen action he could not tolerate.

Suspecting his host wished to dismiss his guests but was unsure how without being accused of disrespect, Chanoch rose. He grabbed a cup of wine that lay untouched on a nearby table, thinking he might revive his abba with it.

As he stepped forward, the early morning sunlight, streaming into the hall from high apertures in the walls, caught Chanoch's eyes. Shielding them, he witnessed Lamech having a stern conversation with Adah. Guilt flickered through Chanoch's gut. Would she suffer because of his actions – again?

Chanoch took three more steps before a different woman stood up from the midst of the crowd. His heart skipped a beat. *Why?* She looked akin to Adah, with black hair falling in braids down her back, but her braids were bejewelled with the white strands of age, rather than flowers, and her umber skin had lost its smoothness.

She hobbled up the steps he hadn't yet reached, walking with a cane curled under her fingers, until she stood near Kayin, still sat on the stool. Kayin glanced up in surprise, recognition crossing his eyes. The woman held Kayin's gaze for a moment, as if exchanging thoughts in a silent conversation, then turned to the onlookers who'd sunk into silence, captivated with curiosity.

Realising she wanted to speak, Chanoch wondered how Lamech would react. Again, he prepared to intervene, but again, Adah beat him to it. Defying her husband, Adah strode forward, held a hushed conversation with the elder woman, then crossed back to Lamech and spoke in his ear. He grunted an irritated reply before standing and addressing his guests.

'Those who wish to leave are free to do so. I shall make it up to you next Shabbat,' Lamech sneered. 'For the remainder, there are wash basins in the courtyard and couches in the adjoining rooms. You may use them to make yourselves comfortable. We shall shortly serve a morning meal to those who have energy left to consume it, as it seems we have another riveting tale to listen to.'

The sarcasm lacing Lamech's voice wasn't lost on Chanoch. Yet, his host had clearly resigned himself to the vexing realisation that many of his guests were willing listeners, or at least wanted to take advantage of his extended hospitality. To disrupt proceedings now would certainly be worse for his reputation than tolerating their continuation. And Lamech had a reputation to preserve – especially after the previous night's audacious announcement.

The audience sat up, then most disbanded to refresh themselves. Chanoch sipped at the wine he hadn't needed and lowered himself onto some cushions, ready to people watch from his new position by an ostentatious stone pillar. He heard a cough at his shoulder. Turning towards it, he saw a man, one young enough to have energy left after staying awake all night.

'May I sit here, sir?' the young man asked. He had one of those faces which exuded enthusiasm, although in his hazel eyes – rimmed with black – intensity was apparent. A light scar traced the line of his right eyebrow.

'Certainly,' Chanoch replied. 'Do you wish to speak with me?'

His companion nodded and passed him some flatbread and olives from a bowl he carried, then they began a conversation which continued throughout the meal. Indeed, they only ceased when the woman with the cane took the centre of the platform once more.

Lamech – who had demanded a couch be brought to the stage during breakfast – now propped himself up with cushions, poured himself a large cup of wine and pulled Tzillah near. Chanoch chuckled at his host's piqued expression. It was indeed going to be a long morning.

The woman began, raising her usually gentle voice above the crowd.

CHAPTER 1

Countless summers have been and gone since the day that changed my life. Even so, the shock of finding the bearer of half my soul caught in twisted thorns still hits me every time I picture his face. Though some memories have faded over time and the outlines of his features have grown indistinct, that image remains: those beautiful eyes turned lifeless.

I had known something was wrong; I had felt it in every fibre of my being long before I found him. Not just because both my older brothers were unaccounted for, but because I sensed a part of myself was missing.

Havel and I had been entwined since our conception; we knew everything about each other, and there was nothing hidden between us. We had rarely been apart for more than a few days, the only exception being those weeks when he had tended the sheep on the northern plains, the winter before this tragedy happened. Those weeks had been miserable for me, but they were nothing compared to the torment to follow.

When Kayin was condemned at the sacrifice and fled, I – along with everyone else – had searched everywhere we thought my eldest brother might be. As dark settled in, Havel and I collapsed together in the hut, but, after a short bout of restless sleep, I woke to find Havel missing. Setting out with my younger brother, Chayim, we walked as far as the forest together before splitting up. Chayim entered the woods while I continued towards the fields.

Havel would not give up looking until he found Kayin, I knew that instinctively. Yet there was no sign of either of them. When the weight in my chest and stomach grew so intense that I could barely walk without it dragging me down, I fell to my knees and cried out for Elohim to have mercy; cried out for Him to show me where Kayin and Havel might be.

As I lifted my tear-stained eyes, a ray of sunlight shone through the haze, lighting up a section of tall grass in the distance. I ran as fast as my weak legs could carry me, stumbling over ditches in the ground and treading through thistles in my desperation to get to the light before it faded. Upon reaching the general area of grass where he lay my soul guided me the rest of the way – drawing me irresistibly to its other half.

Part of me wishes I had never prayed that prayer – that Yahweh Elohim had continued to protect me from a sight that would forever wound me. Yet finding Havel alone gave me precious moments with him that I would not have had if someone else had brought his slumped body home. If Yahweh hadn't led me to the spot, I doubt we would have discovered him before his body had begun to rot in the dust. That would have been a far worse sight and I wouldn't have been able to cradle him and weep for him as I did in those moments. So, the better part of me was grateful for the answered prayer.

When I found Havel I couldn't believe what I saw. Even though I had known something was desperately wrong, even though I already felt the hollow of loss, nothing could have prepared me for the sight of it.

His face was so different without the vivacity that always characterised it. I threw myself beside him, opening his eyelids wider, striving to find him, yet there was no sparkle there, no joy and no fire. Lying in the thorns was a body that used to hold the one I loved, yet I knew that my brother was somewhere else. Suddenly, he was lost to me. He had left me. He had gone as swiftly as the wind blows through the trees. My soul ached at his betrayal.

I set about untangling the thorns from his body, desperately thinking that somehow, if I released him, he might come back to me. I started with those piercing his brow. His lifeblood had dried in drips down his face, some settling on his eyelids, some on his cheeks. Some had run down and filled the cavern in his ear before drying out. His soft, brown curls were stuck in clumps to his ears where they had mingled with the blood. His body was now hard and stiff, and, despite the earth's heat, cold. His coldness mirrored the chill in my bones.

Once he was free from the thorns, I tried to move his body away from them. Wrapping my arms around his chest, I dragged him towards me, into a patch of grass containing fewer weeds. Then, allowing his back to rest upon my knees, I moved one of my arms to cradle his neck.

By then, my tears were flowing and blood was seeping from my own torn hands. As he again failed to stir, I begged him to return to me. My tears fell onto his face and mixed with his blood, causing it to run further. Deep, wretched sobs convulsed my entire body as I sank my head into his neck and squeezed. I could not let go; how could I ever let go?

Time passed in a haze until, when the sun was beginning to set again, I heard someone shouting in the distance. I knew I had to move; I had to let them know I was there, for I would never be able to carry Havel's body alone. So, I gently eased Havel to the ground. This was easier now – the stiffness in his limbs had strangely softened since I first held him. I stood and waved my arms in the air at the figure silhouetted against the setting sun. As he neared, I recognised Abba. When he saw my face, his own instantly changed.

'It is Havel,' I said. When my father looked down and saw his beloved, lifeless son he fell to his knees and cradled the body to his chest, crying in loud wails. I joined him, putting my arms around my abba, breathing his earthy scent and feeling his living warmth. I prayed to Yahweh, pleading for another miracle: that Havel might re-join his body. How could we ever be a family again without the one who had held us all together? Yet He did not answer. Had Yahweh left us too?

At length, my abba spoke in broken tones. 'Where is Kayin?' he asked.

In my torment over Havel, I had completely forgotten about Kayin. 'I don't know. I haven't seen him.'

Abba drew Havel's body away from his chest and studied it all over. He put his fingers into its wounds and gently touched the bruises on its neck. Then, stroking his son's hair, he kissed his bloodied brow.

'Is this where you found him?' Abba asked.

'No, he was stuck in the thorns – just there.' I pointed to the spot a few strides away. Abba looked at it, drew his brows together, and then carefully put down Havel's body. He began to examine the surrounding area, brushing away some of the grass and studying the ground. He picked up some of the thorns and moved them around. He rubbed grasses between his fingers, touched areas of dirt and even smelt them.

'What is it, Abba?' I asked after I could stand watching him no longer. He turned and looked at me. The pain in his eyes seemed to have intensified – if that was possible. I could see he was hesitating before answering.

'There were two people here, Awan. Two track marks beside your own, two scents.'

'What do you mean, Abba?' I asked.

'I hope I am wrong, but I fear that Havel has died at the hands of Kayin.'

'No!' My hand shot to my mouth; I could not believe it.

My father stumbled back to me and placed a gentle hand on my shoulder. Then he stroked the bruises on Havel's neck.

'A man's hand did this. See the shape of his fingers.'

I looked again. The imprint was clear, but my mind could not comprehend it.

'Couldn't it have been a serpent? Kayin had similar markings after he was attacked.'

'Similar, but not the same. And there is no sign of a bite.'

'It could be hidden in the thorns—'

'Awan, I don't want to believe it either, but Kayin is missing and… It is not the first time.'

'What do you mean?'

'Kayin once attacked Shimon in the fields. In the end, he did not hurt him, but the look in his eyes... I think if Chayim and I had not been there, it could have gone differently.'

I shook my head and pushed my father's hand away. I couldn't bear the thought that my beloved Kayin would do such a thing. 'I have never heard this story,' I protested.

'Havel asked me not to tell you.'

I began to pace away from my father.

'Awan, it's true,' he called out behind me.

'No, Abba! Don't say it again. There must be another explanation. I cannot accept it.'

He rushed to me and grasped me. I fought him for a moment, but he did not let go. I began to shake as he held me.

'I cannot, Abba...I cannot...'

'I know, my beautiful girl,' he soothed, holding me and stroking my hair as tears streamed down his cheeks. I relinquished my fight and allowed him to cradle me as together we gave in to the devastation of his discovery.

When my mother saw her son's body approaching the hut, his head and legs dangling over my father's outstretched forearms, she fell into the dust and lay prostrate on the ground. She refused to look at him – could not acknowledge what her eyes beheld.

'What do we do with him?' I asked Abba, as he laid Havel on the ground in the same spot where the ewe, Naomi, had recently died after giving birth.

Abba shrugged. 'I'm not sure. But he cannot stay here.' He was silent for a moment, escaping to a memory, before muttering, '...to dust you shall return.'

I asked him to repeat it, for I had not heard.

'We should dig a hole deep enough to prevent animals scrabbling it,' he said.

My younger siblings appeared. Channah threw herself on Havel's body, wailing, but the others held back in disbelief. Then Chayim's arms closed around me. I fought back the emotion that threatened to consume me – squeezing him, then pulling away.

Avigail tried to drag Channah away from the body. Channah screamed and clawed at her older sister's arms. Then Shimon knelt beside her, and she calmed under the presence of her twin brother. After some time the three of them rose, kissed Havel's brow, and withdrew.

The sounds of Chayim and Abba digging a grave in the dark commenced. Avigail dipped out of the hut, having put the younger ones to bed. We knelt beside our mother, fingers threaded together. Still Ima didn't move or acknowledge us.

Finally, my father came to her and picked her up, carrying her limp body, as he had carried Havel's, to the place where their son lay. He kissed her face and whispered in her ear, gently coaxing her to say goodbye before they covered the body.

She shook her head many times before eventually relenting. My father lowered her to the ground beside Havel, but she just stared at her son's form, still refusing to move. Abba took her hand tenderly and placed it on her son's face. She drew in a cry, pulled her hand away and covered her eyes.

Abba relented and removed the body to the grave. Ima remained unmoving with her hands covering her face until Havel was completely concealed in soil. Then Abba carried her back to the hut and laid her on her pallet.

She was to stay on that pallet for weeks, not saying a word and leaving it only to relieve herself.

In Ima's absence, I became practical, taking over the cooking and organising the household. Avigail helped with the younger ones. I appreciated the distraction from grief, but even so, taking care of Ima's daily tasks as well as my own took all my energy. At the end of each day, I would fall exhausted on my bed and sleep deeply until morning. Every time I woke, I reached for Havel – only to find he was not there.

Soon it was time for the wheat to be harvested and everyone joined Chayim in bringing it in. The work took a lot longer without Kayin's direction and contribution, yet none of us mentioned it. Once the wheat was dry, there was threshing and winnowing to keep us busy, and then the summer fruit to collect.

During that time, nobody spoke or ate much. Occasionally one of us would burst into tears as we went about our tasks. Whoever was closest to them would hold them for a time until tears were wiped from faces, and we carried on as if it hadn't happened.

Due to my mother's silence, my father didn't tell her of his suspicions about Kayin. To my knowledge, he didn't speak of it with anyone else either. Nor had I yet confronted my own feelings about my eldest brother, so confused was my mind on the subject. Grief for Havel's absence so consumed me every time I stopped work that to think of the circumstances surrounding his death was too much for my heart to bear. I could not escape the pit of loneliness even when surrounded by other members of my family.

One evening, after the harvest was over, my mother rose from her pallet and joined us at our meal. We all looked at her in anticipation – this was the first time she had joined us since Havel's death. However, she didn't seem to notice our expectant faces and said nothing about either son during the meal. She barely spoke at all.

Later that night, long after we had retired to our beds, I woke to hear Ima releasing great, agonising wails outside the hut.

CHAPTER 2

As season after season passed, our new reality slowly became normal. We all found our individual ways of coping. I sometimes wandered among the sheep, speaking to them by name and talking about my lost twin brother. Though they could not talk back, I knew they missed him as I did, which brought me comfort. Abba would watch me as I wandered, rarely saying anything.

Although they were subdued, family worship times continued. Abba tried to lead us, but it was not the same without Havel. We continued praising Elohim with words we knew, repeating truths to each other from the lessons we remembered. Most of the time, I was unable to find new words. So I sang the old songs, hoping that if I persisted for long enough, the feelings expressed in them would eventually become real again.

I sang of Elohim – our rock, deliverer and hiding place in times of trouble. I sang of His greatness, although I couldn't comprehend it; I sang of His love, although I couldn't feel it; and I sang of His goodness, although I didn't see it. It wasn't that I had ceased to believe that Yahweh was my salvation; I just felt so numb.

I don't think any of us experienced His presence the way we used to when Havel led us. Perhaps we had been so reliant on Havel's guidance that we were spiritually lost without him. I also suspected that the memory of Yahweh's voice at the sacrifice – when He had condemned Kayin so harshly – had frightened us into not taking risks with our worship. And Abba had always struggled to bring Elohim to life.

Abba's natural reaction to pain had always been sullen frustration, and that did not change, though it seemed deeper-seated and less volatile than it had been in the past. He occasionally lashed out when upset, but he seemed to have lost his fight. Perhaps the agony was so great that he had hidden it deep inside.

After that first period of silence, my mother often spoke of Havel as if he were still with us. Sometimes I would catch her talking with herself like Havel was next to her. Yet she never mentioned her eldest son. It was like Kayin had never existed.

By the time he was eighteen, Chayim was responsible for most of the farming. Although Abba helped in the fields if needed, most of the work – and all the organisation – fell to my younger brother. He aged rapidly as he grew into a man. His persistent cheeriness had departed with Kayin, and worry lines crept into his face. Still, his responsibilities could not entirely squash his nature. He continued to crack small jokes when we were together, though the following chuckle often sounded more like an apology than a laugh.

Avigail also lost some of her gregariousness. Though she had never been a great talker, her natural confidence had tempered. When she reached womanhood, her earlier disdain of Chayim dissipated. She began to crave his company and often spent her time with him tending crops rather than with me. I didn't mind, for his need was more significant than mine, but spending so much time alone didn't help my loneliness. Consequently, I found myself clinging to my mother, even though she gave little back during those initial years.

As for the younger ones, Shimon seemed a little lost, finding nothing he particularly enjoyed except hunting. He often moaned that Havel was not around to help him, making me wince. However, as he matured, he usually did as Abba bid without fussing. By contrast, Channah proved herself a confident shepherdess, perfectly at home tending the sheep just as Havel had been. She was soon quite capable with a sling. Neither of the younger twins spoke with me very much, but they could often be seen huddled together, a reminder of how Havel and I used to be.

I continued to lug the family's laundry to the river regularly. One day I was halfway through scrubbing and rinsing the linens when, as often happened, I found myself staring towards the fields, wondering if Kayin would come to join me. Suddenly aware of my wandering thoughts, I shook my head and screwed up the tunic in my hand.

'Why, Yahweh? Why do I continue to think of him?' I groaned.

Throwing the tunic back on the pile, I climbed onto the ledge that jutted out over the river and dunked my feet into the cool water before leaning back against my growing fig tree. My arm searched for the hand that wasn't there – the hand that had planted this tree.

'Argh!' I cried again, pulling my hand up and sinking my head into it. 'Why? When will this cease?'

Hearing a shuffle behind me, I turned to see Abba standing a few strides away. He gave an apologetic smile and moved to join me.

With my thoughts still on Kayin, I opened my mouth. 'Did you ever talk to Ima about Kayin? She never speaks of him!' I blurted, as if my frustration was all Abba's fault.

His eyes widened and he leaned backwards, taking a moment before shaking his head. 'I once started the conversation, but she refused to hear it and grew so upset that I didn't try again.'

'And the others?' I asked.

He shook his head again.

'Yet, we all know,' I said in exasperation, rising and hastily gathering the linens into a bundle, 'for he never came back! Not talking about it doesn't help, Abba. It just buries the pain deeper!'

'Are you finished?' Abba asked, raising an eyebrow.

'No!' I cried, throwing the laundry back down. I wasn't sure if he referred to it or my attitude.

Abba stood and pulled me into his chest. 'I'm sorry for my failures,' he muttered, kissing the crown of my head. 'Forgive me.'

I grasped him and allowed my shoulders to shake. 'Why would Yahweh allow this, Abba?' I asked. 'I try to praise Him still, but the words stick on my tongue like dry bread.'

'I don't know the answer to that.'

I sighed and pulled away, then crouched down and resumed the washing where I had left off. Abba stayed and helped.

That night, after everyone was asleep, I snuck out and sat near the dying embers of the fire. Taking a half-consumed stick, I swirled the ash about. I tried to lift my voice to my Elohim, yet all that came from my mouth was bitterness.

You have made my teeth grind; my stomach churns.
Bile rises and empties on the ground.
I cower in the ashes, my soul bereft of peace.
I have forgotten what happiness is.
My endurance has perished.
So has my hope from Yahweh.
Will you not remember my affliction?
Or must bitterness and sorrow consume me?

My soul continually bows to the dust.
I long to join him who lies there.
Must I go on in this anguish alone?
When shall I know Your steadfast love again?

The following morning, Abba came to me again. 'I sought you out yesterday to ask you something,' he said.

I was still frustrated with him and only grumbled in response.

He continued anyway. 'The main hut is crowded now the twins are tall. Yet, a space remains in the second hut with Chayim. As the eldest, I think you should take it.'

My chest constricted. That space belonged to Kayin. I swallowed down the bile rising again in my throat and nodded. I would do as he wished.

After collecting my small number of things, I moved them into Chayim's hut. Then I stood staring at Kayin's old pallet for some time. It had been ridiculous to leave it empty, yet none of us had dared ask to take his place.

I slowly lowered myself onto the bed, resting on my side. Burying my nose into it, I deeply inhaled. It smelled of my brother – barley, sweat and a hint of the river. How could it retain his scent after all this time? As I lay there surrounded by his fragrance, Kayin's kindness to me flooded into my memories – his smile, care, love and touch.

The lock on my heart released. Grasping the sheepskin he had laid on, I clutched it to my chest. Fresh tears streamed down my cheeks as I convulsed with the pain of losing Kayin. For whilst Havel had been the keeper of my soul, Kayin had been the victor of my heart. I knew then that I had indeed loved him – as a woman loves a man – and that the struggle of the years since his disappearance had come from an inability to reconcile the person I loved with the man who would murder my Havel.

For I knew that Abba was correct about Kayin. I had seen it too: those flashes of anger, those hints in his eyes of the evil that lay beneath. Yet I had never dreamt he would be capable of murder! I had thought that, with care and patience, he could come around to realise how much we loved him and would submit himself to Yahweh. Indeed, he had shown signs of doing so just before his sacrifice had been scorned.

Perhaps it was my fault? If I had just told him I loved him, instead of insisting he wait for me, maybe none of this would have happened. He might not have been so angry, so jealous. My throat constricted, yet cries of agony broke through, at the realisation that my precious Havel lay in the ground because of me.

At some point during my weeping Chayim must have entered the hut, for he was at my side the moment I cried out, embracing me.

'It still smells of him, Chayim!' I gasped. 'It's like he is here beside me again. Oh, how could he do it? How could he do this to me?' As my body shook, Chayim rubbed my arm, trying to soothe me. 'Why didn't I just tell him?' I moaned.

'Tell him what?' he asked softly.

'Tell him I loved him! If I had just told him, he wouldn't have been so jealous of Havel. It is my fault, Chayim.' I broke into sobs again, and he tightened his hold before speaking.

'No, Awan, you cannot think that. You must not bear this burden. There was something inside our brother that was broken. You couldn't have healed him; only Yahweh could have done that.'

'Then why didn't He? Why did He condemn Kayin's efforts at sacrifice instead of reaching out to him? Oh, forgive me, I don't want to question Yahweh, but I don't understand.'

'I don't either, but we must trust in His wisdom. Havel knew that; he knew we couldn't force Kayin to repent but could only pray for him. He knew we had to trust Yahweh through the circumstances. That is still true, even if none of this makes sense right now. Even if all we can see is darkness.'

I lifted my eyes to Chayim's, unable to say any more. I knew Chayim was right. In the last few years, he must have grown not just in stature but also in closeness to Yahweh, for I heard his words as if Havel himself were speaking. Yet, they still seemed to brush over my heart rather than sink into it. My tears prevailed, tears not just for Havel but now also for Kayin.

Chayim held me, joining with my grief, until at some point during the night, we must have fallen asleep.

I woke at dawn, becoming quickly aware that I was not in my usual bed and that Chayim had his arms around me. It took a few moments for confusion to unwrap itself and for me to remember how we had fallen asleep. Sighing, I sank into his sleepy arms once more.

Then my song finally returned, as if the small ray of sunshine I could see in the doorway symbolised the tiniest sliver of hope. I began to sing to Yahweh in a soft, low voice, trying not to wake my brother.

Satisfy me in the morning with your unfailing love,
That I may sing and be glad in you.
For as many days as you have afflicted me,
May I delight still in your truth.
Only let your work be revealed to me,
And your glorious power be known.
Let your favour be upon me and bless my heart.

As I looked up, I saw my mother standing in the doorway presenting a rare smile. Aware of the position that Chayim and I were lying in, I blushed furiously.

'Good morning, Awan,' she teased.

Chayim rubbed his eyes then sat up, stretching his arms out wide.

'Good morning, Chayim,' Ima continued.

'Morning, Ima,' Chayim replied with a yawn, completely oblivious.

'Breakfast is ready,' she said, 'when you two are.' Then she promptly left.

'Oh no,' I moaned.

'What?' questioned my brother.

'Ima's face,' I replied. 'She saw us lying together. I can tell that it put an idea in her head.'

Chayim let out a big, open laugh that lit up the whole room. I couldn't help but smile and chuckle at him, as his laugh provided medicine to my soul. Then, when he had regained control of himself, he looked at me quite seriously.

'How are you feeling?' he asked, his hand warm on my cheek.

'Better. Thank you for last night.'

He smiled, then said gently, 'I loved him too, you know – Kayin, I mean. Perhaps not in the same way as you did, but… I think it's alright to mourn his loss as well.'

He planted a quick kiss on my forehead, then got up and went outside to wash before breakfast.

Much to my relief, Ima did not immediately act on what she had seen but seemed content to let nature run its course. There was no way my heart was ready for another attempt at love.

CHAPTER 3

It was nine summers after Havel's death before the balance in the family shifted once more. I first became aware of it one night when I was out late, bathing in the river. We had spent a long day in the fields cutting wheat covered in small insects, so Avigail, Chayim and I had gone straight there afterwards to bathe.

My two siblings left earlier than me, walking towards the hut arm in arm with Avigail laughing loudly at something Chayim was telling her. I smiled, deciding to give them time alone and spend longer by the river.

For this time of year always reminded me of Havel's death and that day, my emotions were particularly raw. All afternoon, the sun had cast the same shadows over the earth as when I'd been cradling Havel's lifeless body. Now, the evening sky bore the same colours as it had when I had wept with Abba in the field.

Just before dark, I began meandering home. As I passed a thicket of trees and bushes, I heard voices behind it. I should have walked on, but curiosity got the better of me, and I hid behind a tree and listened. At first, I thought it might be Chayim and Avigail, but I realised it was Abba and Ima when they spoke again.

'Chavah, I'm not sure how much longer I can cope with this. We should build another hut so we can be on our own. The children are all adults now.'

'I don't see why we need to do that; I like having them near us. I know they are safe if they are with me.'

'There are far too many of us in that small space!'

'Yes, it is a little squashed, but we're all comfortable enough. Shimon and Channah don't mind sharing a bed.'

'Chavah, we must lie together again; it is not good for us to be separated like this. And lying together is rather difficult now the twins and Avigail are adults.'

'When will you have time to build another hut? You are too busy, Adam, as is Chayim.'

'In case you hadn't noticed, we have several strong daughters who do not shy away from hard work. Besides, Shimon always wanders around aimlessly. I can teach him how to build.'

'That boy still seems averse to hard work like oil is to water.'

'He will do as I say. He just wants to feel needed. Or, if not, he will do it if Channah asks him.'

My mother laughed. 'That's true. I think they might need a hut of their own soon!'

'So it's settled then. We will build another. Perhaps two.'

There was a chuckle followed by a pause, during which rustling suggested an embrace.

'You are still as beautiful as the day Yahweh gave you to me,' Abba said in a low voice. I suddenly felt embarrassed, as if I had stumbled onto a private moment and shouldn't be there. However, if I moved now, they might hear me.

'Adam, please, I cannot do this now.'

'What? How long will it take for you to have me back in your bed? It's been years, Chavah!'

'Oh, Adam, it's not you. I still love you. It's the thought of the consequences – that there might be another child.'

'Praise Elohim; it would be wonderful if He gave us another child!'

'I fear it.'

'Why?'

Her voice dipped, almost out of hearing. 'I cannot bear the thought of giving my heart to another son who might be taken from me.'

My father sighed. 'My love, I understand. Even so, we have been commanded to multiply and fill the earth. At present, we only have three daughters and two sons, which is not enough to fill our small patch of land, let alone the whole earth. It may be painful, but I believe Yahweh will bless us if we continue to have children. Besides, we will need another son to avoid what happened before.'

'But there would be such an age difference. We can't expect Avigail to marry someone so much younger than herself,' my mother said. 'Even if we had another son in a few seasons, she would have to wait for years.'

'I thought Avigail would marry Chayim? It is Awan I fear for. Her heart has been lonely since Havel was taken.'

'Actually, I think there's a connection between the eldest two. For sure, Awan's heart once belonged to Havel, but I've seen her and Chayim together.'

'They have lain together?'

'They have, more than once.'

'Then we must join them in marriage immediately. It's what Elohim would wish.'

I had to place my hand over my mouth to stop myself from making a noise. *Marry Chayim?*

'Why haven't you told me this before, Chavah?' Abba sounded deeply affronted.

'I just didn't think they were ready, after everything that has happened…'

Perhaps I should have come clean right there and interrupted their conversation, confessed I had heard all and explained what was really happening between my brother and me.

For it was not what my mother thought. Allowing myself to grieve for Kayin had gone some way to helping me during the day, but at night-time my old fears often returned in full force, clawing me back into shadowy places. Chayim knew it, and he'd been wonderful, always willing to sit up and talk or comfort me if I woke during a fitful dream. I was honest with him in a way I dared not be with the rest of my family. We sometimes fell asleep next to each other, exhausted from emotional recollections.

I was grateful for his care. I believe we provided what each other needed: somebody else who had been close to both brothers and understood the pain of their loss and Kayin's betrayal. Even so, I didn't think my mother was correct, and I suspected Chayim's heart truly belonged to Avigail.

Fear stuck my feet to the ground. I didn't dare bluster into my parent's private conversation and confess I'd heard all. So instead, I stayed rooted to the spot, praying that Yahweh would help me.

Abba continued the discussion. 'I will speak to them on the subject tomorrow. We must put this right. However, don't think I have forgotten you, my Chavah. It would be wonderful to have the next generation producing offspring, but I still long for you to re-join me. I love you, and I want to show you that with my soul and my body.'

'I will, Adam. Please just give me a little more time. I still feel so weak of heart. I don't think I am yet strong enough to bear another child. But a grandchild... Perhaps we may hope for some joy in that.'

Shortly afterwards, my parents emerged with their arms around each other, walking back towards our home. I slid further into the bushes in case they turned around and saw me, but they did not.

Now it was very dark, and I would have to walk back alone. I had avoided being out at night since Havel's death. My twin had always known when I was afraid and would slip his hand into mine to strengthen me, offering words of encouragement from Yahweh.

Now, as I hurried along, I had no one, and all the sounds of the night amplified. Crickets chirruped loudly in the long grass; water was rushing in the river just over the ridge. Wolves howled far in the distance and the earth shuddered under my feet. On top of it all, I could barely see where I was going. I stumbled in the direction my parents had taken, trying to stay in a straight line.

A loud noise from the bush startled me. Could there be a predator out here? I knelt on the ground and felt around, trying to find some sticks or stones. My fingers happened on a branch and I swung it around. No response. I broke two twigs off and started rubbing them together to create fire. It was a hopeless endeavour.

The noise came again – it was definitely an animal. No more delay. I ran, stumbling over stones on the ground, trying desperately to keep my sense of direction. My left foot found a hole. It twisted, and I fell to the ground.

I cried out for help, terrified that whatever creature was out there would attack me. I didn't think I was far from the hut. Someone might hear me if I cried loud enough.

The shuffling grew closer. I tried to stand, but my ankle gave way again. Then suddenly, the beast was so close I could feel its breath. I screamed, throwing my hands over my head, shielding myself from harm.

'Awan?' It was Abba. He was holding a flaming stick and looking at me with concern. 'Awan, what's wrong?'

I sat up and looked around me. Just to my right stood a sheep contentedly chewing on some grass. I couldn't believe it. I had run away terrified from a sheep. I let out a slightly hysterical laugh. Abba raised an eyebrow.

'I might have thought that sheep was attacking me,' I mumbled. 'I ran and twisted my ankle.'

Abba continued to look serious for an instant. Then he burst out laughing. He laughed a full and hearty roar, and I couldn't help but join him. For that moment, I forgot all about the conversation I'd heard earlier and the one awaiting me. I forgot about Kayin and Havel. I thought only of the sheep standing there chewing and the ridiculousness of my fear. Abba put his free arm beneath mine and lifted me, then helped me hobble back to the hut.

The next day was Shabbat and we were all together. We had a new story to share. Abba told everyone of the killer sheep that had attacked me in the night. My family found my misfortune hilarious.

Chayim jumped up and began retelling the scene in verse, with facial expressions to match. Avigail joined him, lending her wit to rhyme suggestions.

Hear the story of Awan and the beast –
A more fearsome creature you never did meet –
Fiend of the night, predator swift,
It chased her down when she was at risk!

Poor Awan, will she survive?
Who will save her from those jaws?
Poor Awan. 'Help!' she cries,
As the animal chases even more.

Avigail ran and pulled me up, encouraging me to act out my stumble. I did so pathetically, until Chayim waved his arms for me to retake my seat.

She twisted her foot in a troublesome crack;
Feeble Awan fell with a smack.
She covered her head and screamed aloud.
What will happen to Awan now?

Poor Awan, will she survive?
Who will save her from those jaws?
Poor Awan. 'Help!' she cries,
As the animal chases even more.

Avigail enhanced the tale with dramatic actions and sound effects far better than I. By now we were hooting with laughter.

Wait! Here comes a saviour at last:
Brave Abba with a torch to blast
the terrifying animal to the wind.
But Ho! The saviour merely grins.

Poor Awan, how could she see,
The fearsome creature was just a sheep?
Poor Awan! Only she
Could be so scared of such a —

'Peep?' Avigail finished, scrunching her nose.

Channah, who'd been dancing along, fell on the floor in giggles. Chayim pushed Avigail, who fisted him back before they fell about panting and laughing. I couldn't stop either; it was the first time in years I'd felt my ribs ache.

I glanced around, seeking Havel to share my delight with. Like a cold blast of wind, it to hit me that he was longer with us. But Chayim was, and Avigail was, and Ima was smiling again. *Thank you, Yahweh, for these.*

I wish we had ended the day there, and Abba had never started the following conversation. After we'd eaten, Shimon and Channah withdrew to check that their sheep were still secure. The rest of us were tidying away the remnants of the meal when Abba called Chayim and me together. I suddenly realised what was coming. *Oh, why hadn't I found the courage to speak to him before now?*

'Awan and Chayim. Your mother and I have been talking, and we think it is time we officially honoured your marriage before Elohim.'

Avigail, who was within earshot, spun round in disbelief.

My father was beaming. The joy in what he thought he was announcing was written on his face. I almost didn't want to interrupt and ruin his jubilation, but I couldn't allow him to continue.

'Abba,' I interjected softly, 'please don't go on. I believe you have the wrong impression of our relationship. May we speak alone?'

'That isn't necessary. You have been sharing a hut for years now, and it's become clear that we should have joined you in marriage some time ago. I am sorry I didn't realise earlier,' he replied – gently but firmly.

Chayim looked at me wide-eyed. I tried again.

'Abba, Chayim and I do not have the relationship you imagine.'

'Haven't you lain together?'

'No, Abba. I mean, yes, but not in the way you think. We have only offered each other comfort.'

'Are you aware of how a man and a woman lie together?'

My cheeks warmed. I was not entirely ignorant – I had shared a hut with my parents – but it was uncomfortable to talk about.

'Not precisely Abba, but I believe it goes beyond what we have done. And requires a different kind of love than we have.'

Avigail was glaring at me. Although not looking directly at her, I could feel her eyes boring holes in the side of my head.

'I see we should have discussed this before now,' Ima interjected. 'However, I have found the two of you in each other's beds several times; you have clearly spent the night together and developed an intimacy.'

Abba nodded. 'Just because there is no one else to witness it doesn't mean we should abandon Yahweh's commands. He wants a man to leave his mother and father and formally unite with his wife. Chayim, what do you say? Will you confess your devotion to Awan?'

Chayim flushed a colour I had never seen him turn before. 'Abba, I can't deny what you are saying. However, I don't think I love Awan the same way I love Avigail,' he replied, looking at the ground.

Avigail turned her attention from me and fixed it on Chayim. Her jaw had dropped wide open.

'What we are trying to say is,' I continued, 'If Avigail agrees, I believe she should marry Chayim.'

'No,' said my father, firmly. 'That is not acceptable. If he has lain with you, he must marry you. Elohim told us that when you unite as one flesh, you must stay that way for life!' My father was getting increasingly irate at the unexpected turn of his special announcement. This was not what any of us wanted.

'But she clearly does not *want* him, and I do!' Avigail suddenly screamed. 'Oh, how could you do this to me?' she shouted at Chayim. Then, 'How could you betray me like this?' she spat at me. Avigail stormed off, running from our treachery with tears streaming down her face.

My parents looked at each other in shock.

'Well done, Abba. You have just succeeded in repeating the episode with Kayin and Havel,' Chayim muttered under his breath, kicking a stone that lay on the ground. I'd never heard Chayim criticise anyone before but couldn't deny it was justified.

Hearing Chayim's words, my mother began to cry.

'Oh, Ima, please don't cry. He didn't mean it like that,' I said gently, going to her and wrapping my arms around her shoulders.

My father looked at Chayim with a mixture of disbelief and disgust. 'It is precisely that situation I am trying to avoid, and I would appreciate it if you would pay me more respect. I have not brought this on – it is your indiscretion. Why is Avigail so upset? Have you been playing games both their hearts?'

'No! At least, I have done nothing intentionally,' Chayim cried.

'Which do you choose then?' my father thundered.

'Abba, can't we just let this go? Think, talk and pray about it for a while?' Chayim pleaded. 'I don't want to leave either of my sisters on their own. They are both dear to me. You put me in an impossible situation.'

'One which is easily resolved,' I interjected. 'You must marry Avigail, for you love her, not me. I am certain we have not been 'united as one flesh'. In addition, my heart has not yet healed, so I have no desire to marry.'

'That may be the case, Awan, but you are the eldest, and you cannot remain unwed forever. Besides which, I still maintain you must be responsible for your actions.'

'Abba, didn't you hear her? We have done nothing.' Chayim yelled in exasperation and began to pace.

'You have done enough!' Abba shouted to Chayim's back. 'I believe – no, I have decided – the only solution is for you to wed both girls.'

Chayim spun around. We all stared at Abba with complete astonishment. Silence reigned for a few moments until I plucked up the courage to speak.

'No, Abba. Please. I mean you no disrespect, but I don't believe that is Elohim's design.'

'None of this is His design!' he exclaimed, throwing his hands in the air. 'It was not His design that we were banished from the Garden. It was not His design that your mother should have excruciating pain in childbirth or that we should have endless toil while farming. It was not His design that Kayin should murder Havel. Yet here we are!'

If our shock could have worsened any further, it did then. Ima – who had neither asked nor allowed herself to imagine what had really happened to Havel – began to wail in anguish as Abba's words sunk in. She tore her tunic and hurled herself to the ground, planting her face in the dust.

My father realised what he had said. He groaned and sank to my mother's side. 'Chavah, I'm sorry, I didn't mean to say those things. Chavah, please, I'm so sorry…'

I breathed deeply and rose. I needed a walk and time to pray.

CHAPTER 4

As I left my parents, I heard Chayim follow me. 'Awan, may we talk?' he asked as I headed towards the river.

'Of course,' I said, wiping the sweat from my brow.

He grabbed hold of my hands, stopping me in my tracks. His touch felt strange after what we'd just been through. 'How are you, after hearing that? About Kayin, I mean.'

I was surprised that was his first question; I'd thought he would want to talk about the other thing.

I briefly thought before answering. 'In truth, I have known it for many years. Though, I wish Abba hadn't spoken in such a way. Poor Ima! I've never known him to be so unreasonable. I didn't consider he would come down on us like that. I think— Oh, I need to spend time with Yahweh,' I sighed.

'I shan't keep you. I just want to make sure – did you mean what you said about your heart? Because I want to do the right thing, but I'm not certain what it is.'

He was so sweet – the kindest of men. 'Chayim, you know me. You have helped me grieve, guided me through so much heartache. You have been the best companion I could have wished for, showing maturity and love for me at every turn. Yet, I have never interpreted it as anything more than brotherly love, and I never felt like we did something we shouldn't have.

'I am perplexed Abba has reacted this way. I don't know what's behind it, but I hope it will work out if we wait and talk it through once things have calmed down. As for my heart, who knows? I have no idea how to interpret anything.'

'Nor I. For how do I know whom I love and in what way? I care about you both dearly – and truly, I would not object to joining my life with yours if it is what *you* want. Yet, it is Avigail who I… Who—'

'Takes your breath away and consumes your thoughts?'

'Yes, something like that.' He gave me one of his lopsided smiles.

'I'm not sure I'm qualified to tell you what love between a man and woman is like, but that's how I felt about Kayin. Even though Havel was everything to me, and I could not imagine life without him, it was Kayin that I blushed to think of. Havel was comforting, but Kayin— Kayin made my heart beat like a wolf was chasing me.'

'Or a sheep?' Chayim grinned.

'Or a sheep!' I laughed.

'Is that love though? Or is it something else – something less enduring than the kind of relationship we have? I mean, we get on well; I think we could live together and be happy. Whereas perhaps after several years, my feelings for Avigail will have changed.'

'That is something I don't know and perhaps will never find out. I feel that love and passion must be related somehow. Yet, if passionate love for me led Kayin to kill Havel, perhaps it is not a good thing at all? Perhaps it's madness to assume those kinds of feelings lead anywhere good. How are we supposed to know? It's no use asking our parents, for they hardly had a choice: they married each other or nobody.'

'Abba says he was besotted with Ima instantly.'

'Well, she is beautiful and probably a lot more appealing than all the animals.' I grinned. 'I wonder if she would say the same about him, though?'

We chuckled together, glad that we could feel at ease once more. After walking on a while in companionable silence, Chayim spoke again.

'I'm going to go and find Avigail now… attempt to smooth over the rocky ground.'

'That sounds like a good idea. If it feels appropriate, tell her I love her.'

'I shall.' And with that, he scampered off, returned to his wonderful, lively self. Not for the first time, I marvelled at how aptly he was named. Chayim means *life*, and he exuded joyous, bountiful life.

My thoughts returned to turmoil immediately after Chayim left. The idea of marrying him had shocked me at first. I was determined not to upset my sister, who clearly felt she had the prior claim. Indeed, I had been happy to watch their growing affection until the possibility of my own marriage had been dangled before me.

The confrontation with my father had made me uncomfortably aware that rejecting Chayim meant sentencing myself to life without a companion. Especially if Ima never agreed to have another child.

Snippets of their private conversation came back to me. Abba had mentioned avoiding a repeat of Kayin and Havel's rivalry before Ima told him about Chayim and me. So why had he chosen to push his point about us lying together so fervently? Why not take our word for it and let the matter rest? And what was his last statement tonight all about? Did he somehow think that Chayim having us both as wives would prevent rivalry? As far as I could see, it would only lead to further trouble, for how could there cease to be a struggle between two wives of the same man? I started to speak my questions aloud in prayer as I walked.

'Yahweh Elohim, please, in Your mercy, help me understand. You have placed the capacity for love and passion in our hearts. You designed us to fit together and gave us a desire to have children.

'Why did you choose to make only one family? Why didn't you create more people so we wouldn't have to fight amongst our siblings? It's proving nothing but a burden. What are we supposed to do when we are unevenly matched? Previously two men desired me, and now there are two women to one man!

'You told us it is not good to be alone, yet what other option is there? If I disagree with Abba, will I be destined to loneliness?

'And speaking of being alone – where is Kayin? I don't know whether You put him to death for his sin or whether he ran away. Is he alone somewhere in the wild? Will he ever return? Did I truly love him once, or was it just some passing infatuation? When I think of him now, I am furious at him for betraying me. Confusion tightens around me like twine when I'm reminded of him by a sight or a smell, or sometimes by Chayim's laugh, which has the same tone to it. My only relief is indulging in fantasy: imagining some impossible scenario where we are reconciled…'

I stopped, reached my hand out and grasped the slender trunk of a tree.

'How do I know what love is? Yet, I do know Chayim. I know he is warm, dependable and decent.

Most importantly, I know he loves You. Should those things be all that matters, or should I seek more? Should I desire what I felt for Kayin? I certainly didn't know Kayin fully – or what was in his heart – so how can I trust any of those feelings? He destroyed our family. He took a life with no just cause; he took my Havel!'

Tears prickled at my eyes as I strode forward again and before long, I could taste their saltiness on my tongue.

'Oh, my Havel! He was light, love and all that was good in the world. Why was he taken from me? He drew us all closer to You. He stood up for Kayin before Abba, did not push me to make any choice, and never tried to claim anything for himself but always gave freely. He sacrificed for the sake of us all, yet Kayin repaid him with hatred!

'Did Kayin think of me when he killed my brother? Perhaps it was only about the sacrifice and nothing to do with me? I do not know! Shall I ever find the answers, or must I live my life forever wondering?'

I had reached the river. I sat down on the bank and cast my feet into the water.

'Should I marry Chayim? Is it right or not? Please, Yahweh, tell me what to do.'

My question was met with silence. I sighed, realising how ridiculous I must sound to Him. Then a picture entered my mind of Havel chastising me for forgetting how awesome and holy Elohim is. Suddenly, remembering Elohim's righteous fury at Kayin's sacrifice, I trembled in fear. I pulled my feet out of the water and tucked them beneath me, kneeling in repentance.

'Forgive me, my Elohim, for I am guilty of reducing You to my level when You are Yahweh, the Most High!

Praise be to Your name! Please help me be content knowing my place before You and living in Your will, whatever that may be. Let me desire no more than I need. Show me what is sufficient for me.'

After a few moments, a gentle wind blew over me and sent a shiver into my body. Then Ruach Elohim whispered on the wind.

'Ehyeh: I am.

I remained kneeling on the riverbank for some time, allowing my mind to quieten in the presence of Yahweh. When peace had fully descended, I dwelt there a moment more, before reluctantly making my way home. It was almost dark, yet I knew no fear, for Yahweh was near. He was listening, and despite my irreverent ramblings, He had given me an answer. Not the one I expected, but the one I needed. A new song came to me as I walked:

> *I sang of despair, eyes flowing without ceasing;*
> *Yahweh from heaven looked down and saw.*
> *I called on His name from the depths of the pit;*
> *He heard my plea and took up my cause.*

> *Redeemer of life, all-sufficient one,*
> *Help me grasp the heights of your love for me.*
> *Quieten my thoughts, fill me anew*
> *With songs of your goodness, faithfulness, truth.*

> *My soul continues to remember its pain.*
> *It stays bowed down 'til I call to mind*
> *That the steadfast love of Yahweh never ceases;*
> *His mercies are new every moment of time.*

'Yahweh is my portion,' says my soul;
Therefore, I will trust and hope in you.
For you do good to those who wait;
Perfect salvation, you will demonstrate.

Despair turns into hope.
Food for my soul; food for my soul.
Despair turns into hope.
Yahweh make me whole; make me whole!

Redeemer of life, all-sufficient one,
Help me grasp the heights of your love for me.
Quieten my thoughts, fill me anew
With songs of your goodness, faithfulness, truth.

When I arrived home, my mother and father were sitting outside waiting for me. Abba stood as I approached. He closed the distance between us and grasped my hands.

'Awan, I have wronged you. Will you please allow me to explain?'

'Yes, Abba.' We sat down together. Ima also took my hands and squeezed them tightly. Her eyes were red from weeping, but her face had calmed.

My father began to speak. 'I fell into old sins earlier. I allowed shame about my failures to take over my thoughts, and I wouldn't hear what you and Chayim were trying to tell me. I have always felt responsible for what happened to our boys. For many years I mistreated Kayin – I projected onto him the guilt for my failure in the Garden. I then allowed his anger about it to fester and grow when it was within my power to speak with him and help him. By the time I finally managed to be honest, it was too late – bitterness had consumed his heart, and there was no longer any way back.

'I do not cope well with guilt. Nor shame. Shame has dominated me since the day we first sinned. I have never given it entirely to Yahweh and accepted His forgiveness. Perhaps it is because I walked so closely with Him that I find it so hard to believe He could ever accept me again after I betrayed Him. Havel used to beg me to stop carrying the shame of that first sin. I still don't understand where that boy got his wisdom from – how he could comprehend both the condition of my heart and the goodness of Yahweh so instinctively.'

'Havel spent every moment walking with Yahweh, Abba; he never wandered away. And yet, he was still aware of his sin, his humble place before Elohim's holiness.'

'You too, daughter, are wiser than I. And you were right earlier, where I was wrong. I allowed my guilt about the situation with you, Kayin and Havel to cloud my judgement. When the opportunity came to see you married safely to Chayim, I presumed Yahweh was providing a solution. I thought it might lessen the pain that the rivalry between your elder brothers had caused.

'I see now I was mistaken. Your Ima has confirmed that she doesn't know whether you and Chayim have been united in flesh and that you were always clothed when she came upon you. So, we have decided to trust your word.

'You were also right regarding two wives. Yahweh told me that being united with my wife would mean her body belonging to me and mine to her. This does not fit well with having two wives, and I shouldn't have commanded it. I was so worried about another rift in the family that I acted irrationally to prevent one.'

'Yet, disobeying our Elohim is not the right way to prevent anything,' my mother chipped in.

'Exactly,' Abba said, smiling at his wife. 'So, I must beg your forgiveness, Awan, and ask that we put all this behind us.'

I breathed a sigh of relief. 'Of course, Abba. You will always have my forgiveness and my love.' I threw my arms around his neck and kissed him on the cheek. He wiped a tear away and gave me a small smile. 'Abba?' I asked. 'Can you promise me something in return?'

'Name it.'

'Promise me you will honour Havel's memory by doing as he asked. No more guilt, no more shame. Accept mercy from Yahweh and accept Havel's sacrifices to pay for our sin. Yahweh accepted them, so you have been forgiven. You just need to believe it.'

He looked into my eyes as another tear slid down his cheek.

'Thank you, my precious girl. I shall endeavour to try.'

Then my mother spoke. 'We have just talked with Avigail and Chayim, and they have confirmed they do desire to wed. Are you sure you are content with that?' she asked, looking me straight in the face.

I briefly felt a rush of panic. My questions were being answered so swiftly. Was I sure they were the answers I was happy with? Could I cope if my companion was taken from me to begin a new union with Avigail?

Then I remembered the word spoken to me by Yahweh: **'Ehyeh.** Yes, He was sufficient for me, and I must trust Him to be so.

'I am content,' I confirmed. Then I beamed as the image of a gloriously happy Chayim and Avigail entered my mind. 'More than that. I am glad.'

CHAPTER 5

The wedding day, a few weeks later, was beautiful. The blazing sun was offset by a gentle wind, providing a perfect level of warmth and a dazzling sky. We had no traditions to draw on, for this had never been done before. All we knew was that the beauty of life and love should be celebrated before the Creator who had given it all.

Avigail's face was radiant with excitement. Early in the morning, Ima brought clay and pasted it over Avigail's face to cleanse her, then washed it off and smoothed olive oil into her skin, along with scent I'd pressed from the hillside herbs.

I'd woven Avigail a new tunic with a belt to accentuate her tiny waist above her well-curved hips. She glowed as she put it on. Then I braided her long, dark hair, twisting flowers into her locks before pulling a few curls out to frame her face.

I had already moved out of Chayim's hut and squeezed back into my parents' one. The hut had been cleaned and refreshed ready for his bride, erasing all traces of Kayin, though I kept the sheepskin. We were only partway through building the new hut that sat a little further from our original one and would become the couple's family home when complete.

When we emerged from Avigail's preparations, Chayim was waiting outside with the rest of the family. A feast of lamb, fresh bread and the most excellent fruit from the harvest was spread out.

As Avigail neared him, Chayim's smile resembled her own; it spread wide from ear to ear, putting a sparkle in his eyes like the reflection of a moonlit night on the water.

My father said a few simple words of praise to Elohim. Then He asked Yahweh to fill Chayim and Avigail with tenderness for each other as great as the love Elohim has for us.

'May you guide them in righteous living for all their days. May they be delighted by each other each day of their lives and may you bless them with children,' he concluded.

We all joined our voices in repeating the words, affirming our desire for the same. Then the couple made promises of faithfulness to each other before Elohim. Afterwards, we joined together in a simple song I had composed for the occasion:

Praise Yahweh from the heavens and heights,
Praise Him on the earth and above it.
For He has done great things,
His mercies never end,
and His goodness never fails.

Honour Him with your lives forever,
Walk in His paths of righteousness.
And bless His name,
As He blesses those
Who will love and honour Him.

May the man who fears Yahweh rejoice,
And his wife be a vine, fruitful every season.
May Yahweh bless you both,
All the days of your lives.
With the birth of many generations.

Honour Him with your lives forever,
Walk in His paths of righteousness.
And bless His name,
As He blesses those
Who will love and honour Him.

After singing, Ima served the food. While she did so, Channah and Shimon acted a sketch, imagining the married couple in a few years.

'Avigail, it's your turn to change these soggy linens,' Shimon screeched.

'I am sure it is your turn, husband dear,' Channah countered, tutting away. 'I have done it the last sixty-seven times.'

And so they continued, pretending to bicker with snotty children running around their feet. It had always been Chayim and Avigail who had acted out scenes for their younger siblings. To see the twins indulging in their own impressions was hilarious.

Once we had overindulged on Ima's feast, the couple went off for a walk while we cleared the food away. I knew my parents had spoken to them separately about what to expect when they were joined together physically. Now, they were supposed to talk about it and get comfortable with each other before going into the hut by themselves.

That time soon came, and I watched as my little sister nervously entered her new home hand in hand with her husband. As I imagined her taking the place once slept in by Kayin and then myself, I couldn't help dwelling on it. What if it had been us joining together instead of them?

I brushed the thought away, determined not to consider it. Kayin had murdered my brother; I should never think of him that way again. Yahweh alone was sufficient for me.

Within a few cycles of the moon, it became clear that Avigail was carrying her first child. When Ima had carried my siblings, I had been too young to fully notice what pregnancy entailed. Now I was a grown woman, seeing Avigail struggle shed a whole new light on the matter. I didn't envy her at all. At first, she was violently sick every morning then, as her time drew near, her back ached and she couldn't sleep. Fortunately, Chayim maintained his sunny disposition. He cradled her closely at every opportunity and laughed it off when she threw a tantrum or pushed him away.

When the day of the birth came, Avigail walked around the huts sweating and panting for half a day before water streamed down her legs, and Ima decided it was time for her to recline inside. She called me in to assist. I had assisted in birthing lambs before but having my sister's life in the balance made it terrifying.

Chayim stayed outside at first, though his face turned pale, and he paced around nervously. When Avigail felt the urge to push, she screamed for him. He came inside at once, running to her side and clutching her hand. She squeezed it tightly as she cried out with every contraction.

After what seemed like an eternity of pain, a tiny infant was finally born.

My mother's face was radiant as she lifted the girl and cradled her. I tied the cord with a sliver of twine, then cut it off. Ima handed the babe to its mother, and instantaneously the whole toil was worth it. Sickness, discomfort and pain disappeared from Avigail's face as she held her baby daughter in her arms for the first time. The tiny girl immediately nuzzled, and Ima helped her find her way to suckle.

Yet, the pain was not entirely over. A short while later, when dusk was setting in, Chayim was passed his swaddled babe as lesser contractions restarted, and Ima helped Avigail deliver the afterbirth.

Then she didn't stop bleeding. I had to fetch more linens which Ima packed into Avigail's body, trying to stem the flow. My mother's own blood drained from her face.

'This shouldn't be happening,' she said in a hushed voice. 'You must call on Elohim.' I nodded. Avigail's eyes started to roll, and her head tilted. Chayim looked from Ima to me with questions in his eyes. I led him and the babe outside. The other three family members were all there, waiting for news.

One look at our faces, and Abba knelt to the ground. We all followed. We pleaded for our Avigail; crying to Yahweh as we knelt in the dust, begging Him for her life. Several times, Chayim returned to the threshold of the hut still clutching his child, his face an agonising mix of powerlessness, impatience and faith. Each time he returned to resume prayer.

As the evening wore on with no news and the moon lifted in the sky, we continued to wrestle in prayer, sometimes with spoken words, other times with words unspoken. When the moon had passed halfway over the sky, the babe in arms grew restless and whimpered for her mother. Chayim rose again and entered the hut. We all watched nervously, not knowing whether our sister was still with us. Several moments later, Ima emerged.

'She lives,' she sighed, 'but she is frail, and her lifeblood all but spent. I still fear for her.'

Abba gathered his wife into his arms where she released her pain, crying in silent sobs as tears soaked into her husband's tunic.

I rose and joined Chayim. He had placed the babe on her mother's chest and wrapped Avigail's limp arms around her, supporting them with rolled-up fabrics at her sides. My sister slept as if half of her remained in this world and half had moved on to the next, unaware of the suckling child. Chayim's face was destitute. Fear punctuated every line of it, and his cheeks were wet with tears. I drew him into my arms for comfort and we knelt beside the bed, powerless to do anything but pray.

CHAPTER 6

Avigail made it through the night. We kept a vigil by her bed, taking turns watching over her and giving her water. Ima told us she must consume twice the usual amount to feed the baby and regain her strength. So, we kept dripping it into her mouth, sip by sip. The babe seemed to know her mother was not well, for she fussed only when she was hungry or soiled and otherwise slept in contentment next to whichever one of us was trying to get a few moments rest.

The next day Avigail remained weak, unable to open her eyes for more than a glance. She would moan in her sleep and, if she had been strong enough, might have flailed about. As it was, she only lifted her hands slightly or turned her head. When she woke, we tried to give her some broth from a bowl, but it spilt down her chin.

The next few days continued in much the same way. Chayim never left her side, sleeping next to her when he needed rest and kneeling before her while he was keeping watch – usually with his child in his arms. I often stayed with him, though I left the couple alone when Avigail seemed conscious enough to be aware of her husband's presence. At those times, I would take the baby's soiled linens to the river to clean them.

At one point, Ima came into the hut with a reed in her hand.

'I have an idea,' she said, showing me the reed, a fingers-breath wide. 'It's hollow. Perhaps we can get her to suck through it.'

The idea worked. Avigail soon realised what we were trying to do and was able to drink some water and crushed broth through the reed without it spilling. Chayim tenderly lifted her shoulders and supported her head just enough for it to pass down her throat without her choking.

Slowly, day by day, my sister grew stronger. On the second Shabbat after the birth, she managed to sit up in bed. The colour had returned to her face, and she smiled at us for the first time. Chayim was jubilant. He passed her the child then climbed on to the bed behind her. Letting Avigail rest on his chest, he wrapped his arms around hers and sat his chin on her shoulder. I left them alone to stare at the loveliness of their daughter together.

They named her Dorit, for she was the first of her generation. Once Avigail could be carried outside, we held a special ceremony for Dorit's naming day. Abba spoke words of blessing over the child, and we all promised to care for her and help her grow in the knowledge of Yahweh.

Dorit continued to develop in size, strength and lung capacity, making us aware of her presence at every opportunity. As she strengthened, so did her mother. After four weeks, Avigail was able to walk, and after a season, she had almost returned to her former vigour. She also held maturity in her eyes that hadn't been there before.

By this time we had completed the third hut, so the new family moved into it. As a result, I retook Kayin's pallet in his old hut, and Channah and Shimon moved in with me. I noticed that my parents didn't press them to marry even though my siblings were well into adulthood and still sleeping next to each other.

Dorit did us all good. Seeing a new life flourish lifted our spirits, and we enjoyed having a child around again. Ima particularly doted on her, and as soon as she began to walk, Dorit followed her grandmother around incessantly.

I noticed a change in my mother and father around this time. They seemed happier together again and more affectionate. At first, I attributed it to their granddaughter, until I noticed Ima expanding around her waist. I caught her on her own one morning near the well and questioned her.

'Yes, Awan, you are correct. I am expecting a child again,' she smiled tentatively as she dipped dishes into a pot of water.

'How are you feeling about that?' I asked, remembering her conversation with Abba some time ago – the one I shouldn't have overheard.

'I am well,' she said, interpreting my question as being about her health.

'And is your heart?' I continued, grabbing a linen cloth to dry.

Her eyebrows drew together then she smiled again, more openly this time. 'You've always been perceptive – I shouldn't be surprised. I was scared at first; scared to have another child after Havel died. Yet having Dorit around has made me long for one again.

Seeing Avigail nursing her kindled a longing in my breast. I believe the time is right.'

She laid a hand on mine. 'Your dear brother can never be replaced, Awan. You must not think I mean to do that.'

'Don't worry, Ima. I would never assume you meant to replace Havel. I know how irreplaceable he is in my heart. I would love to welcome another brother or sister into the world.' Putting down the bowl I held, I gave her a firm hug and kissed her cheek.

'I'm glad you know. Now I feel I can tell everyone else. I was most afraid that you would be angry with me. I feel my part in neglecting you after Havel's death. You spent that time looking after me, when it should have been the other way round.'

'Don't blame yourself, Ima, for I lay no blame on your shoulders. We all had to cope in our own way and find a journey through the grief.'

She squeezed me again. I suddenly had a nagging feeling inside my chest – it was time to confess.

'Ima, I need to tell you something. I heard you and Abba having a private conversation some time ago, the night I was *chased* by a sheep.'

She looked at me, puzzled, before submerging another bowl. 'I can't think what that would have been about.'

'You were talking about your need for a hut of your own and about not wanting another child. And then you spoke about Chayim and me and our relationship.'

Realisation dawned in my mother's eyes. 'Ah, I remember. Well, that explains why you knew to ask me about the baby.'

My cheeks warmed. 'I'm sorry. I should have told you I was there. I shouldn't have kept it from you all this time—'

'Awan, no harm has been done. You are an adult now; I'm sure you can manage what you heard.'

'It nearly led to problems with Chayim—'

'No, that was my doing, not yours. I told your father I had seen you two together. I truly thought you had feelings for each other, and I desperately want you to be happy, sweet one. I know how lonely you've been. I suppose that too stemmed from guilt about neglecting you. Regardless, I should have checked with you first. Thank Yahweh, it turned out all right in the end.'

'Yes, it did.' A great weight lifted from my shoulders that I hadn't realised I'd been carrying. I thought the conversation was over, but Ima continued.

'Unless you are still sad and just being brave? Awan, how is *your* heart?'

The question set me back and I found myself drying something twice. 'I confess I do miss my brothers, even after all this time. When Havel died, it ripped me in two. I didn't know how to live without him; he had always been there, you know?'

Ima nodded. 'I remember well feeling the two of you kicking about together in my womb. It felt like I was carrying a couple of jackals!'

I smiled. 'Even when we were apart, I still felt Havel's presence in my life. But the day I found him in the field, I knew he was gone. I knew his soul had departed, and I couldn't go with him. It felt like I was starting life all over again, yet I didn't know where to start, and I wasn't even sure I wanted to.'

My mother's eyes roamed over the distant hills.

'I have slowly learnt to live again,' I said. 'Chayim helped me so much. I suppose that's why you noticed a connection between us. Mostly though, Yahweh helped me. I wasn't sure how to talk to Him with Havel gone. Havel had always taken the lead; known what to pray and what to do. I was content living in his shadow, for indeed, it was no shadow at all but felt like permanent daylight.'

She turned to me and I caught a glimpse of something else – longing?

'It took time to build my own connection with Yahweh,' I continued. 'I spent a while feeling like I was wandering. But Yahweh kept me safe, and He came to me when I eventually asked Him to. He has been my companion since then. Although I may never marry, at least I will have Yahweh. I am content.'

A smile tugged at one side of Ima's mouth. 'I am glad for that. And what about Kayin?'

'What of him?' I asked with trepidation.

'You said that you missed your *brothers*. You have only mentioned Havel.'

'Oh, you heard that.' I stared at the cloth in my hand. 'I don't know if I should speak about it.'

Ima sighed and dried her hands on her tunic. 'I fear that is also my fault. I haven't spoken to you of Kayin since that day. I couldn't process my feelings about what happened, so I tried to forget him. It was easier than coming to terms with what he did. But it didn't work. The day your father had his outburst, it all hit me. Denying Kayin's actions and pretending he hadn't left had harmed us all.'

Tears prickled at my eyes. Perhaps in relief she had finally admitted it, perhaps something else.

Ima continued. 'While you were away from the hut that afternoon, your father and I grieved together for

Kayin and wept for his sin. It was still raw when you returned, but things have grown easier since. I now feel able to talk about him again. So please, speak.'

I took a deep breath. 'I loved him, Ima. I was aware of his flaws – which sometimes frightened me – but I still loved him. Although you all thought I would marry Havel, if I had been forced to choose between them back then, I believe I would have chosen Kayin. For it was Kayin that consumed my thoughts and my dreams, even while Havel was by my side. I held back from him because I wasn't sure whether he loved Yahweh. I don't know whether that was wise or foolish, given how it turned out.'

Ima couldn't hide the surprise on her features, though she was trying to, so I pressed on.

'Like you, I didn't know how to process what Kayin did. I needed to grieve for him, but I didn't know how. And I was so angry! I still swing from being furious with him to feeling despair at my heart's constant longing. Although time has settled the rawness of my emotions, no matter how much I pray against it, I am bitter he took my future away. Even so, I miss him still.'

'As do I, Awan,' Ima said. 'I had eighteen summers with Kayin before the rest of you were born. I loved him ferociously and would have defended him to the death. Yet, in the latter years, he never seemed to see that. He was always so far from us, as if some world existed in his mind that we weren't part of.

'I have spent some time considering this. I now believe we all have struggles that we need to lay down before Yahweh. Your father, as you know, likes to hold on to shame and fails to lay it down, even when he has been forgiven. I am discontented: always thirsty for something more to fill my life when I should find my satisfaction in Yahweh. I seek too much purpose in serving my children rather than my Elohim.

'Kayin craved being needed and loved, as I do. Yet he sought recognition and praise for what he did, and when he didn't get what he thought he deserved, he allowed resentment to consume goodness. Pride is a terrible thing. Even Havel struggled with it.'

Indignation tugged my heart. 'Havel wasn't proud!'

'He wasn't perfect, Awan. You told your father Havel knew his sin and was humble before Yahweh. You were correct. You see, Havel was disposed to sin just like the rest of us. You may not remember much of his childhood, but he was by far my most wilful child! He began to change the day he nearly lost his life, when Kayin rescued him on the cliff face. He realised his lowly position before Elohim and repented. But he still struggled. After he began leading worship, he came to me and asked me to pray with him. We'd regularly pray for Yahweh to protect him from possessiveness and pride.'

'I knew about the cliff face, but I never knew that. I thought I'd known everything about him.'

'We can never know everything about somebody. But love accepts, compromises and endures – even through the surprises and the imperfections. Love is not proud; it is not self-seeking. Love forgives and moves forward. This is the love Yahweh models for us, is it not? You are naturally compassionate, Awan. But, as you have confessed, anger still grips your heart. Don't fall into the same trap Kayin did, my love. Don't let that anger fester – even if it is justified. Try to open your heart some more and lay it down before Yahweh.'

CHAPTER 7

The season after my talk with Ima, she gave birth to her eighth child. We were all thrilled to see the ruddy little boy emerge and delighted the delivery was relatively simple. Ima had feared she might struggle after such a long time, but it was not the case.

The following Shabbat, Abba called me to him after an enthusiastic time of worship. His excitement at having a new child was evident for all to see. As I sat next to him he opened his arms wide, and I gladly snuggled into them.

'I have been wanting to thank you,' he said softly, kissing my forehead.

'What for Abba?' I asked.

'You don't know what a gift you gave me the day you stood up to me and told me to lay aside my guilt and shame. I have been working on it, spending more time with Yahweh, and He is healing me. You were right that my sin had been paid for, and I should no longer carry it around. Now I am reconciled with your mother and my new son has been born, I feel as joyful as I did the day we named Avigail.'

'I am so pleased for you, Abba, and only glad I could help.'

'Times have been hard, but you did well by standing up to me.'

'I never wanted to disrespect you.'

'I know. Yet sometimes, Yahweh calls us to speak the truth lovingly, and in those times it is right to put aside our fears and obey Him. I am proud of you, Awan.'

I choked back a sob. 'I love you, Abba.'

'And I love you, my precious girl. Please, don't hold in all your emotions. I'm not unaware that you've lost a confidante in your brother, Chayim. Your mother and I are here; speak to us when you need a shoulder to cry on.'

I thanked him and snuggled further into his arms.

Two days later, when their son was eight days old, we held a naming ceremony like the one we had for Dorit. When Abba asked what name Ima had chosen, she stood, held the baby out and pronounced his name Set.

'Elohim has appointed me another son in place of Havel,' she said. 'For Kayin killed him.'

My mouth turned dry. Ima had assured me no child could ever replace Havel and then named her new son specifically as a substitute for him? Moreover, she'd announced Kayin had killed Havel so boldly, so soon after wailing and crying when Abba did the same. She really must have moved on. I turned my face away to hide the heat spreading from my cheeks to my neck and spent the rest of that day in a sullen mood, the joy of the new child spoilt completely by his name.

I had been trying to challenge the bitterness that remained in my heart, praying to Elohim that I would lay down my anger against Kayin. I never expected to need to do that for Ima too. She was the one who had challenged me to do so, yet here she was naming her child Set. I could not comprehend it.

Why would she do this, Yahweh? If she is not bitter? Oh, protect me from these feelings. Soften my heart towards my mother again.

The next day I decided to make some new linens for my little brother's bottom. Dorit's were hopelessly soiled and I could no longer get them clean. I set up my sticks, tying flax fibres to either end and tightly weaving threads over and under, creating a close-knit fabric that would be sure to catch anything Set produced.

It took most of the day to construct three squares of fabric and sew them together with a bone needle and flax thread, but I was glad to be doing something proactively for Set. It took my mind off his name.

A week later I presented Ima with six new wraps for her baby.

She gladly took them from me, then pressed my hands and thanked me. 'Praise Elohim for giving you to me, Awan. You are truly a blessing.'

I held Set while she examined the fibres. He was wide awake and staring up at me. His little almond eyes reminded me of Havel. He cooed, as if replying to my thoughts, and clasped my little finger. Then he drew it towards his mouth and suckled the end of it. I laughed, causing him to startle and open his eyes wider. Set considered my face awhile then having exhausted himself, promptly fell asleep – still suckling my little finger.

'He's finally sleeping. You have the touch, Awan,' Ima said.

Just a shame I shall never have one of my own, I thought, recognising the fluttering in my chest for maternal longing.

'Perhaps someday Elohim shall give you a child,' Ima continued, like she'd read my mind.

'Perhaps,' I replied, dropping a kiss on my sleeping brother's forehead. But I didn't believe it. What did she expect me to do, wait twenty years and then marry this infant in my arms? No, it was far more likely that Set would marry Dorit when the time came. Still, I was glad to bond with this baby; there was no reason why I couldn't enjoy him.

Determined not to feel further resentment about Set's name, I decided to question my mother. 'Ima, why did you call Set a substitute when you said no one could replace Havel?'

'Do you feel like he's replaced Havel?' she asked back.

'Not at all. I love him, of course, but he could never be the same to me as my twin.'

'I too was confused when I received the vision. Yet because it was clear, I obeyed Yahweh.'

I looked at her nonplussed, so she continued.

'The night before Set's naming day, I had a vision from Elohim. Havel was there, standing before me. I tried to reach out to him, desperate to hold him again, but I couldn't stretch far enough. I saw him standing over a young boy. The boy had fairer hair, but his brother's eyes.

'I recognised in him the babe in my arms – seen in years to come. Then Havel passed the boy a jar of oil. After that, he smiled at me and mouthed 'goodbye' before he faded away, leaving only the boy. Then I heard a voice say one word: ***Set***.'

Her vision set my mind racing. I didn't understand what the jar of oil meant for a start. Could it be that Set was meant to lead our family in some way? A symbol, perhaps, that he was intended as a spiritual guide, as Havel had been? It seemed odd he would be chosen rather than Chayim or myself.

Ima answered my thoughts. 'We cannot discern the mind of Yahweh, Awan. We can only obey. We do not see what He sees. We do not know why He had a close relationship with Havel rather than Kayin, or why He would choose Set now when you and Chayim are walking with Him still. We must simply wait on Yahweh and see what He intends. Perhaps in time, we shall understand.'

As if confirming the name Himself, a wave of peace from Elohim washed over me as she spoke. 'If Yahweh gave you the name, then who am I to question His wisdom?' I murmured to little Set.

Ima squeezed my hand in response. 'Awan, a while ago we spoke about your feelings towards Kayin. How are you getting on with that?'

I sighed and considered it as Set nestled further into my arms. 'I am trying not to be angry, Ima. Yet when I think of Kayin, I struggle with resentment. I'm trying to lay it down before Yahweh, but I'm unsure how to do that. How can I forgive him when he's not here to ask for forgiveness? I don't know who he is anymore – if he is even alive. He turned out to be so different from the man I thought he was – the man I thought I loved. I hate that he took away my Havel; I hate the man who deceived me.'

'Are you sure he was different? Or were those things we saw as broken as much a part of him as those things we loved?'

'I could not love someone capable of murder, Ima!'

'Perhaps not. Yet how different was he from you or me? When Yahweh spoke at Kayin's sacrifice, I suspect he felt like the ground he'd built his life on was pulled away from under him – for he based his worth on what he could grow, and his produce was rejected.

'If someone took away what I find my purpose in, might I not be capable of the same? If Kayin had been anyone other than my son, I would have hunted him down for what he did to Havel. Sometimes, I wish I had. Because you children are the ground I build my life on, and having Havel taken away from me stole the earth from under my feet. You saw what it did to me.

'I suspect it comes down to trust. I struggle because I do not truly trust my life to Elohim. I try to lay it down, then I snatch it back again. I want to trust Elohim with you all too, but I continually fail. What are you holding back from Him, Awan?'

'I don't know. I suppose I do keep trying to take back the bitterness, but it is so hard not to when I cannot see Kayin; when I don't know what truly happened. And Ima, surely it cannot be *good* to love Kayin still – to love evil, to love the things that make people wrong before Yahweh?'

'To love evil? No, of course not. But to love people even though they hold evil in their hearts? Yes, we must. For we are all the same, my love; we all hold evil in our hearts. We all struggle with sins – some are simply more obvious or destructive than others. I'm not sure that makes any of us better or worse, just different. We are all under the same judgement. We all need forgiveness.'

My body suddenly felt heavy and I wanted to lie down. 'I will consider what you have said, Ima. I don't deny I need forgiveness also, and I shall examine my heart. Although I do not see how my lack of forgiveness for Kayin makes any difference.'

'Perhaps not to him, for as you said, he is not here to receive it. But it may make a difference to you, child, and your future walk with Yahweh.'

I sighed. I was convinced that, even if Kayin lived, he had no place in my future: he was never coming back. Nevertheless, she did have a point about my suffering from bitterness. It pushed down on me like a stone in my gut and I now wanted to expel it.

Whilst Kayin did not deserve forgiveness – I could never excuse what he had done – perhaps forgiving did not have to mean excusing the offence. Maybe it meant accepting that we are all guilty of something, and I was as undeserving of Elohim's mercy as Kayin was.

A few weeks later, my mother was trying to lift a pot from the fire when she squealed, dropped the pot and clutched her back. I rushed to steady the pot before all its contents emptied on the ground.

'Why were you lifting this, Ima?' I cried, 'It is far too heavy for you; you've only just had a child.'

I flushed, realising I sounded like a mother scolding her infant. Fortunately, Ima saw the funny side and began laughing but this was cut short by another spasm of pain. I placed the pot down and rushed to her side.

'Let me help you,' I said as I gently took her weight and lowered her onto the wicker chair that Avigail had made for Kayin.

Ima took several weeks to recover from her injury, so I looked after Set during that time. I strapped him to my chest and carried him about with me as I ground grain, prepared meals and washed linens, only taking him back to his mother when he needed nursing.

It was the time of the barley harvest, and my other siblings were out in the fields all day. At midday, I filled a skin with water from the well and carried it out with a basket of bread and cheese. Little Dorit toddled along behind me. Once we reached the fields, we stopped to eat with the workers. I placed Set on top of his wrap on the floor, where he contentedly grasped hold of his toes and sucked them.

Chayim habitually played a game with Dorit, hiding among the sheaves that stood drying, and calling out for his daughter to come and find him. When it was her turn to hide, she sat in one place, covered her eyes and called out, 'Babba, Babba,' in words barely formed.

Of course, he pretended he couldn't see her, as if by covering her eyes, she had made herself invisible. 'Dorit? Oh where is Dorit?' he said, looking behind every sheath. After a while, she opened her hands and fell into hysterics at his mock surprise.

While Chayim and Dorit were playing their game, Avigail and I found ourselves with a moment of privacy. Set was still content, and Shimon and Channah were sitting a way off, deep in a conversation of their own as they shared the bread I had freshly baked. Avigail stroked her stomach and locked eyes with me.

'Awan, I have something I need to ask you,' she began. She looked serious, her earnest eyes piercing me. 'You may have noticed I am with child again.'

'Avigail, that's wonderful!' I exclaimed. I stopped my praise when she looked to the ground and drew in the dust with a finger.

At length, she spoke again. 'I am scared, sister. I think back on what happened when I was birthing Dorit, and I wonder if I shall make it through the next labour.'

'Avigail, you must not think that way,' I said, grasping her hand and drawing it to my mouth to kiss it.

She pulled it away. 'Yes, I must. It may well be the end of my life, and I must be prepared for that. Awan, I want you to promise me something—'

I tried to protest, but the intensity of her face stopped me.

'You must promise me that if the worst happens you will marry Chayim and take my children as your own.'

My chest tightened. 'Avigail, you cannot say such a thing. Please believe that Elohim will protect you!'

'I have no basis for believing that. It's not that I don't trust Him, Awan, for I do. I just know that His plans may be different from ours. It may be His will to cut short my time on this earth. I shall suffer less than you if it is, for I shall depart just as Havel did. Whereas you shall all be left with another grief to bear.'

I could barely believe her words. I had rarely heard her speak of Elohim, let alone talk with such conviction. I couldn't argue with her, for I had seen her blood after the labour and her death-like pallor.

She had only just made it through, and who could be sure she would do so again?

Realising that she knew this and had still consented to have another child filled me with even more admiration for her. There was only one way I could reply.

'I don't want to make this promise, and I shall pray every day that I do not have to fulfil it. However, if the time comes and you do depart from us, then I will do as you say: I will take your children and love them as my own. You have my word.'

'Thank you, Awan,' Avigail breathed out. Then she allowed me to retake her hand and kiss it.

'What are you two looking so serious about?' asked Chayim as he came to join us with little Dorit sitting on his shoulders, legs dangling over his chest. He swung her into his arms and tickled her tummy as he sat next to his wife. Avigail smiled at him, all traces of our conversation vanishing from her face, then leant over and kissed him firmly on the mouth.

Chayim forgot his question and enjoyed his wife's embrace while I averted my eyes and found a reason to fuss over Set. The baby gave a little start when Dorit threw herself next to him and poked him in the nose. As his eyes began to crease and well up, I scooped him into my arms and planted kisses all over his neck. When I drew my face away, his mouth twitched to one side and then the other, as he graced me with his first smile.

CHAPTER 8

As Avigail's pregnancy wore on, we all became nervous. While Set and my mother grew in strength, Avigail weakened. I kept the first part of my promise to my sister: I prayed for her every day. I prayed that Yahweh would strengthen and keep her through her pregnancy, labour and beyond. I tried not to doubt, I tried to trust in Him, yet as Avigail became confined to her bed after only a few cycles of the moon, I couldn't help but begin considering a different future.

It felt so wrong to think about having Chayim to myself again, yet the thoughts kept entering my head, and they were not unpleasant. I pushed them away in respect and love for my sister. At the same time, I began to see little Dorit in a different light and tried to build a stronger bond with her – just in case.

There was no apparent reason why Avigail should become weak before the birth, yet she did, to the point where she could barely rise from her pallet to relieve herself. Thought Dorit spent the night in her mother's bed, cradled in her arms, during the day, she was a bundle of energy needing to be entertained. So I helped, keeping her with me whenever she wasn't following Ima. Indeed, I often extracted her from her grandmother's side and took her and Set off to play.

One day I was in the vineyard with both children, picking grapes and testing them for ripeness. We had a basket half full of clusters from the sunniest part of the glade, and Dorit was sitting next to it, helping herself. Occasionally, she bit one in half and squeezed it to a pulp between her fingers. Set was lying on his tummy, arms tucked beneath his chest and legs sprawled behind him, trying desperately to pull himself towards the grapes.

I heard someone shout my name and looked up to see Channah sprinting towards me.

'It's Avigail's time,' she said, leaning over and resting her hands on her knees as she panted.

'So early? How far along is her labour?' I asked, aware that I had been out the whole morning.

'The first pains only started a short while ago, but they are already intense and close together. Ima thinks it will come soon.'

'Carry Set,' I said, kneeling in front of Dorit who climbed onto my back automatically, aware by now of our routine.

We jogged towards Avigail and Chayim's hut as quickly as we could. It wasn't fast enough. When we arrived, screams from inside were already piercing the air. Shimon must have fetched Abba because he was pacing outside with brows drawn and lips tightly pressed.

I swung Dorit round, passed her to my father, and went straight in. Ima was kneeling on the floor at the end of a limp Avigail. My younger sister was covered in sweat and tears, her hair damp and strewn over her face. Blood was already seeping from her, though the babe had not yet been born.

Chayim was cradling Avigail's head, and she held one of his hands, though it looked liked she had no strength left even for that. Chayim's face was pale; his eyes penetrated me as I looked at him. I knew he was preparing himself for the worst.

'What can I do?' I asked Ima.

'Pass me that bowl of water,' she said. 'Then sing. Give us hope, Awan.'

I saw a tiny head crowning between my mother's hands as I passed the water. I saw the faces of those dearest to me in the world, hopeless and filled with pain. How would Avigail have the power to continue? I lifted my quivering voice to Elohim, the deliverer.

> *To you, my Elohim, I call.*
> *My Rock, be not deaf to me,*
> *For if You are silent, we fall.*
> *Hear now my plea for mercy.*
>
> *I cry to my Yahweh for grace:*
> *Don't crush this life to the ground!*
> *I lift my hands to Your dwelling place.*
> *I ask that life would come down.*
>
> *Deliver us. Deliver us!*
> *Deliver us from the jaws of death.*
> *Deliver us. Deliver us!*
> *In You is found all our strength.*
>
> *For You are the source of all life;*
> *By Your breath, you caused us to be.*
> *Declare Your purpose and might;*
> *Birth this child of Yours in safety.*
>
> *For the sake of Your name, Yahweh,*

Honour Your holiness here.
As we are fruitful and multiply,
Bless us by now drawing near.

Deliver us. Deliver us!
Deliver us from the jaws of death.
Deliver us. Deliver us!
In You is found all our strength.

The room wasn't silent as I sang. Amid the song Avigail felt another contraction and pushed, shrieking as she did. Yet, despite the noise, a tranquillity came upon the room that had been previously absent. The tiny head slid out with that push, and Ima turned the babe slightly, ready for the next one.

I continued to sing. Chayim's soft voice joined mine, singing the words into his wife's ear as he held her weak body – willing them to give her life and strength. Avigail brightened a little; just a tiny amount of pink presented on her cheeks. The next contraction came.

'This is the last one,' Ima said softly. 'Perseverance, my daughter; it's nearly over.'

My voice rang out as Avigail pushed and gave a loud cry. Chayim focused on her while Ima concentrated on the form that slid into her arms. The infant didn't cry. Ima turned her upside down and smacked her bottom. Still nothing. I had finished a chorus and for a moment we all held our breath, waiting for a sound of life. Ima's tears accompanied the silence.

Without explanation, I knew what to do. I moved towards Ima and knelt. Laying the infant along my forearms, I lowered my face to hers and covered her nose and mouth with my lips. Praying my breath could channel the ruach of Elohim, I exhaled: once, twice, three times. The child moved; spluttered; and lastly, wailed; drawing her tiny arms up and fisting her fingers in protest.

My mother and I wept with relief, tears flooding our faces.

'Ima,' came an agonised voice from the other end of the bed. We looked up. Chayim was still holding Avigail's head, but her eyes were closed and it tilted back. Tilted like Havel's had. Had she given her child the last of her energy then departed?

'No!' I cried and ran round to where she lay. I grasped her. Gently I shook her shoulders, yet still she did not move. 'No, Yahweh! No!' I wailed, losing all composure as reality struck me like a branch in the wind. I could not lose another; I could not bear it! I threw my arms around Avigail and clutched her to myself. 'Pray, brother,' I commanded. 'Do not lose hope.'

Chayim shook his head gently, but as he did so, Avigail whimpered. Her body stiffened slightly in my arms, her eyelids flickered and she looked up at me.

'You're still with us,' I whispered as warmth flooded my chest. 'So is your daughter.'

She gave me a gentle smile, too weak to offer any other response, and then relaxed again and fell asleep. I gently laid her down on the pallet, checking twice that she she still breathed. Chayim sat shaking his head, as though unable to decide whether he had lost his wife or not.

'Come and see your little girl,' I said, taking his hand and leading him to where Ima stood swaddling the baby. She was so small that when Chayim put his large hands out to stroke her he almost covered her body.

'I don't know how to feel,' he said, still not taking the child in his arms. 'Should I be joyful for the birth when life still feels so fragile? What if she is too small to live long? What if Avigail never wakes?'

'Enjoy the time you have,' Ima replied as she manoeuvred the little girl into her son's arms. 'It may yet be extended but, if it is not, you don't want to regret a single moment.'

Chayim stared down at his new daughter, who was now squirming in his arms. He gave her his smallest finger to grasp onto, and immediately – just as Set had done to me – she drew it to her mouth and suckled it. His face softened; his mouth even twitched at the sight of his large finger in her tiny mouth.

'She will need nursing immediately, yet I fear Avigail is too weak,' Ima said. 'I will feed her myself until her mother is strong enough.' I was immediately grateful for Elohim's provision. What would we have done if Ima had not still been nursing Set? I had no idea if babies could thrive on sheep's milk.

For the first few days, my mother and I kept vigil over Avigail's bed – as we had done after Dorit's birth – taking turns to sit with her and feed her. This time, mercifully, she had a normal amount of bleeding after labour. Indeed, her health began to quickly return, as if delivering the baby had stemmed the tide of her fleeing life.

Channah regularly brought in fresh fruit, trying to ask Chayim questions about the harvest. However, Chayim was still in a daze and unwilling to leave his wife's side for one moment. On the second day we heard the bleating of sheep who had been penned in nearby, presumably so Abba could direct the work in the fields instead of watching the livestock.

By the third day, Ima decided Avigail must nurse to prevent her milk drying up. So, we laid the little girl beside her mother to suckle and kept watch to ensure Avigail did not roll on her. This we continued thrice a day – just enough to ensure her milk came in without draining Avigail of too much fluid and strength. As soon as Avigail could get out of bed, we placed the wicker chair outside her hut so she could sit there during the day. Chayim was still reluctant to leave her but he made himself useful grinding grain within eyeshot and sorting through the produce the others brought in.

By the time the little one was four weeks old, Ima was satisfied that she had put on enough weight to survive on her mother's milk. Indeed she had doubled in size since her birth. Avigail wanted to celebrate with her naming day, which we had put off until they were both strong enough.

Originally Chayim had called his daughter Zilpah, meaning *frailty*, for she was so small. However on the day of the celebration, her parents announced that they had changed her name.

'She shall be called Techiyah,' Avigail said. 'For she and I have both seen revival.'

CHAPTER 9

A little while after Techiyah was born, Avigail asked me to pray that Yahweh would close her womb.

'I cannot bear to keep Chayim away from my bed, yet we both know I cannot survive another birth,' she said, when I asked if she was sure. I didn't know whether it was within Elohim's will that my sister's womb be closed, but I promised her I would pray for it.

Yahweh must have listened, for Avigail never bore another child. The same could not be said for my mother. Before Set was four, Liora joined us on a wintry morning when the sunlight was low. Nadav, Raham and Shalom – triplet boys – came two summers after that. 'Elohim is generous to us and His mercy brings peace,' said Ima on their naming day.

One morning, when the triplets had seen three full moons, I crept into my mother's hut with some warm milk for her. She was reclining backwards, propped up at the end of the pallet with a boy on each breast. The third was squirming beside her legs. I sat near her, put down the drink and picked up Nadav to settle him.

'Thank you, my love,' said Ima, who looked beyond exhausted. 'I thought twins were hard. But triplets – ah! I need an extra breast.'

I laughed at her, then cooed at Nadav, whom I'd startled. 'What can I do to help?' I asked.

'Exactly what you are doing. Bring me refreshment and hold the extra one,' she smiled. I stroked the soft, downy hair covering the baby's head. The other two began suckling intermittently. 'They are pretending now while their brother goes hungry.' Ima unlatched one babe at a time and placed them down next to her, then I handed her my bundle, who grasped at his mother hungrily. Raham and Shalom protested at the cold, then instinctively snuggled in together, entwining their limbs. A pang shot through my stomach and stopped my breath.

Ima didn't miss a thing. She stretched out her free hand and grasped mine. 'They are just like you and Havel were. They cannot bear to be alone but are always seeking each other.'

I nodded as a tear slid down my cheek. Ima kissed my hand.

'How can it still hurt so much after all this time?' I asked. 'When will the pain cease and leave me be?'

'If you ever find the answer to that, I'd love to know,' she replied. I sniffed and kissed her hand back.

The triplets proved exhausting, yet my mother wasn't quite finished. When Set was twelve and the triplets almost four, she bore another child. A dove had tangled itself in a thorny thicket near our home on the morning of Ima's labour, so she called her daughter Yemima.

Around this time, I started to understand the vision Ima had seen when Set was a newborn. Set did not seem to hear Yahweh the same way Havel had done, but he walked in humility as if he knew his place before Elohim and was content in it.

As much as I adored Chayim, he had always been a natural follower rather than a leader. In contrast to Chayim, Set was quite solemn – more solemn than Havel too – but he participated actively in our worship, asking many questions about Yahweh and showing signs of spiritual maturity beyond his age. We often made up songs whilst working together, and the better ones we performed to the family on Shabbat.

My fondness for Set increased as he grew older. He regularly sought out my company, usually joining me at the river, for he loved fishing and swimming. He asked me to tell him stories of the older brothers he had never met; he seemed fascinated by the power of sin and its destructive force. It had been long enough that I could now speak of the good times without being consumed by the bad ones. Even so, I shared discerningly. I only revealed details of the rivalry between the brothers when hairs started gracing Set's chin and his voice deepened. And so, despite his name, I was ultimately glad for Set's company.

As they grew up, Chayim's daughters, Dorit and Techiyah, formed a formidable threesome with my sister, Liora. By the time she reached eighteen years, Dorit was tall and elegant. She had the same long, beautifully soft hair as her mother and grandmother and loved to occupy herself by tying it into all sorts of styles. Techiyah was smaller and more timid, but she looked up to her elder sister in awe and copied everything she did. Liora, at thirteen, enjoyed the company of Chayim's daughters far more than her triplet brothers, so she also tagged along behind Dorit.

The three began to spend considerable time braiding each other's hair and even experimenting with painting cold charcoal from the fire around their eyelids. One day they insisted on braiding my hair. They spent half a day on it, plaiting many tiny strands into my tight curls and weaving into it flax fibres they had prepared. Once finished, they stood back to admire their handiwork and exclaimed in one voice how wonderful it was.

My head felt strange; I wasn't used to the tightness and weight. When they tried to attack me with some sticks of charcoal, I flatly refused.

'No, thank you!' I laughed. 'I'll leave the face drawings to you three.' However, when I saw my reflection in a bowl of water, I agreed that the hair looked good. Perhaps I would wear it this way from here on.

My younger triplet brothers were full of mischief that didn't change as they passed into their second decade. They reminded me of Chayim who, as a child, had constantly tormented Avigail with little tricks. Unfortunately for my youngest sister, Yemima – the victim of most of their jokes – there were three of them to endure! Still, I consoled myself that if they turned out like Chayim it would be no bad thing.

Chayim had sobered further as he bore the responsibility of raising his own family, yet he was still the wonderful light he'd always been. I enjoyed seeing him whenever I got the chance and missed him when I didn't. As for Avigail, she never fully recovered her previous vigour and increasingly spent time inside her hut, rather than with the rest of us. As well as being an excellent weaver, she had recently become adept at spinning wool from the sheep and turning it into blankets, which was extremely time-consuming. At first I tried to call in on her regularly, but as life became busier, her company was missed too.

Around the time Dorit turned twenty-three, Shimon and Channah announced they had decided to marry. They wished to live together in the old cave in the hills. When questioned why, Shimon said he disliked farming and preferred hunting, which was more accessible from the cave.

I was still sharing a hut with the twins at this time, yet I didn't have much to do with them as they had always kept to themselves. Even so, I hadn't noticed much physical intimacy between them, and I wondered what had prompted the decision now. I could tell that Chayim was disappointed, as his careful training of Shimon in the fields would go to waste. But he didn't complain. At least Set was now a capable apprentice.

'Might you find a different cave, Channah?' my father asked. 'We're still using that one for storing food.'

'I was thinking, if you agree, Abba, that I might take a small flock with me. The cave we know is in an advantageous position.'

'Yes, but there are predators in that area. That's the reason we moved to the plain,' Abba replied. 'And I'd rather keep the flock together.'

'Most predators have moved east,' Shimon responded, a little tersely. 'Besides, they'll be safe with me to protect them.'

Abba looked unsure, but Channah smiled up at Shimon. 'It's true we've had less trouble with wolves recently,' she said.

'Alright,' Abba agreed, reluctantly. 'If we can find another suitable cave close by, you may have the old one. But I still don't like it.'

Set and I volunteered to search for a new storage cave so our siblings could have what they desired. One day we were searching on the hill over the stream when Set called out that he had found somewhere.

'It is the strangest thing,' he said as I approached. 'Someone has been here before.'

I pulled back the vines covering the mouth of the cave and peered inside. It was dark, but just inside the entrance the remains of a charred torch lay on the ground and, beyond that, an animal skin. We lit a fire outside and, as it took, discussed what might lie deeper inside the cave. Once the fire was sufficient to remove a torch from it, we ventured in, only to find far more there than we had imagined.

There was a bed of sorts – although it looked like there had been more to it once upon a time, for strips of linen lay ripped and discarded alongside tufts of fleece. At the back of the cave were several food baskets. One held dried barley that was so old it crumbled in my fingers. I lifted the lid off another basket and flies swarmed out of it. The contents had decomposed to the extent that there was only a blackish mush on the bottom. The smell of rot was so intense that Set and I had to cover our noses. I quickly put the lid back on.

'Who could have lived here?' Set asked in confusion. I glanced around again. Pictures began to form in my mind as I bent down and picked things up. I gathered up the remains of the bed and took it outside the cave into the light of day. I smelled it, wondering if the scent would confirm my thoughts, but any human traces had long disappeared.

'I believe this is your eldest brother's handiwork,' I said to Set when he squatted beside me. 'See, this is his stitching – I would recognise it anywhere. Clearly nobody has been here for an age. I think he must have retained this cave for himself, keeping it a secret from the rest of us.'

We decided to clear out the dry baskets and dispose of the mouldy ones. We swept out the cave, ready to move our family's supplies into it within the following days. As we walked home we were both silent. Thoughts of what might have transpired in that cave long ago pervaded my mind causing confusion and a longing for the truth. Yet bitterness did not consume me. I realised that I had held the work of Kayin's hands and thought about him without anger becoming my primary emotion.

Thank you, Yahweh.

We celebrated Shimon and Channah's marriage the following Shabbat, in much the same way we had for Chayim and Avigail. That night they went up into the hills and started their new lives away from the principal family.

Shortly after Shimon and Channah moved out, Abba asked me if Set and Liora could take the other bed in my hut. I gladly agreed. It had been uncomfortably quiet sleeping on my own and did my bouts of loneliness no favours. Liora was thrilled at moving away from Ima and Abba, relishing any opportunity to show she was more grown-up than her younger siblings.

Unfortunately, Set and Liora did not appreciate lying close to each other on the extended pallet, and they argued every night. If Set placed even a finger on her side, Liora picked up the rolled cloth from under her head and whipped Set with it. The atmosphere was somewhat different than it had been with Shimon and Channah, who never argued. Nonetheless, tiresome as their bickering sometimes was, it was better than the isolated alternative.

When Set was alone with me, he often complained about his sister. 'She is so obsessed with how she looks; all those girls are. When will they grow up and consider more important things?'

I reminded him that they were still young and not everyone could be as mature as he.

'Dorit is older than me,' he said, one summer's day when we were working in the fields. 'Yet she acts just like Liora. Last week when we were swimming in the river, she pretended to catch her foot in a weed. When I swam to help, the weed miraculously disappeared.' He rolled his eyes as I stifled a giggle. 'What?' he asked.

'Perhaps Dorit was trying to get your attention, Set.'

'Why would she do that?'

'Well, you are the only unmarried man, and there are three young women. It's hardly surprising there might be some competition to catch your eye.'

'Ugh, I don't want any of those girls. I would far rather spend my days with you, Awan. You don't act as they do. You work hard and are more serious.'

I raised an eyebrow at him and smirked. 'I have had little choice in my life, Set. At their age, I had many responsibilities looking after the family. They don't have so many.'

'They could help – they just choose not to. They are idle,' he said.

'Don't be unkind, brother; it doesn't suit you. Perhaps you could take some time to get to know them rather than getting annoyed with them. They might bother you less if you gave them some attention.'

'I spend plenty enough time with Liora, thank you. However, perhaps you are right about Dorit and Techiyah. I will try to do as you say,' he said, lifting his chin, 'though I would far rather be with you. You also love Yahweh, but I never hear a word about Him from them. They used to listen on rest days when they were younger, but now they seem to spend the whole time tittering behind Abba's back.'

'Then continue to set them a good example. We cannot force people to love Yahweh, Set, but we can encourage them to see how wonderful He is by displaying His relationship with us. Why not ask Abba if you can lead worship sometimes? He used to love letting Havel do it. And when you spend time with the girls, why not ask them how they feel about Yahweh? You may be surprised by their answers when they are alone rather than showing off to each other.'

I arranged some vegetables for dinner into a basket. 'I am old, Set. Far too old for you. Invest in those girls, and one day you may realise one of them is good for you.'

'You are not old! You look the same as you did the day I was born.'

'You remember that do you?' I laughed. 'Perhaps it is true, though. None of us knows how long we have been appointed to remain on the earth. Yahweh did say we would die as part of the banishment, but we don't know when that will be. Ima and Abba also look just the same to me as they always have – perhaps with just a few more laughter lines on their faces.'

'So, you confess you are not old? I am a grown man now, Awan; I have seen twenty-one winters. We are not so different.'

'Except I used to change your soiled linens and carry you around in a sling,' I laughed again, ruffling his light brown hair with its sun-lit flecks. The chest that had puffed out as he stood up to his 'twenty-one winters' deflated slightly. I worried I'd upset him until a broad smile filled his face.

'One day, you might forget that and see me as a man. I will look forward to that day,' he replied. Then he picked up the basket we'd finished with and started making his way home, throwing another grin over his shoulder at me.

I sighed as he wandered off. I adored my younger brother but could not imagine seeing him as anything other than the babe I had helped deliver. I would hope and pray that his eyes and heart would be drawn to one of Chayim's daughters.

CHAPTER 10

T he following year, we had a terrible grain harvest. The river had not effectively filled up the dug channels, and the crops dried out before they matured. After taking in all the salvageable barley and wheat, Chayim became despondent, blaming himself for not maintaining the channels properly. He said we wouldn't have enough for the winter or next season's seed. I even heard him mutter something about Kayin not making this mistake.

I felt for Chayim, who had always enjoyed tending vegetables more than grain but had been tasked with managing everything and rarely got to do what he loved. Work in the larger fields was backbreaking. Kayin, with his size and strength, had been well suited to it, but Chayim found it more exhausting, and he lacked Kayin's remarkable foresight and ingenuity.

The main difficulty was that Shimon had left. Since moving to the cave, he had completely stopped farming. He had even stopped joining us at the Shabbat meal, though Channah always came and made excuses for him. As intended, Channah had taken a portion of the flock into the hills with her, so Abba was always busy tending the sheep left on the plains and ventured into the fields even less. Nadav had shown interest in shepherding and stayed with

Abba but wasn't responsible enough to be left alone for long.

Fortunately, Set was competent managing the seasonal fruit, vines and trees, so he had taken over this task from Abba. Raham and Shalom had come into their own as labourers, but they couldn't be left alone either. They needed constant instruction, or they might descend into wrestling rather than working.

Ima was expecting a child again, so I was busy at home and found it challenging to get out and help my brother. Fortunately, my youngest sister, Yemima, was now twelve and very helpful. I felt confident leaving her with simple tasks.

Nevertheless, I decided to speak to the older girls and encourage them to work with their father in the fields, at least until things improved. I wasn't sure Avigail would appreciate me interfering, yet I was now frustrated with their idleness too, while the rest of us worked hard constantly.

Avigail herself had not ventured into the fields for some time. She tended to the physical needs of her little family and had taught her girls the skills they would need to set up their own homes, yet she didn't enforce work on them often.

One day, when I could see Chayim looking particularly despondent, I took Dorit, Techiyah and Liora aside and asked them, as gently as I could, if they could assist with the farming.

'But I am working on a project with my Ima!' Dorit exclaimed. 'And Techiyah is too weak. She is not allowed to work with Abba.'

I was surprised. Techiyah was small, but she was no longer weak. When I caught her eye, Techiyah looked a little embarrassed and nodded. I suspected Dorit of making excuses.

'Where is the project you are working on? Is your Ima doing it alone? I see no evidence of it,' I said.

At this, Dorit became enraged and stormed off to complain to Avigail. Liora watched Dorit's reaction and attempted to emulate it. Mercifully Ima, who was only a short way away and had heard the exchange, affirmed that it was about time Liora learnt to pull her weight.

Later Chayim came to me alone.

'Avigail is upset that you have told the girls to work,' he explained, looking sheepish. 'I have been asked to reprimand you.'

'Do you desire to reprimand me, brother?' I asked Chayim, with a slight upturn of my mouth.

'No, I desire to hug you,' he exclaimed, drawing me into a tight squeeze. I laughed in his arms and squeezed him back. 'I am so glad someone has spoken to my daughters; I was beginning to despair of them.'

'Forgive me, Chayim, but as their Abba, is it not your job to speak to them?' I asked, almost reprovingly if it weren't for the lilt in my voice.

'Ah, if only it were that simple,' he replied, releasing me from his arms. 'Avigail has become… Oh, I don't want to criticise her; she just wants to protect the girls. But I don't think she realises how hard it's been for us. She is very firm about the girls not working too much. I argue with her on pain of death.' He allowed his tongue to loll out of one side of his mouth after speaking.

'Since when did you pander to Avigail?' I chuckled. 'You always stood up to her when you were young.'

'Then I was a foolish child, free from the consequences of her wrath. Now I am a peacemaker,

Awan. I will do anything to avoid a fight with my wife.'

'Well, if you will take my advice: I suggest you pick Avigail the most beautiful flowers the hills have to offer and kneel before her telling her how much you adore her, before gently suggesting that on this point, she may be wrong. Perhaps try to explain how things have been. I'm sure she will come around.'

He chuckled and gave me a quick kiss on the cheek. 'I wish I had your courage. I will try. Pray for me, Awan!'

And with that, he left, taking his smile with him.

Somehow, he must have succeeded in winning Avigail around, for, the following day, his daughters begrudgingly accompanied him to the fields to help re-dig the water channels. Liora joined them. I couldn't help but be amused as the young women used all their strength on the digging sticks and barely made a mark in the ground.

After a while Set took the sticks from Dorit and Techiyah, handed them to Raham and Shalom, and instructed the girls to help me with crops we had harvested instead. Dorit simpered at Set but glared at me as I approached. I showed her how to grind the grain on the flat stones and I showed Techiyah how to press the early olives for oil. Only Liora continued to dig with her brothers.

The next day the girls would not stop complaining that their whole bodies ached, but at least they turned up. Over the next few weeks, our moods improved. The water channels flowed again, and all the summer fruit was brought in and processed. There wasn't as much as we had harvested in previous seasons, but we could make it last.

Despite this, it was clear that Abba would have to take the sheep away over the winter as there was no spare barley for their food. Indeed, on the following Shabbat, he informed us that he and Channah had decided to combine forces that winter and try crossing the river to head south with the flocks. Ima looked worried. She was nearing her sixth month of pregnancy and their journey would likely mean my father's absence for the arrival of their baby.

'I will do my best to return before the little one arrives,' he said, putting his arms around my mother's shoulders and kissing her on the cheek.

'How will you feel about leaving Shimon?' I asked Channah.

'Oh, he'll be alright. I told him he should come and stay down here with the rest of you, but he likes his own space. If he misses me too much, he can come and find me,' she grinned. 'In the meantime, Abba and I shall enjoy having some time to ourselves with the sheep, like we used to.'

I eyed Channah's body, trying to discern if she was carrying a child, but I couldn't see signs of it.

The next few weeks flew by as late olives and vegetables were brought in and next year's barley seed was sown. Dorit seemed to be settling into her tasks. One day, when Set and I were by the river soaking barley, Set told me Dorit had actually smiled once or twice whilst she had been sowing the seed. However, most of his words were reserved for Techiyah, whom he seemed to have grown fond of whilst training her in the vineyard.

'She lives in her sister's shadow, but I have discovered that hidden behind, there is a sensitive soul. Thank you for encouraging me to look deeper. I even asked her about Elohim yesterday, and she said the best thing about her week was hearing us sing songs to Him.'

'That is good, Set,' I replied. 'Perhaps you could sing with her to help her take the words to her heart?'

A handful of winter figs were ready to pick on my tree near the river. I gently cupped and pulled them off, then cradled them to my heart.

'Your tree is better than Abba's,' Set commented.

'Yes. Kayin said this was a perfect spot for a tree. It is so close to the water that the roots are constantly nourished. She is bearing the fruit of her good planting,' I added, affectionately stroking the trunk.

Shabbat was bittersweet as we gathered for the last time before saying farewell to Abba and Channah. Even Shimon joined us. Set must have spoken with Abba, for he was encouraged to lead a time of devotion to Yahweh.

Set spoke of how, many years ago, Havel and I had crossed the river on the entwined trees and how it showed that Elohim always listens if we will only ask Him. I smiled in encouragement as he related one of the stories I had told him in our times together and drew a lesson from it even though it wasn't his own experience.

When he finished speaking, Set sat beside Techiyah, who flushed at the attention. Dorit glared in jealousy, but Set ignored her as he took her sister's hand and began to sing. Slowly, Techiyah joined him, looking into his eyes as he spurred her on. They must have written the song together, for it wasn't one of mine. My heart warmed as the timid young woman bloomed before my eyes:

Blessed are those whose delight is in Yahweh.

They are like trees planted by water,
Where leaves do not wither, and fruits do not fail.
Whatever they do shall prosper.

Not so those who fail to trust Him.
They are chaff blown on the wind, reaching the sky.
Yahweh Elohim, grant that we may be
Delighted in you, the Most High.

Silence reigned for a few moments after they sang and then everyone, except Dorit, began exclaiming how wonderful it was to hear them sing together and how beautifully their voices blended. A tear ran down Avigail's cheek, and Chayim put an arm around her. Warmth and peace flooded my heart. We seemed to finally be moving on and bringing up a new generation bearing Yahweh's image.

The next day, I said goodbye to Abba and Channah with tears in my eyes. It reminded me of the winter that Havel travelled north and how much I had missed him. The atmosphere was subdued for the rest of that day, everyone feeling their loss.

There wasn't so much for us to do when the winter set in. Between chores, I noticed Set and Techiyah often disappeared together. I was pleased for them, though I was once again losing a companion. When I spotted Dorit skulking about looking miserable, I drew alongside her and tried to make conversation.

'Is it hard being alone when you are used to having your sister by your side?' I asked.

Dorit clucked her tongue and rolled her eyes, replying nothing. I persevered.

'You know, when you were a girl you were fascinated with faces. You used to climb onto my lap and play with mine, giggling at how my features changed when you pressed my nose in different directions. But you were particularly interested in the little interloper who threatened to steal attention away from you. You often made Set jump by suddenly poking him.' I was chuckling, but Dorit did not return a smile.

'You mean Set has always despised me, and I was a fool not to see it before,' she bit back. 'You think my wish to be the centre of attention has never changed. I know you consider me selfish.'

I was taken aback. 'No, Dorit, I meant none of those things; I was just trying to encourage you to laugh. Every child thinks they are the centre of the world; you were no more selfish than anyone else.'

'Don't try to pretend that you like me, Awan. I know you don't. No one does.'

'Where is this coming from, my love? Of course I like you – I love you! I am sorry I interfered in asking you to work, but truly I did it for your good and ours. I bear you no ill will.'

'What would you know of ill will? Everyone loves you, Awan; you can do no wrong! You go about being so exemplary, leaving the rest of us looking like dust. I am sick of you and your high standards. It is not just my ima that suffers for it; we all do.'

Her words stung like a slap in the face. Where were these sentiments coming from? I took a deep breath before I managed to reply. 'What do you mean, Dorit? How does your mother suffer?'

'Because my abba never stops singing your praises!' she squealed. 'He talks about you day and night, and Ima is left feeling miserable. Every time he mentions you, we all wonder why he didn't just marry you.'

Alarm quickened my pulse. 'That can't be true. I have never seen anyone love with such devotion as Chayim shows your ima. He chose her, not me, and I blessed their union. Besides, you didn't see how he behaved when she was with child: Chayim remained devoted to you all throughout.'

Dorit scoffed and began walking away, then threw back a further comment. 'It's you who does not see. You are blind to the truth, Awan. Do you know what my biggest fear is? Why I am angry that Techiyah has abandoned me? I am scared of being left alone and… and turning out like you!'

With that, Dorit stormed off and left me gaping at her back.

CHAPTER 11

Dorit's words whirled around my head for the next few days. I could focus on little else and found myself growing increasingly irritated. I kept asking myself how she could perceive me in such a way. I was alone. I often felt alone – even when surrounded by others – yet thought I'd learned to deal with that. I believed I was walking with Yahweh and finding companionship in Him, not seeking attention from others.

How could she accuse me of being a source of strife between her parents? Hadn't I given up a life with Chayim for Avigail's sake? Hadn't I stood by them both through their trials, even agreeing to take their daughter as my own if necessary? Now, that same daughter despised me and accused me of acting superior to everybody.

I didn't feel superior to them. I had spent my whole life serving others, rarely taking anything for myself but always giving out. And what had been my reward? Losing the two people I had loved most in the world. And still, I had continued serving my parents and the next generation, trying to do good despite the suffering I had borne.

How could she think of me that way? What was it about me that she feared becoming – self-righteous?

She was well on the way to that already! I had meant what I said to her: she was young, and I could excuse a measure of selfishness. However, even if I allowed her that grace, she was still the most conceited person in the family. Dorit cared for none but herself. She tried to capture Set's attention all the time. I didn't begrudge her the boy, yet she certainly held a grudge against her sister. Surely that was where all this stemmed from: she felt rejected because Set had chosen Techiyah and, for some reason, she was taking that out on me.

I displayed none of my troubled thoughts to my family. I smiled at Dorit and pretended our exchange had never taken place. She, however, showed no such restraint and continued to scowl at me.

However, when I spent time with Avigail and Chayim on Shabbat, I struggled to act normal around them. Chayim had always been the easiest person to get along with, yet now I couldn't help but feel uncomfortable. It was difficult not to interpret his actions differently in the light of what Dorit had said.

I could not hold his gaze. When he smiled at me, I looked to the ground; when he squeezed my hand, I pulled it away. He noticed, of course, and looked at me quizzically, yet said nothing, for I didn't give him the opportunity to be alone with me.

Unanswerable questions quickly spiralled as a week turned into several, and still, the winter continued. Remembering Abba's words, I wished I could confide in him, but he was absent, and I couldn't burden Ima with this in her late stage of pregnancy.

As the awkwardness continued, I longed again for deeper human companionship and simultaneously despaired at my longing for it. I fell back into old contemplations about the purpose of love and desire. The beauty of love shrank in the face of the pain that rivalry caused. What would this rivalry lead to once man filled the earth, as Yahweh had foretold? Surely it wouldn't end in Havel's death but in the demise of countless others.

As the second month of my father's absence wore on, contentment in anything evaded me. I even avoided Set, seeing no point investing in relationships. Bitterness gnarled my bones when I considered Shimon, selfishly serving his own interests instead of helping the family.

What is the point of life, Yahweh? Why did You create us? We're doomed to continue this trajectory, despite efforts to the contrary. We shall never be Your image-bearers.

He didn't answer me. His absence shouted louder than my words as I cried out to Him at night, desiring His presence. He had moved far away and I could not feel Him anymore. My soul was downcast and troubled.

If You too leave me, what hope is there?

One day, I finally smelled spring in the air. Ensuring Ima was well before I left, I ventured to the beckoning hills to collect fresh herbs. Most of the plants had begun to sprout again, and the new growth was fragrant and flavourful. The air always felt fresher in the hills, where the scent of thyme carried on a breeze that gently ruffled the longer grasses.

I stood on the highest plateau before the mountain trail began and surveyed the land to the east. The sun glittered off the winding Tigris as if the water were dancing for my benefit. I could just make out a small family of behemoths – tiny in the distance – descending from the wooded area, close to where Havel and I must have seen them all those years ago.

It took my mind back to that journey, reminding me what it had felt like to be out in the wild, not knowing exactly where we were going but just following Yahweh's lead. I had loved that journey – spending time alone with Havel, walking with him and knowing I was also walking with Yahweh. In the darkness we had held each other, keeping warm, safe in the knowledge that He who created the stars was watching over us.

Thinking of it brought a longing for those days – not just for that journey but for a new one. I knew that without Havel, it would never be the same. Yet I suddenly desired to explore further and see again those great animals whose vastness seemed to reach the heavens. Perhaps removing myself from this awkward situation was just what I needed.

I wasn't sure how to leave behind my family and responsibilities, nor who might come on the journey with me this time. Would Set? I doubted it for, in Techiyah, he had reason to stay behind. Besides, no one else walked in Yahweh's presence as Havel had done; could anyone accompany me the way he had?

The longing didn't leave me as I returned home. It grew stronger with each uncomfortable moment spent in the company of Dorit or Chayim. So, I began to enquire of Yahweh. The question filled my prayers over the next week. I didn't hear any words of response, yet slowly I began to experience something that felt like confirmation. I kept recalling when Havel had overwintered the sheep alone in the northern pastures. Afterwards, he had spoken of how he felt closer to Elohim when alone with Him; how time away from the bustle of family life had been good for his soul.

I kept returning to our journey in my dreams, watching the trees grow together and seeing the whirlwind before me. Was Yahweh beckoning me to come? The distance I'd lately experienced gave me such a hunger for Him that the appeal of journeying to find Him became irresistible.

One day, I gathered the courage to speak to Set about it. Still unsure about going alone, I asked him if he would consider accompanying me.

'Why leave, Awan? Everyone that you love is here,' he replied.

'I only mean to go for a short while, Set. I thought you might enjoy the chance to see a bit more of the creation. There is so much wonder beyond these lands that you've never experienced.'

He looked around. 'I can't right now,' he whispered. 'I have just asked Chayim if I can marry Techiyah, and he has given me his blessing.'

I lifted my brows in surprise. 'That was quick,' I said, with no condemnation in my voice, only surprise.

Set smiled, 'I must confess it's become a little difficult... What I mean is, we wish to be united as husband and wife, and we see no reason to wait.'

'I am pleased for you both. I had a suspicion you would rather stay here anyway.'

'You're not upset with me?'

'Of course not. When do you plan to wed?

'Chayim will speak to Abba as soon as he returns with the flocks.'

'Good. I wouldn't leave without seeing Abba in any case.'

'You would still go on your trip – alone?'

In truth, I was nervous of going alone. I wondered how I might defend myself against wild beasts, for a start. Even so, it gave me the best chance of finding Yahweh.

'Perhaps,' I answered.

'You could ask Dorit; it might do her good to see the world.'

I was even less keen on going with Dorit, and I highly doubted she would want to come, but I agreed to think about it.

Abba and Channah returned three days later which was just as well, for Ima was about ready to burst. We had a special rest day to celebrate being reunited, which Set led. He'd grown into leading our family worship while Abba had been gone, proving how hard he'd been listening and thinking by leading us with strength of purpose and wisdom. He seemed so young to assume the position; I had to remind myself that Havel had been younger when he did the same.

It was wonderful to have Abba back, and in such good spirits. He and Set soon settled into an easy camaraderie.

After we ate together, Channah excitedly told us what it was like south of the river. 'The land turns into a marsh further south, with water seeping over it, completely flooding the area. Enormous birds with long legs wade there, hunting for fish and insects.'

'We only observed this from a distance,' Abba said. 'As that land wasn't suitable for grazing, we couldn't take the sheep there and quickly turned back to remain in the area between our river and the marshland.'

Channah nodded. 'We had to be on our guard, though, for jackals and other predators had their eyes on the sheep. We took it in turns to keep watch, always keeping a fire going and a sling in hand.'

'I don't think we'll go south again,' Abba said. 'The northern hills are safer.'

'But we did find some goats!' Channah exclaimed, jumping up.

'What are goats?' Techiyah asked.

'They have wiry, double-skinned coats and long, floppy ears. We succeeded in herding them into our flock. You must come see.' So we all followed Channah to the field to inspect them.

Their stories added further fuel to the fire in my heart, but I couldn't ask to leave straight away for Ima went into labour that night. I didn't envy her the suffering, yet I did envy her the child. My mind had been in such turmoil that it was pathetically weak. As much as I tried to resist, my body knew it wanted an infant of its own, and it betrayed me. As soon as I had delivered the baby and passed it to my mother, I had to escape. Once alone at the river, I allowed the tears of a lost future to flow freely.

They called my youngest sibling Ronel, *Song of Elohim*. He was a sturdy boy with a big head, and I was not at all surprised he'd taken so much effort to push out. Forgetting the pain as soon as she held her baby, Ima laughed at the size of him and praised Elohim that he hadn't been her first.

We observed Ronel's naming the same week that we celebrated Set and Techiyah being joined in marriage. The beginning of new life was everywhere. And my heart ached.

CHAPTER 12

Unable to wait any longer, I announced my intention to leave when we were all together on Shabbat, asking if anyone wanted to join me. My siblings and nieces looked surprised and unsure how to respond. None of them volunteered to come.

The following day, I spoke with Ima to check she didn't mind me going when the baby was so young. She gave me a warm embrace, stroked my cheek and told me that she knew I had to go, and it was fine. Tears glistened in her eyes as she looked deeply into mine.

'You are the best daughter a woman could wish for, Awan. You have been my constant support and companion. I will miss you more than I can say, but I know this must happen and that Yahweh will guide you and care for you.'

She kissed me and held me for some time before letting go. Abba came then, offering words of support and love. I gained the impression they knew something about my journey that I didn't. I only expected to be gone for a few weeks. Perhaps, despite their assurances, they worried something might happen to me on the journey.

I packed enough supplies to last several nights, including one of Avigail's wool blankets, a spare tunic and a short spear for protection (I had never mastered the sling). Then I tied the bundle to my back and went around saying goodbye to my family.

The triplets all looked embarrassed when asked to hug me but did so begrudgingly. Yemima kissed me and wailed that I wasn't allowed to leave, before Abba pulled her from my arms and held her tightly. Liora and Techiyah clung to me too. Set gave me a warm embrace and wished me well.

Dorit stood awkwardly and said nothing, so I wrapped my arms around her and whispered, 'Whatever you think of me, I still love you.' If anything did happen to me on the journey, I wouldn't have her regretting our last moments together in years to come.

Finally, I reached Avigail and Chayim. My closest sister looked into my eyes, and I suddenly saw all that Dorit had told me – she was in pain, and I had been blind to it. My stomach churned. I wished I had more time to speak with her properly, yet was hopeful my time away would benefit her relationship with Chayim.

'Dearest one,' I said quietly to her, 'trust in Yahweh with all your heart; love Him with all your strength; and allow Him to heal you. Your husband adores you – never disbelieve it. I go praying every blessing upon you, and hopeful that when I return, we may be true sisters in heart again.'

Avigail's eyes warmed, and she offered me a small smile before I kissed her. Chayim must have heard my words, though gently spoken. Nevertheless, he barely raised his eyebrows before diving in to give me a hug and a squeeze.

With that, I turned to leave. I made my way towards the hills, intending to call on Channah and Shimon on the way. I had walked about half the distance to their cave when I heard someone calling behind me.

'Awan, wait.' I turned around – it was Chayim, running to catch up, water-skin in hand.

'Chayim, what is it? Is something wrong?'

'No,' he panted, trying to catch back his breath. 'I've decided to come with you. I'm not happy with you going alone.'

'Chayim, you cannot,' I responded, trying to fight the pleasure his announcement created. 'You must stay with Avigail; she needs you.'

'She doesn't need me. She's perfectly capable of running our household for a short while. Whereas you – anything could happen to you out here.'

'Elohim will protect me.'

'I don't doubt that. Yet perhaps He wishes to use me for that purpose?' He gave me one of his lopsided grins, and my resolve waned. I drew in a deep breath to strengthen it.

'No, Chayim, there is more going on than you realise. Your coming will hurt Avigail.'

'I asked her about it. She said it was fine.'

'Fine?' I questioned, aware of the many times I had said I was fine when that was precisely the opposite of how I felt.

'Yes, she said it was fine.'

'What about the crops then?' I asked, trying a different tactic.

'Oh, the triplets can handle the weeds for a while. As long as I'm back to pull the flax, it'll be alright.'

I tried to picture the flax when I had last seen it; it was not far off being ready. I might be gone longer than Chayim realised. I knew I should insist he go home, yet the thought of spending quality time with him was enticing. I hesitated for just a few moments before relenting. 'Perhaps for a few days then. But you must turn back and leave me if I wish to go further.'

'Agreed,' he said.

As we walked, I prayed silently, asking for forgiveness and protection over Avigail's heart. Around midday, we reached the cave and greeted Shimon, who was standing outside sharpening a spear. He was clothed only in animal skin with no tunic over his body.

'Awan. Chayim. Come and see the cave!' he enthused, leading us inside. They had successfully made it a home. A comfortable pallet lay at one end. A seating area to the side surrounded a small fire burning steadily just within the entrance – enough to give some light whilst ensuring the smoke was drawn outside. Baskets on the floor lined the wall opposite the pallet. Herbs tied with twine hung from the ceiling, along with the skins of several mammals and snakes.

'I found those shortly after we moved here,' Shimon said, noticing my attention had been drawn to the snakeskins. 'A family of serpents. I hunted them and speared them all. We enjoyed their flesh; it's surprisingly delicious roasted over the fire.'

They'd eaten serpent? It didn't seem right somehow, but I said nothing. Channah entered and ran over to hug us both.

'How do you like my home?' she asked.

We both expressed admiration for it, although I still wasn't sure about the snakeskins.

'Please sit; have something to eat,' Channah said. As we perched on a boulder each, she brought out some fresh bread and fruit.

'So, you're really going then, Awan? And why are you with her?' she pointed at Chayim.

'She wants to see the mountains again. I'm not keen on her falling down a cliff, like last time, without me there to catch her,' Chayim replied. We all laughed, though it felt slightly forced. Channah sat down with us, but Shimon moved outside and continued sharpening his spear.

After we had eaten, I rose to leave. 'We better be going so we can make some progress before dark. Farewell, Channah. See you soon.'

Shimon patted our backs as we walked outside. 'I might see you around. I often go into the mountains. If I don't, enjoy the views. And stay away from the giants.' He grinned.

Channah kissed us both on the cheek then we left, ascending the hillside where her flock grazed contentedly in the afternoon sun.

As we continued through the forest, climbing gradually into the higher hills, the tension between Chayim and me started to ease. We spoke first of our family, laughing at some of the pranks the triplets had recently played on Yemima.

'A few mornings ago, I heard a scream at dawn and rushed into their hut to find our parents fishing frogs out of Yemima's bed whilst the boys sniggered in the corner,' I said.

As it grew dark, we made camp near a stream. After lighting a fire, we ate some of the food I had in my pack and then lay down to sleep. I was careful to ensure I was a respectable distance from Chayim, even though it meant feeling the chill of night.

The next morning, after a quick breakfast of fruit and soaked barley, we set off again. The miraculously entwined trees soon became visible. Chayim ran around them, touching them to check they were real. Unlike my last time here, the path was well-trodden, suggesting Shimon used the trees to traverse the river. One at a time, Chayim and I crossed. I tried not to look down at the gushing torrents below until I'd successfully made it to the other side of the Tigris.

We pressed on. Although there was no urgency, excitement hastened our steps. Before the day grew dark, we were into the hill country bordering the eastern mountains. These hills were far higher than those that housed our caves and they contained an incredible array of wildlife. Chayim began to leap about like a young lamb, pointing at all the creatures he had never seen before.

'I can't believe this place!' he said as he grabbed my hands and twirled me around in a circle. 'Why have I never been up here?' I laughed joyfully at him. He looked like a boy again as he marvelled and skipped, his thick floppy hair bouncing on the breeze. It warmed my heart, taking me back to a time before worry and trouble marred our lives, when Chayim had often been seen charging around the fields in excitement and wonder.

As we climbed further, the air grew lighter. The atmosphere emboldened me to address the issues at home. 'How have things been since the girls started working with us?'

'Oh, much better,' he replied. 'Dorit skulks around much of the time, but her idle chatter has decreased. I know that in time, she'll be grateful of the skills she's learnt. She's even offered to help Avigail more.'

'That's good. Although, I suppose it shall be hard for Dorit now Techiyah lives with Set?'

'Yes, I was unsure about that, but I had no decent reason to withhold my blessing. The couple are clearly besotted with each other and needed to wed sooner rather than later.' He tilted his mouth in a comedic grimace. 'However, I fear it has hit Dorit hard.'

'She always had her eye on Set for herself.'

'She did?' he asked in surprise.

'Did you never notice it? For several years she's been trying to get his attention. He was never interested. In fact, I think he disliked her efforts. Then, once affection grew between him and Techiyah, Dorit was sadly left behind. I fear she is heartbroken.'

'I didn't realise. She is my own daughter; how could I have been so blind? I should have spoken to her before I gave my consent to Set.'

'Perhaps that would have been wise, but I imagine it would have made little difference to the outcome. We cannot choose whom the children fall in love with any more than we can choose whom we love ourselves.'

Chayim looked at me intensely and I glanced away.

'So, what can we do to help Dorit feel better?' I continued, determined to change the subject.

'I fear the terrible triplets may take longer than most to grow up,' Chayim chuckled, the intensity leaving his face as swiftly as it had arrived. 'It'll be some time before they'll consider marriage. I shall speak to Dorit about what she most enjoys, to ensure she keeps occupied and happy. I can spend more time with her now that she's working with us.' He paused. 'I often think it's a shame there are not more of us around by now.'

His sentiments echoed mine. 'Do you ever wonder why Elohim chose to create just one man and one woman? I often think it would have been better if there were many of us so we could have chosen partners from different families.'

Chayim laughed. 'You think having more choice would have made us more content?'

I had never considered that. 'Perhaps not; perhaps it would have made things worse! Though I do wish I had not been left alone – and I fear the same fate for Dorit.' I scuffed my foot into the ground.

'I would have taken you as my wife,' Chayim exclaimed, turning and grasping my hands.

'No, Chayim.' I pulled them away. 'We did what was right. It was good for you to marry Avigail.'

'And yet we only had two children. I don't mean that I don't love them; I wouldn't change them for anything. Just that— I wonder whether Elohim hasn't blessed me because I made the wrong choice.'

'He has blessed you! He has blessed you with two daughters and a wife who loves you. Chayim, you must not think of me. You must love your wife.'

He stopped walking and sat on a boulder.

'I do love her; truly I do,' he said in a broken voice. 'It is just hard sometimes… We fight so often! She is still the same Avigail: strong-willed and resolute. I have always ceded to her and tried to make her happy, but she only seems to grow sadder as time passes. Her strong character hides behind a kind of… veil of mourning. It only comes out to scream at me when I misstep. I don't know what to do with her. I haven't been in her bed for several seasons. I try to hold her, but half the time she refuses me as if I have done something wrong – but I don't know what it is.'

Chayim sunk his head into his hands, and tears seeped through his fingers. What had happened to my joyous, carefree, brother? How long had there been a problem in their marriage I had been blind to?

I sat down next to him. 'It's interesting you mention mourning. I heard Ima speak that way once before. I wonder if it might relate to Avigail's trials in bearing children.' I didn't know how to voice my suspicions that it might also relate to Chayim's affection for me. 'Have you spoken to Abba about it?' I asked. 'I believe he has also experienced this kind of… distancing.'

'I haven't. I think I've been embarrassed about admitting anything is wrong. But it's a good idea; I shall try to do so on my return.' He looked up at me, his eyelids rimmed with red. 'I must confess, Awan, I wanted to come on this journey to get away for a while. I needed a break.'

'Then let's enjoy our time together and think no more of sadness,' I said, standing and pulling his arm. I could do nothing to shift his weight, but he took the hint and stood with me. I smoothed a tear from his cheek and we began walking again.

It didn't take long for our mood to lighten again as we surveyed our surroundings. The lowering sun threw beautiful colours across the sky. The great eagle was screeching and soaring up ahead. Rabbits lolloped over the grass around us, nibbling at shoots and guarding their young. When the eagle neared the earth, the rabbits dashed into their burrows. He swung majestically back into the sky then, righting himself, dived again a little further off, returning with something caught in his talons and flying towards the mountains.

Songbirds chorused in the trees, singing delightful melodies that enticed me to join them, offering praises to the Creator. In my heart, I prayed for Chayim and Avigail; aloud, I sang songs about the beauty of creation and the wonder of the mountains.

Before the mountains were born
Or You brought forth the world,
From everlasting to everlasting, You're Elohim.
You are radiant with light;
More majestic than the eagle.
A thousand years in Your sight
Are like the day that just went by.

Teach us to see what You see;
Give us eyes to know Your goodness.
Forgive our sin, that we may be
Covered in Your glorious mercy.
I cannot see what You see;
I do not understand the eagle.
Yet I will praise You as he does,
Maker of the mountains and the sea.

That night, we came across a cave just before darkness fell. Chayim caught some grasshoppers which we toasted over flames. Then we lay straight down to sleep, exhaustion claiming us.

CHAPTER 13

The following morning, I woke to find Chayim was already up and had taken the waterskins. He returned before long and I was thrilled to see a lopsided smile gracing his face once more.

'Good morning,' I said. 'You slept well?'

'Very well,' he replied, passing me a fig from our supplies and some water. We ate in companionable silence, occasionally smiling at each other.

'We should reach the mountain forest today,' I said as we packed our few things, which Chayim then slung over his back. As we walked, distant trees formed a dense covering over the first mountain ahead. The sky was so brightly blue we could barely look at it; it contrasted brilliantly with the greenery of the peaks.

While I was admiring the view, Chayim caught me off guard, tickling my waist and causing me to jump in the air. In revenge, I tossed grass at him, laughing aloud when the sticky stalks of some weeds caught in the unruly hair that always flopped over his face. He looked ridiculous with weeds for locks, dangling down his tunic. As he tried to pull them out, he got into more sticky mess.

Once free of the weeds, it was his turn for revenge. He threw them back at me but, fortunately, not much stuck to my braids. So, he resorted to chasing after me with a handful of grass, stuffing it down my tunic when he inevitably caught me. I squirmed, struggling to get all the itchy grass out as Chayim clutched his stomach, chortling in victory. When I fisted his arm, he pulled me close then knuckled my head.

'I am not one of the boys!' I giggled, trying to escape his clutches. He continued holding me, tickling me even more until I could barely breathe.

Abruptly, Chayim stopped and grasped my arm. 'Awan, quiet.'

Shocked by his altered manner, I followed his line of sight. Emerging from a thicket not far ahead padded a predator we had never seen before, moving silently on large, soft paws. Its rump reached to half of Chayim's height, and a short tail with a black tip curled behind it. Its coat was short and tan-coloured, with darker spots scattered all over. Its face was round and flatter than a wolf's, with a triangular nose in the centre and a mouth curled beneath in both directions. Most captivating were the two sharp fangs on either side of its jaw.

As it spotted us, the cat's pupils narrowed to black slits, and its jaw opened to reveal a row of sharply pointed teeth, bared in our direction. The dark tips of its ears flickered. It emitted a low growl, then lowered its chest towards the ground, raising its hind quarters.

The hairs on my arms prickled.

'Don't try to run,' Chayim whispered, 'we shall never beat it.' He slowly pushed me behind his back then grasped his sling and felt around for a stone.

Three tiny cubs followed their mother from the thicket. A chill ran through me.

'Try not to hurt her,' I whispered. 'She is defending her young.'

'I shall kill her if she hurts you,' he replied. Then he raised his sling as if warning the creature, who surely couldn't know what he meant by it. Unaware of the danger, her cubs bounded forward and wound around her legs. She softened her stance slightly, raising her shoulders as they slid beneath her, but didn't take her eyes off us.

I backed away, as slowly as possible, reaching for the spear strapped to my back. The creature's ears twitched again as she considered me. Chayim followed, keeping his sling at the ready and his eyes locked on hers. When she didn't react to his movement, I released the breath I'd been holding, hoping she'd decided to leave us alone.

As my hand relaxed down, one of the cubs ran forwards, straight towards us. The mother started and, within a flash, she was almost upon us, jumping in front of the cub. Her rear end spun as she pushed the young one back. When she turned her head, fear shone in her eyes. With ears pinned back, she bared her teeth again.

A stone hit her rump.

'What are you doing?' I hissed at Chayim.

'I must protect you,' he murmured.

The cat screeched in fury, twisting her body around and lifting her front paws with claws open. She was going to attack us! Her front legs lowered again, getting ready to pounce. My heart raced.

Another stone sank into her upper leg, making her skitter in pain.

Despising the thought, I abandoned self-defence and ran for the nearest tree. Chayim, however, stood firm. He primed the sling again, daring the creature to pursue me.

The muscles on the cat's rear twitched as I reached the tree. With my pulse racing, I climbed swiftly, certain of her attack. What would happen to Chayim? But as the next stone hit her, instead of leaping for Chayim, she picked up her cub by its scruff and scampered back towards the thicket. The other two cubs followed and soon were gone.

By now, I had climbed halfway up the tree. Chayim continued to watch the thicket, his muscles not relaxing until he was satisfied the cat would not return. Then he came to the bottom of the tree, holding up a hand to me. I shook my head. Grinning at my refusal, he placed his foot into a hold on the trunk and swung himself up with a couple of bounds.

'I hope you didn't injure her,' I whispered as he sat on a branch behind me. My voice was shaking, my displeasure clear.

'I don't think the stones went deep,' he replied. 'They were warning blows.'

'Yahweh Elohim, Creator of all,' I muttered, 'thank you for sparing our lives. Please do the same for that beautiful creature who was just trying to protect her young.'

Chayim voiced his agreement with my prayer. When I continued trembling, he shifted closer and wrapped a strong arm around me. I was still cross, but his arm felt good nonetheless.

'I'm sorry if I upset you,' he said, placing his head against mine. 'Forgive me?' He began to murmur comfort into my ear, just as he used to many years ago when we lay on my pallet during my nights of terror. My body softened into his as warmth returned to it.

We stayed there for some time until my heart had stopped racing. Then Chayim swung himself back to the ground and caught me as I jumped. Stumbling into his arms, I stayed there for a few more moments, forgiving him fully as I basked in the comfort they provided. When I looked up at him, he was studying my face, sorrow having settled on his features.

'What is it?' I asked.

'I've realised how much you mean to me; how much it would have broken me if you had been hurt.'

He put his hand behind my head and pulled me into his chest, then placed a kiss on my hair. After a while, he spoke again. 'Do you remember the conversation we had years ago, the day Abba announced I should marry you?'

'Of course, how could I forget?' My heart began to beat faster again as I stayed pressed to him. I could hear his heartbeat too, mirroring my own.

'I asked you then what love was – as if either of us had any real experience of it. Even then, I knew it was possible my feelings for you would be more enduring than those for Avigail. That you might be a better wife for me.'

'Chayim, please don't say such things,' I said, forcing myself to pull away. 'I thought you still loved Avigail?'

'I do! Oh, I do. And yet, I don't know how I can continue to live with her. She exasperates me. The feelings she produces now don't encourage goodness. They leave me incensed in a way that I never thought possible. Whereas you? I have never quarrelled with you; you bring out the best in me.' He stroked my face as my eyes wandered back to find his. 'You are beautiful in every way, Awan. It's not right that you're alone. Perhaps I chose wrongly. Perhaps I should have waited, and then I might have seen the truth more clearly.'

Sadness mingled with longing. 'It is too late now, Chayim. You made your choice. You made a home with Avigail.'

'And yet, being here with you and feeling all the difficulties melt away… It is you that feels like home to me, Awan.' He looked down at me. Eyes the colour of cut pine studied me under lighter brows that stopped just short of joining in the centre. Wisps of hair fell over those eyes and ruffled in the breeze. Solemnity closed his lips.

As I studied those lips, another voice whispered to me. I don't know where it came from; it was a voice I hadn't heard before. It sounded seductively sweet as it spoke the words I longed to hear:

You could kiss him now. Take this opportunity to see what it feels like.

My breath caught as I considered it.

You might never get another chance. You could be lonely forever if you don't.

I breathed in deeply. Chayim's familiar scent, mixed with a hint of grass, was now enticing as well as comforting.

It is just the two of you here. No one will ever know. What harm could it do?

I leaned towards Chayim until our foreheads were touching. He had never had the emotional power over me that Kayin had possessed. Yet his warmth was consoling, his compassion was tender, and his presence so affirming that I longed for a piece of him to be mine. As our skin touched and our noses drew together, my chest betrayed me and began to flutter like a butterfly was trapped inside it.

Just a little further and you can have what you've always wanted.

Chayim didn't seem to hear the voice, but his eyes closed and his mouth reduced the small gap remaining between us.

No.

This was a different voice, commanding and firm.

You shall not have him.

Shocked by the warring voices, I jumped back from Chayim. He looked at me quizzically then put his hand behind my head and pulled me closer.

No.

'Yahweh?' I whispered, recognising the second voice as one I had heard a long time ago. A burning warmth filled my body, like the day Yahweh had declared He was sufficient for me.

Chayim paused, his lips a fraction from mine. 'He is here?'

The burning ignited my soul and with it, truth dawned. 'He is everywhere,' I confirmed, taking a step backwards. 'If we go up to the mountains, He is there; if we go down to the depths, He will be there.' How foolish I'd been to think he'd left me, to think I had to find him.

Chayim released his hold on me and moved another step away. Alarm overtook his eyes as realisation dawned. They widened in terror.

'I thought I could have you and nobody would know,' I said, dropping my head in shame. 'But Yahweh knows. And it is wrong to have you.'

Chayim's eyebrows drew together and his eyes welled. He fell to his knees and planted his hands on the ground. 'Forgive me!' he cried to the heavens. 'I deserve nothing from you. I can only beg, please have mercy on me.' He sank his face into the dust as his body shook with the comprehension of his offence.

I knelt on the ground a short way from him and silently begged forgiveness. I did not feel the same level of fear. To me, Yahweh's presence was here as a beautiful warning rather than an act of condemnation. Yet, even so, I began to feel the shame of what I had done taking hold. I knew I had encouraged Chayim; I had delighted in spending time alone with him and drawing his attention for myself. I should have refused his company from the outset. I had cruelly betrayed Avigail by allowing him to come when I knew her fears. Fears that, it now seemed, were justified.

As we knelt in the dust, a pair of white doves flew down and stopped on the ground just in front of us. Showing unusual placidity, they didn't seem bothered by our presence. In due course, Chayim raised his head and considered the birds. He quietly retrieved some grain from his pack and scattered it on the ground beside him.

The doves drew nearer to peck the grain and, as they did so, he scooped them up with a swift movement. Holding them close to his face, he spoke to them gently. 'I am sorry. Your lives are no less valuable than my wretched one. Yet Yahweh has given you to us for a sacrifice.'

Chayim passed one of the birds to me, not daring to look me in the eye. As soon as he had a spare hand, he wrung the neck of the one he was holding before laying it tenderly on the ground. He held out his hand for the second bird, but I hesitated.

'We must,' Chayim said, with a zeal in his eyes that I had only seen before in Havel's. I couldn't deny that look; I knew it held divine instruction. I passed him the bird and after another swift movement, its life was forfeit.

We made a fire and burnt the doves on it. Watching the flames consume the stack of wood, we recalled together the words Havel had prayed to Elohim at that first sacrifice – words that had often since been part of our family chorus. As the smoke rose into the air and the tongues of flame devoured the birds, Chayim spoke to the Eternal One:

> O Mighty One, Yahweh Elohim,
>> You speak and summon the earth
>> From the rising of the sun to its setting!
> You determine the ways of the beasts,
>> And direct the course of the sun.
> The heavens declare Your righteousness,
>> For You alone are our judge!
> Forgive us our every inclination to evil!
> We have dishonoured Your holy name.
> In your mercy, save us, we pray,
>> For we call out to You in our distress.
> Accept this sacrifice of blood;
>> Deliver us for the sake of Your holy name.
> For You are a devouring fire,
>> You are a mighty whirlwind,
>> And we cannot stand before You.
> Yet still, we plead with You to be merciful.

As the flames licked the last of the birds, and the burning in my chest reduced to a comfortable level, I continued:

> We praise You for Your steadfast love.
> We praise You for the deliverance of Your
>> voice.

We praise You for Your faithfulness to Your
    children.
We plead with You to gather Your faithful ones
    As a mother gathers her cubs.
Bless us that we may honour You again
    Even though we deserve nothing.
Bless us according to Your great mercy.

When the fire had burnt out, I turned to Chayim and spoke to him. 'You must go home now, to your wife.'

'I know,' he replied. 'Are you coming back with me?'

'No. I'll stay away for a while, giving time for healing.'

'I'm sure that's not necessary.'

'Yes, it is. Avigail is not unaware of your conflict, Chayim. If I am not there, things will be better between you.'

He looked at me and searched my face, then he sighed. 'You are right, though I shall miss you.'

'And I you.'

We stood and cautiously embraced, then drew away from each other. Chayim handed me the pack of supplies. 'I will manage without,' he said, keeping only his water skin. Then he turned to leave. As I watched his back descend the hill we had recently climbed, the voice of Yahweh returned, speaking softly this time.

Daughter, it is time to find Kayin.

CHAPTER 14

Istood motionless. Had I heard Yahweh correctly? Did He really say it was time to find Kayin? He wanted me to locate my missing brother – the murderer? Then Kayin *was* still alive! But what about my feelings towards him? I had chosen to forgive him; I had tried to lay it down before Yahweh; but facing him again? Could I cope with that?

As I questioned the instruction, the warmth filling my chest burned intensely as if the very fire of God was pressing my heart onwards. I knew what I must do. But first, I ran after Chayim.

'Wait,' I shouted.

He turned towards me as I threw my arms around him, now unembarrassed. 'I don't know how long it will be before I see you again.'

'What do you mean?'

'I am going to find Kayin.'

'Kayin?' he asked, grasping my shoulders.

'Yahweh just told me to; I heard His voice as you walked away.'

'But why?'

'I don't know, but after what we have just done – after all my disobedience… I am listening to Yahweh this time, Chayim. I will obey, no matter what it costs.'

'How will you find Kayin? Do you know where he is?'

'No! But Yahweh will lead me. Please, Chayim, tell everyone I love them.'

Realisation dawned and displaced the confusion from his face. 'I cannot bear the thought of losing you, but I trust Yahweh.' He held a breath as he studied me. 'Be careful, Awan. When you find Kayin, he may not be as you remember him.' A single tear rolled down his cheek as he kissed mine gently. Then he turned to go.

'Chayim?'

'Yes?'

'I'm scared. What if I can't cope with seeing him? What if my heart cannot bear it? What if I am consumed by anger – or worse, desire – even after what he's done? I don't know whether it's better for him to be different or the same.'

Chayim took my hands and closed his eyes.

'Yahweh Elohim,' he prayed, 'quieten Awan's soul. Fill her with peace in Your goodness and love. May she know that You will never ask her to endure more than she can bear, and You will give her the strength to face all things.'

He released me with a small, encouraging smile, and continued walking back down the hill. I watched him go, aching to retrieve his protective embrace, but the burning in my chest kept my feet firmly planted.

As Chayim's jolty stride traversed the next hill, all my earthly comfort edged away. Chayim did not turn to look back at me. My heart began to weep as fear grew.

Once he'd disappeared from view the burning in my chest began to subside until it was once again a pleasant warmth. I picked up my pack, slung it over my shoulders and headed back to the trail that Havel and I had taken so long ago.

Fearing to think of Kayin just yet, I considered Dorit's words instead. I had been indignant – so sure she was wrong. Perhaps Yahweh's distance of late was due to my stubborn refusal to see my sin. For my actions that morning proved Dorit had been right.

I was as selfish as she was; I just hid it behind a veil of service. I still desired my comfort above the welfare of others. If I really cared, I would have spoken to Avigail before interfering with her daughters. The truth was, at least part of me had wanted to impress Chayim. I had cared for that more than for my sister.

I had come so close to taking what I desired, with barely a thought for what was right or wrong, nor the ramifications. I had listened to the deceptive whisper because it had spoken words I longed to hear.

Thank Yahweh that He stepped in to prevent us from going further. Not only that, but He provided the doves to make the blood sacrifice. In awe of His graciousness, I adapted the previous day's song as I walked, trying to accept the undeserved forgiveness I knew was mine through that offering.

> *Teach me to see what You see.*
> *Thank You for Your endless goodness.*
> *Forgive my sin that I may be*
> *Covered in Your glorious mercy.*

When the sun had lowered sufficiently that it was too late to turn back, I allowed my thoughts to return to Kayin and what it might be like to see him again. Although bitterness no longer consumed me, I had never reconciled his actions with the person I'd thought he was. Also, Chayim was right: he might be different now, even unrecognisable. Trepidation mounted as I anticipated seeing him again.

I came to a stream and stopped to drink the cool fresh water. When I dipped my feet into it, the sensation took me back to our river and my times with Kayin when we would paddle and talk, and he would help me with the laundry and fishing. I remembered the feel of his large hands holding mine; how he entwined his fingers with my own when we were alone.

I had feared the river until I associated it with Kayin, and it became a special place. I'd been so shy as a young girl. He'd encouraged me to emerge from my cocoon like a butterfly, and my confidence had grown. Was that confidence misplaced? Had it contributed to my selfishness; was it wrong?

I considered what I'd been taught about Elohim. He'd made the abundance of the earth, forming living things with His words; watching them flourish and conclusively calling them good. Havel had said this showed Yahweh was concerned not just for creation's objects but also their beauty and enrichment. Whilst He'd made all things, Elohim had only breathed His ruach into humankind. He wanted us to be image bearers: people who showed His character to all creation. Havel once told me,

> Yahweh is love, goodness, kindness, joy, peace and patience. He is complete in justice and mercy; He is always faithful and true. This is what we are supposed to replicate.

At the time, I had been young and had eagerly accepted those words. Recently, it felt impossible.

How could I ever hope to display Yahweh's goodness if my every thought was selfish? Yet, it remained true that Elohim did not want us just to survive but to live life fully. How could I achieve this? I closed my eyes, saw Havel and heard his words again:

> It's only possible if we acknowledge the Creator at the centre of creation. Trying to live without the source of life is like pouring water into a skin with holes in it. The water quickly runs out and is worthless. If I place myself at the centre of my life, instead of allowing Elohim to be there, then every act of worship or service will be fleeting, unsatisfying and ultimately fail to change my heart.

'Yahweh Elohim,' I prayed aloud, 'forgive me for placing myself in the centre of a life that was given by You, for You. I see that I have acted in ignorance, desiring what wasn't beneficial. I know that filling my life with anything – loved ones, children, or even hard work – will fail to satisfy unless you are at the centre. I desire to flourish, but on your terms. I crave blossoming into your image – that of goodness and faithfulness.

'Please, Yahweh, replace my leaking water-skin with something new. Rebirth my heart. Remind me daily how indebted I am to You for everything. Open my eyes to see the beauty of Your holiness and to desire You above all else.'

I stopped where I was and knelt on the ground. Then I sang again as a new song formed in my heart and sprang to my lips:

Why, soul, are you downcast? Why disturbed within?
Put your hope in Elohim; give all praise to Him.
You asked to hear Him. You asked for His voice.
Now that He has spoken, obey and rejoice.
I need Your help now; I need You to be
All that You have promised – sufficient for me.
I need You, Yahweh, so walk by my side,
And lead me onwards until I arrive.

I will bend my knees, and I shall bow my heart;
Yahweh, make me humble, in full, not in part.
I turn my life from the evil inside;
Cast it to the wind, for in You I'll abide.

I need Your help now; I need You to be
All that You have promised – sufficient for me.
I need You, Yahweh, so walk by my side,
And lead me onwards until I arrive.

I'm so prone to wander, so bind me as Yours;
Claim my life, seal it, with all that endures.
Supply me a heart that delights in the truth,
Not desiring another; choosing only You.

I need Your help now; I need You to be
All that You have promised – sufficient for me.
I need You, Yahweh, so walk by my side,
And lead me onwards until I arrive.

I reached the edge of the forest just before it got dark. Choosing a thicket to shelter in, I set about lighting a fire. As the night crept in the noises of wild animals grew louder and I couldn't help wishing Chayim was still with me. I pushed the thought aside. Hadn't I just been praying about filling my life with Elohim and not needing another? Oh, my wandering heart!

As the fire took hold, and its warmth washed over me, my nerves about the darkness calmed. I was able to eat a small amount of food from my pack and then lay down to rest. A deep peace settled on my body and mind as I closed my eyes.

'Thank you, Yahweh,' I whispered.

I followed the trail further into the mountains for the next few days. At first I recognised where I was going, but once I had passed the medicinal trees used to save Kayin's life, I no longer knew the way. I made sure to gather more pieces of those trees and put them in my pack in case of injury.

Once, I reached for some berries on a bush and felt a physical force staying my hand. I knew it was Elohim. Another time I found some mushrooms and toasted them over a fire. They were delicious; meaty in flavour. The next day I saw some that looked virtually identical and tried to collect them, but the force again stopped me. I didn't know how one could be good for food and the other not, but – despite my hunger – I chose to trust Elohim.

Occasionally at night, I saw a flicker of light, as if someone else had lit a fire in the distance. I wasn't sure what it meant: perhaps it was a trick of the night or the reflection of a star on a pool of water. I hoped it was Kayin – then I wouldn't have to go far to find him – but the fire seemed to be in the wrong direction.

I had no idea how long I'd be searching – Kayin could be anywhere. When the well-worn animal trail I had been following stopped, the thought of being in the wild for an extended time invaded my mind. There was no obvious way to turn. Hearing a trickle of water, I made my way towards it and found a stream meandering slowly down the mountain. For the next two days I followed that stream, enjoying walking downhill and hoping I wouldn't have to climb up again on the other side.

Eventually, the stream joined a river below. I supposed it was another tributary of the Tigris. Whilst the water itself didn't look challenging to cross, a steep bank, covered in dense woodland, climbed as far as the eye could see on the other side. This mountain might be bigger than the first. Indecision continued. It was only mid-afternoon but, as I simply didn't know which way to walk, I made camp, thinking I'd explore the area first.

I had run out of all the food I'd brought from home. Feeling at the bottom of an oak tree, I found a stash of acorns presumably hidden there by an animal. After cracking the acorns against some rocks to break the shells I set them to boil over a fire. Then I started looking around for clues as to where I might go next. Turning left, I went upstream, looking for areas which might allow a climb out of the valley.

I spied a bank that looked frequented by gigantic creatures. Footprints five times the size of mine were squelched into well-trodden mud, with markings suggesting enormous claws. I nervously glanced around, expecting a two-legged predator like the one that attacked the herd Havel and I had seen. I neither saw nor heard anything. Other footprints were longer, and more pointed, but had been smudged by the drag of low bodies along the ground.

Tiptoeing to the river's edge, I gingerly dipped my hand in the water. It was icy cold, befitting the cooler air here. I shivered at the thought of swimming through those waters.

Just then, I heard a branch snap in the forest behind me. Turning away from the river, I peered into the trees to see if anything was hiding in the shrub. The sun was behind the treetops, and the forest so dense I couldn't see far. Even so, sweat beaded on my lip. I reached for my spear.

A cry echoed from the woods. 'Awan, behind you!'

I was so startled to hear a human voice that I didn't register the instruction. Peering into the trees, I forced my arm up, wielded the spear behind my shoulder. Then a mighty splash sounded from the river. I spun around.

A huge tannin lunged, upside down, out of the water, its back twisting as it shifted its trajectory towards me. Its mouth gaped wide, revealing a vast set of jaws with double rows of needle-like teeth running along them. I should have moved instantly but my knees wobbled. Paralysed with fear, I stood gaping.

'Awan!'

A spear flew from the woods. The world slowed. I threw my body forwards, letting go of my own weapon, which splattered uselessly into the water as I tripped on a rock. The other spear hurtled past me and sank into the eye of the creature. Recoiling backwards, it twisted its spine again and crashed into the river.

As I hit the ground, pain seared through my shoulder, reaching my fingertips and shooting into my chest. There was a loud thud. Then everything went black.

CHAPTER 15

Intense heat seared my face. Where was I, and what had happened? I forced my eyes open. Tongues of fire licked close by, vaguely highlighting surroundings otherwise dark with night. I tried to sit, but pain pierced through my upper body, making me cry out.

'Awan, you're safe,' came a voice.

I tried to focus eyes too dry from the fire's heat. The blurry image of a man materialised with a voice I recognised, but couldn't quite place. 'Move me backwards?' I stuttered. 'Fire…hot.'

'Sorry,' the man said. After walking behind me, he put his hands under my chest and shuffled me back. The spear of pain shot deep into my shoulder, pulling another shriek from my lips.

'I'll help you up,' he said.

I leaned into him and gritted my teeth as he lifted me to sitting. Then he came round to face me. I blinked my eyes until they gained enough moisture that I could see who it was.

'Shimon.'

'Yes, and a good thing too. You were almost a tasty snack for that tannin.'

I groaned. 'What happened to my shoulder?'

'You landed on it when you fell. It looks strange. I tried to shift it back into place while you were sleeping, but I'm afraid I may have made it worse.'

I lightly probed around its unnatural shape. It throbbed down my arm and across my chest. Surely my arm was displaced from the joint?

Shimon sat casually on the other side of the fire and picked up a stick with cooked meat on the end. He peeled off scales with his teeth and spat them out before biting into the flesh.

'What is that?' I asked, horrified. 'Are you eating the tannin? Did you kill it?'

'Oh, not the big one,' he laughed. 'The one that wanted you for supper is the father of the river dwellers. He's a huge beast but doesn't compare in skill to the two legs – he's too slow. Even you got out of his way.'

Remembering the fall, I pressed a hand gingerly to my head, but contact increased the pain and my palm came away sticky with blood. I tried to think how Shimon was even here as recollections of the incident swam in my mind.

Shimon was still talking. 'I've seen him, sitting on that bank and basking in the sun, as if he owns the whole river. No, this,' he waved the stick at me, 'isn't he. He sank back into the water, taking my spear with him.'

Watching Shimon ripping at more meat made my stomach churn. 'Next time I see you, you owe me a spear,' he said with his mouth full. After choking a little on his own laughter, Shimon cleared his throat. 'This was a young tannin. I had hunted it down shortly before I found you.'

'Is it safe to eat?' I asked, swallowing down the rising bile. 'I thought Yahweh said—'

'Oh, I wouldn't worry about that. I've been eating whatever I can hunt for ages and I'm none the worse for it.'

He swept a hand across his broad chest, which he puffed out to show his bulging muscles. His top half was bare, except for a smattering of curly, black chest hair. I stretched my lips into a smile, though I took no pleasure in what he said. It seemed our family worship wasn't the only thing my brother had abandoned.

'If you won't eat this, then you'd better have your pitiful acorns,' he said, passing me my clay bowl containing the nuts which, having long since boiled dry, appeared to have been roasted in the fire. 'I finished cooking them for you.'

'Thank you,' I said gratefully, putting them down and feeling for my water skin. My shoulder throbbed mercilessly as I raised the skin to my lips but as the liquid slid down my throat, my stomach settled.

'How did you find me?' I asked.

Shimon waved a hand. 'Pure chance. I've been tracking a new species in this forest recently. Egg layers – ones that might suit Channah's little farm.'

'You must be away from home a lot. Is Channah not likely to have a child soon?' I asked, peeling the acorn and chewing the bitterness beneath.

Shimon's face clouded over. 'No, and I'd rather not speak about it.'

I studied my bowl, regretting my words.

Then Shimon seemed to change his mind. 'I don't know why she hasn't conceived. She used to refuse me, saying she loved me only as her twin and not in another way. Then, one day, she abruptly had a change of heart, saying she would marry me. I thought she might relax a bit once we were away from the family, but since we've been in the cave, she keeps complaining of pains where a baby should be. Although her cycles sometimes cease, she never seems to expand. Then the blood returns.'

I wasn't sure what to say, having no experience of childbearing. 'Have you brought your trouble to Elohim?' I tentatively asked.

'What would He care? He abandoned us long ago,' Shimon scoffed, poking at the fire with his stick. The remaining scaly flesh caught aflame and acrid-smelling smoke reached my nostrils.

'Why would you say that?' I asked, partly to distract myself from the sickening stench and my own sickening pain.

Without looking up, Shimon answered, 'Havel. Avigail. Channah. Isn't it obvious?'

His words cut my heart. My head felt too heavy for deep conversation, but I didn't want to waste this rare opportunity with Shimon. 'I can see you no longer believe in Yahweh's goodness,' I responded. 'I have struggled with it too. Yet, I have chosen to trust Him despite our trials. I shall pray for you both: that Channah's body may be healed and that you shall have a child.'

Shimon huffed and continued to stare into the fire. We sat in silence until, without apparent reason, Shimon seemed to recover from his sullenness and considered me again.

'What brings you this far out into the woods, anyway? I thought you'd have turned back by now. And where is Chayim? Has he abandoned you already?'

As Shimon spoke, there was a glint in his eye – not of mischief, but something else. I knew that Elohim was Truth, and my parents had taught me never to lie, yet something about Shimon's face gave me pause. He had just been honest with me so I wanted to trust him. Yet to tell him what had transpired between Chayim and me could endanger Chayim's marriage, and I couldn't risk that.

As for the reason I'd travelled this far? A knot deep in my gut told me that telling Shimon about Kayin was a bad idea. He had never liked his oldest brother. The only words I'd ever heard from his lips regarding Kayin showed disdain and contempt.

I chose my answer carefully, trying to steer a course between truth and secrecy. 'Chayim needed to return to his family and the flax harvest. I wasn't ready to go home yet – I've been longing to spend more time in the wild.'

Shimon stared at me for a few moments, piercing through my half-truths, before shrugging and saying, 'Well, that longing almost got you eaten. Perhaps I should abandon my hunt and escort you home.'

'No,' I cried, too quickly. 'That is to say, I am still enjoying being alone. I came here to spend time with Elohim, knowing He would protect me. And so far He has. I am truly grateful, Shimon, for your kind offer, but I wish to stay longer.'

He narrowed his eyes and continued watching my face, willing me to reveal the truth. I could feel my cheeks warming.

'What about your shoulder?' he asked, pointing at it with what remained of his stick. A good point. 'I'd pray for you, but I don't think it would do much good,' he smirked. I was grateful for the change in his expression and chuckled with him, albeit insincerely.

I placed the hand from my good arm onto my dislocated shoulder. Closing my eyes, I braced for discomfort as I felt deeper into the joint. I began mumbling words of prayer, keeping my voice low enough that Shimon couldn't make them out. Would Yahweh listen to me now I had withheld the truth from my brother? Was being secretive to protect others acceptable, or should I have confessed and trusted Him with the consequences?

'Yahweh Elohim, forgive my wretchedness,' I whispered. 'Please take pity and heal me from pain so I may do Your will for the glory of Your name.' The discomfort slowly eased as tingling descended on my shoulder. Simultaneously, my head cleared. I tried to move my arm but couldn't. Yet, Elohim had answered my exact request and healed me from the pain. I smiled, opened my eyes and looked up at my brother.

'It's still broken,' said Shimon.

'Yes, but the pain is gone,' I countered.

He looked unconvinced, 'You won't be much use in the wild with one arm. And you've a gash on your head.'

I chuckled back at him, 'I'm not much use in the wild anyway! Although, I have some of the medicinal tree in my pack. Would you make me a poultice and bind my arm?'

'Fair enough,' he said, holding up his hands. 'I'll make your poultice! But if you insist on staying out here on your own and getting yourself killed, it's not my fault. As Elohim is my witness, I tried.'

'I absolve you of any responsibility, Shimon. You have saved me once and are free to leave me with a clean conscience.'

After he had treated my wound and bound my arm to my chest with my spare tunic, Shimon gathered leaves and rushes to make a bed. Then he refuelled the fire and we settled down to sleep.

The morning chorus woke me. It was louder here, where birds inhabited the dense concentration of trees, enjoying the gradual filtering of sunlight through the foliage. I tried to push myself up, which was surprisingly tricky on a bed of leaves with one good arm. My body was stiff from the cold and ached generally from my fall, but the pain in my dislodged shoulder remained miraculously absent. Shimon's eyes flickered open as soon as I moved; he was accustomed to sleeping with his ears tuned to danger.

I stood and started gathering the things scattered around. Shimon fetched water from the stream, warning me not to attempt getting any from the tannin's river. I longed to ask him how I could cross the river without getting eaten and if he knew the way to the forest's edge. Yet, I didn't want to risk more questions about the trajectory of my journey or how far I intended to go.

Once the area was clear and my pack restored to my good shoulder, we said our goodbyes.

'I suppose I can't change your mind about coming back with me?' Shimon asked.

'Thank you, but no,' I replied. I leaned in to embrace him, perhaps for the last time.

'Ok, big sister,' he said, 'I hope you make it out alive.' And with that, he was gone, disappearing silently into the woods.

I was alone again and still had no idea where I was going. Added to which, I'd forgotten to ask Shimon if he had a spare weapon, so I was now defenceless. Singing my morning song, I asked Elohim for guidance.

Whilst still in prayer, I heard the noise of heavy footfall and breathing coming from the vicinity of the stream. A large, black bear came into view, descending from a tree. It began striding towards me, careless at first. I slowly lowered behind the boulder I'd been perching on, but the movement attracted the creature's attention, and she met my eye.

We froze, pondering each other, each considering if the other might be a threat. Then, promptly, she decided. Charging at an incredible speed, the bear thundered her colossal legs in my direction. I ran.

I darted past the nearby trees, knowing she could climb better than I, and approached the riverbank. There I could largely avoid low branches, but risked the tanninim. Being slight and nimble, I moved swiftly, hopping over obstacles and dodging the remaining trees. The bear crashed behind me, tearing down the barriers in her way. Despite my head-start, she was getting closer.

A claw swiped at my back; she just missed. I stumbled and thought this might be the end but, when no blow came, sprang forwards again. Risking a backwards glance, I saw a tannin rising from the river, threatening the bear, gnashing at her legs. He drove her back from the shoreline, distracting her and delaying her pursuit. I kept running downhill, but it wasn't long before she found a way around and sprung from a clump of trees to my right.

My chest was burning, my legs shook and the pack on my good shoulder dug painfully into my flesh. The one thing keeping me going was my racing heart. All the same, I knew I was slowing down and the bear was not. Would I die out here alone, moments after leaving the safety of my brother's company?

I could run no further. I stopped, gasping, as a fallen tree came into view, traversing the river's width mere paces in front of me. Having no time to consider if it was safe, I stepped onto the trunk and leaped across it in single strides. The bear skidded to a halt, hesitating at the water's edge.

Greeting me on the far side was an opening in the trees where the trunk had fallen. I tucked in behind an adjacent pine and peered around it. The bear was staring in my direction but, mindful of the tannin, she had not yet attempted the river.

I breathed deeply, praying she would give up the chase, for I could run no further. Then she gave a final growl, showing me the full measure of her teeth, before retreating the way we'd come.

I had made it to the other side of the river. It had taken a near-death experience, but Yahweh had once again answered my prayers in the most unexpected way.

Once I'd regained some energy, I tried scrambling a little way up a huge tree to get a view of where I was. I was grateful for my experience fetching nuts, which usually required climbing one-handed with a basket tucked under the other arm. Even so, my endeavours now proved pointless: the forest was so thick that the higher I got, the less I saw. It was almost impossible to make out anything on the forest floor or to see any distinctive landmarks.

Eventually, I gave up, exhausted. Settling in a nook part way up the tree, I laid my head on my pack and closed my eyes for a few moments of rest.

I'm unsure whether I fell asleep during that time or had a vision whilst still awake, but I had barely settled before a bright light shone behind my eyelids, like I was staring directly into the sun.

The forest came into view, but it was nothing like what I had seen from my vantage point in the tree. On the contrary, I felt like the great eagle soaring above the mountains. I simultaneously saw the tallest mountain peak, the ends of the earth in the distance, and the tiniest rodent running in the grass below.

Firstly, I recognised the edge of the hill country and the mountain I had just crossed. Then the vision zoomed in and I saw the great bear sniffing at the spent fire and debris of last night's camp. My sight then swept over the river, through the trees, and found a pathway – one made not by man but by a herd of behemoths. The path ran around my present mountain and down the other side until it reached a spring where multiple footprints congealed in the mud surrounding a deep pool of water.

A smaller animal track was visible on the other side of the pool. This path was harder to follow, yet I was shown specific landmarks: a tree with a split trunk on the left, another stream cascading over mossy stones, a cave with ivy growing over it, among others. Eventually, the trail led out of the woods, down a rocky mountainside and onto a plain.

My view swept wide, encapsulating the open plain which stretched to the horizon. I was drawn to a lake full of deep, blue water and surrounded by luscious trees. From the lake ran several streams and, beside one, I saw a man's tall and muscular figure. His back was to me, and his hair was tied in a loose bundle of matted strands that fell to his waist. Though I could not see his face, everything about his figure was recognisable.

Yahweh had shown me how to find Kayin.

CHAPTER 16

The vision cleared and I sat up. I now had a route in my head; I just had to remember it whilst avoiding creatures baying for my blood. Firstly, I had to seek out the behemoth trail. How hard could it be to find something so big? And yet, the density of the forest prevented me from seeing more than a few strides ahead. I tuned my ears to listen for behemoth cries. Far in the distance, I thought I heard something, so I started in that direction, collecting food along the way. I was famished.

It was dark long before I reached the trail. I decided not to light a fire as I dared not stay out in the open after the incident with the bear. Instead, I hunted around for a thicket I could crawl inside. Despite feeling cold and nervous, I was exhausted from the long day of uphill hiking, and it wasn't long before I drifted into an uneasy sleep.

A noise woke me during the night. A small creature with a spiky back ran through the bush ahead. Watching it, I noticed a light visible through the leaves of the thicket. It was no natural light, but rather like a shimmering cloud. I stared into it and could just make out the outline of a person sitting on the ground with his back to me. In his hand he held an enormous sword. The man was still, but I wavered in fear, glancing around. The light encircled the area in which I'd been sleeping.

Years ago, Ima had told me about the banishment from Eden and the heavenly being with the flaming sword that guarded the way to the tree of life. Could this be him? She had spoken in terror of the blade. Yet, as I watched, my fear dissipated. For it seemed to me that this being, if he was indeed the same, embodied both the will and the mercy of Elohim. Whilst Elohim could not permit imperfect people to enter His eternal paradise, He had not abandoned us to live our mortal lives alone. Even now, this spirit being protected me. Yahweh was watching over me. I fell back into a peaceful, dreamless sleep.

The behemoths woke before me the next day, their tremendous calls rousing me from slumber. That morning, it was easy to follow the noise. When it was almost unbearably loud, I happened upon the trail and nearly ran into the midst of them. They were stomping through the woods, unconcerned with the chaos they left behind, destroying all shoots that dared to attempt growth. Raising their huge necks to the leaves of the tallest trees, their comparatively small mouths grazed as they lumbered along. I slipped back into a shrub and watched as they passed by on the trail they had created.

I was just about to step onto the path when several smaller creatures came into view, bringing up the rear of the herd. They ran on two legs behind the behemoths, living in the safety of giant shadows. Some were also plant-eaters with flat mouths and horns along their heads or tails. Others looked like small predators. Often these would stop to snatch something up from the sides of the trail: a small bird or passing rodent. There might be squawks of protest from other members of this strange herd or the prey themselves.

I waited until I was sure the way was clear, then snuck behind them. I spent the entire day following the herd along the uneven route around the mountain. Just before nightfall, a small stream crossed the path, so I took the chance to refill my water skins. There, the sweet scent of almond blossom reminded me of home. The delicate pink flowers always came out when the flax was ready. Chayim had probably made it back just in time.

I could hear the herd in the distance, carrying on their march in the dark, and I wondered at what point they would stop to rest. After scraping together a few edible leaves and stalks to take the edge off my gnawing stomach, I found an area of boulders, squeezed into a mossy groove in their midst, and slept the night there.

The following day I was alone on the Behemoth trail, and it passed without event. I took the opportunity to gather as much food as possible. I dared to make a small fire that night, boiling roots and toasting pine nuts I'd shaken from gathered cones. By now, my head wound was healing well, but my arm was frustrating me, having become very itchy under its tight wrap. Placing my hands into the joint again, I prayed for healing. Nothing happened. Fortunately, Shimon had left some poultice in my clay pot which relieved the itch when I rubbed it under the wrap.

The next day, others joined me. I had to make myself scarce at one point as large, four-legged creatures with plates running down their backs and spikes on their tails trundled along the path. Beyond a mild curiosity, they didn't seem concerned with me, but I didn't want to be swiped by one of those spikes.

Other creatures appeared as the day wore on and, eventually, I realised why the trail was getting so busy: we were nearing the spring-fed watering hole.

The cacophony of animal noises could be heard long before I saw the water. Deciding it would be safest, I clambered into a tree which afforded a good view. The spring bubbled up between boulders protruding from the side of the mountain. Most of the water trickled into the pool below but some spurted out, creating a crescent moon over the rocks. In the sunlight, a myriad of colours glimmered over the water's surface, creating a light display for the animals.

A great variety of creatures had come seeking respite from their trudge along the mountain trail. One massive behemoth stood in the centre of the pool, his neck and tail almost reaching either end as he drank from the deepest water below the spring. Not just reptiles were here either: various birds and mammals assembled on the other side of the water. I recognised several from the descriptions my father had given me of the animals he'd named in the Garden. Several deer were there – similar to those that frequented the woods near home – along with large, grey creatures that waded in the water, sifting through the reeds with tusks.

I remained in that tree until dusk settled in. As the creatures gradually withdrew from the watering hole, I slid down and tentatively made my way to the water's edge then scrambled up the rocks until I reached the crescent spring.

Heat steamed from the water. I hadn't realised these were hot springs. With the sudden urge to duck my head under, I did so and immediately relished its soothing warmth on my neglected scalp. Unable to resist the opportunity to bathe, I attempted to strip off my tunic but the binding prevented me.

Sighing, I slid closer to the water's edge and dipped my feet in the pool instead. It was almost as warm as the crescent spring and felt glorious around my chapped heels.

Relaxing into liberation, verse sprang readily to my lips, and I murmured over the water.

My soul magnifies Elohim,
My spirit rejoices in Yahweh, my Saviour.
He stretches out the heavens with His hand,
And commands the springs to sprout water.

Like an ant on His fingertips
He sets in place the mighty behemoth.
He commands the mountains to grow up,
And provides all creatures with enough.

I cried to Yahweh, my Elohim;
He sent a bear to decide my way.
I surrendered to Yahweh Almighty;
A sword and spirit did obey.

Yahweh, Yahweh, who is like you:
Awesome in power; mighty in deed?
Yahweh, Yahweh, who is like my Elohim:
Boundless in mercy, supplying all I need?

Dawn started with a scuffle. I woke to find a small monkey ruffling through my pack, with gangly arms and legs, beady black eyes and a long tail curled up behind it. It was removing everything and trying it for taste. A beard of berry juice surrounded its lips, and its hands were full of nuts. My discarded clay pot was on the ground beside the burnt-out fire.

'No,' I shouted, waving my arms at the monkey. It didn't move but opened its mouth wide, displaying my breakfast between its teeth. Grabbing a stick from the ground, I poked it in the scavenger's direction. 'Go away.'

It hooted in laughter then danced – were my actions no more threatening than a dance? I stood up and shook myself off, then, retrieving my bag, I shoved my things back inside. The monkey started launching bits of nut towards me.

'Stop that,' I muttered as a pistachio shell hit my cheek. He whooped and swung into the tree but continued. I drew myself up to my full height, imagining one of my brothers in an imposing stance. 'Hand them over!'

The monkey chuckled. Sighing, I retrieved my clay bowl from the ground and finished packing.

Then I heard the call of a tannin: a screech I recognised as a giant predator. The monkey recognised it too. Dropping the remaining nuts, it swung into the trees and disappeared. The beast was headed this way.

I thought of the vision and the small path I had to find next. Remembering it was on the other bank, I swung my pack onto my back and clambered onto the rocks. I was grateful they were broad and firm unlike the cliff faces near our home, which I would never have managed to climb with one hand.

As I dipped beneath the crescent of water, and a few droplets splattered my face, a solitary killer careered into view, his gigantic head emerging first from the trees. This creature was different from the one

I'd seen as a young woman. I held my breath and ducked behind a boulder. One side of my face remained in view.

No others came to water with him. They all knew to wait for his retreat before attempting their own refreshment.

As he waded into the water, he lifted his head and opened his jaws. His side teeth were each the same span as my hand. His scaly snout was long, as was the enormous sail that dominated his back. I couldn't fathom the purpose of his tiny, clawed hands, yet I knew Elohim had designed each kind with perfect function and adaptability to their environment.

After a few glugs of water, the beast ventured deeper. I stayed completely still, trying to calm my breathing and praying he wouldn't spot me. As he took another step forwards, the ripples lapped at his thighs. His tiny eyes searched the silence.

CHAPTER 17

The monster lunged. His neck scooped into the water, catching a massive fish. The prey was bigger than me, with a spear-like mouth and two-pronged tail, but he shook it in his jaws, easily killing it. I hid my face from the gore, breathing a sigh of relief that I hadn't gone swimming the previous night.

Chatter came from the other side of the pool: the monkeys felt safe again. Then a colossal tail swept round, almost knocking the boulder I stood behind, as the beast turned and stomped up the bank.

When he no longer faced me, I dared to breathe. Carefully navigating the slippery rocks, I crept towards the chatter on the other side of the pool. When I reached some overhanging branches, I grasped one gratefully and tiptoed the rest of the way.

By the time my feet squelched onto the bank, the two-legged tannin had ascended the opposite one and was feasting contentedly. I sank into the cover of a thicket.

Finding an animal trail consistent with the one in the vision took me a little while, but it was easy to follow once found. As I wandered the rest of that day, I recognised several signs confirming I was on the right path.

Though it was early in the year, the trees differed from those on the first mountain. They were populated with seeds, nuts and fruit ripe for harvest. Multicoloured berries peeped out among the leaves, tempting a variety of wildlife. Monkeys swung about hooting, and brightly adorned birds flew between branches and squawked. There was never a quiet moment in this jungle.

Before dark, I had found the stream and cave I'd seen in the vision. The following morning, I didn't continue walking but rested, realising I must have missed Shabbat at some point in my journey.

I enjoyed the small piece of paradise so much that I decided to stay awhile. The plentiful sustenance and lack of predators meant I could enjoy time with Yahweh in relative comfort and safety. I knew I must prepare my heart to see Kayin again.

One night, as I slept in the cave, I woke in a fit of shivers. The place on my arm where Kayin grabbed me years ago throbbed – I'd been dreaming of it. At the time, I'd only felt a sliver of fear, but, faced with seeing him again, and knowing what he was capable of, I couldn't shake my distress away. I sat, cuddling my legs in the suffocating darkness, while fear morphed into terror. What if Kayin hurt me? What if he was filled with violence he couldn't control? I had no assurance he would be pleased to see me – he might treat me as he had treated Havel.

I cried out as distrust of Kayin led to mistrust in Yahweh's calling. A tiny flicker of light broke through, with the words:

Peace. Be still.

'How? How can I be still when my body convulses at the thought of seeing him?' I asked.

I will look after you.

'Like You looked after Havel?' I cried. Then I trembled and threw my face to the ground. 'Oh, my Elohim, my Yahweh, forgive me, forgive me… I should not have shouted at You.'

Do not fear. I am with you. Trust me.

It was hard to trust Him; hard to shake the trembling. I spent the rest of that night in indecision: sitting in the cave's entrance with my pack on my shoulders, almost ready to turn around and go home.

I tried to picture the details of Kayin's face, determined to consider the good rather than the evil. After so many seasons his image had grown hazy. In contrast, the features that intermittently haunted my dreams – those of my dead brother – remained clear. When I tried to place a face on the broad shoulders from the vision, Havel's lifeless one appeared rather than Kayin's. This brought on tears as fresh as the day I'd found Havel in the thorns.

How could I hope to spend time with Kayin if all I saw when I looked at him was Havel? Would I ever be able to forget what he did? Part of me longed to know the truth of what had transpired between them on that terrible day. My mind had conjured so many scenarios that I couldn't discern reality from falsehood. Perhaps hearing the truth from Kayin – having him fill in the details of it – would clarify my thoughts and enable me to move on.

Would Kayin be willing to speak of it, though? How would his decades of loneliness have changed him? How had Elohim dealt with him during this time? Would Elohim's justice – the same that my parents had endured in their banishment from the Garden – have punished him for his sin against my dear brother? Did I want that? Only this much was clear – Elohim had neither killed nor forgotten Kayin. For I'd been summoned to find him.

For what – what did Yahweh require of me? Was it for my benefit, or Kayin's, or both? Was I to take him home or leave him in the wild?

All these questions and more I wrestled with. Yet I did not turn back. For I desperately wanted to trust Yahweh, even if my inmost being screamed in turmoil. As morning dawned and the light streamed into the cave, hope filled my heart again.

For several nights I experienced the same. Yahweh did not give me any fresh revelation. He did not give me any other visions. I simply felt Him in my heart, where He whispered repeatedly,

Trust me.

After almost two weeks in the luscious forest, I knew I must leave the mountains for the plain. I collected as much food into my pack as possible then began the rocky descent down the slopes. I lost my grip and slid down at places, landing on my backside on the stones and berating my useless arm. A family of mountain goats watched my journey. They looked amused as if wondering why I was incapable of balancing. Their kids galloped over the rocks with ease, putting me to shame.

About halfway down the mountainside, I caught sight of a glimmer of water far off. I adjusted my route in the direction of the lake. No doubt I wouldn't be able to see it at the bottom and walking slightly off course could mean I missed it entirely.

I reached the foot of the mountain as the sun was setting in the sky. The back of my legs ached. There was a dappling of tree cover, but I could see no water and my skins were almost empty. That night I ate fruit and went without a fire to prevent a parched tongue.

In the morning, I looked towards the arid plain and saw a gazelle coming my way, panting like she hadn't seen water for some time. I realised I must find some before continuing, and the best way to do that was to follow the gazelle.

After she passed me, I rose and tiptoed as quietly as possible some paces behind her. She twitched her ears, conscious of my movement but too exhausted to take flight. I followed her for some time around the foot of the mountain.

My instincts proved correct. Eventually, I heard the trickle of water. There wasn't enough current for the brook to continue along the dry plain, so it pooled between mossy rocks. I allowed the gazelle to drink her fill first then, when she had moved on, held my waterskins beneath the trickle. Then I dipped my mouth in and drank as much as I could stomach, hoping it would sustain me for the long walk ahead. Finally, I turned back the way I had come, retracing my steps until I reached the place I had slept, hoping from there I'd be heading towards the lake.

And so began my journey onto the arid plain. The earth was dust with no moisture to hold it down. Whenever a gust of wind blew, fine sand would rise, and I had to cover my eyes and nose. The sun's rays created a hazy mist over the earth and I sometimes fancied I saw something in the distance: a tree, an animal, or even a man. Then moments later, it would be gone.

Halfway through the second day, I could make out a line of trees far in the distance. My heart soared; where trees stood there must be water. I tried to focus my dry eyes on that line of trees and progressed towards it. It didn't disappear.

The sun set before I reached the trees. I pressed my exhausted body on in the darkness, praying I wouldn't go off course. The moon was scarcely a crescent, yet it was enough to highlight the tallest leaves and reassure me I was headed the correct way.

I knew I had been successful when the air changed. Moisture tickled my tongue. Then I heard the rustle of leaves in the wind and I was suddenly amongst the trees, enveloped by several comforting trunks. I leaned against one and slid to the ground. Then I shook my waterskin so the final droplets fell into my mouth. It would have to be enough for tonight; I could walk no further.

Upon opening my eyes the following day, I was greeted by a haven of life in the wilderness. Birds sang above my head, grass covered the ground and various desert mammals were hopping within reach of where I sat, still upright against the tree. I had fallen asleep without even lying down, so great had been my exhaustion. To my right I saw the water – a shimmering stretch of azure as far as the eye could see.

I stood and hobbled towards it, unable to resist its allure as my tongue stuck to the roof of my mouth. Tall birds were wading in the water, some standing on one leg. Smaller birds swam on its surface, occasionally ducking their heads to search for food in the weeds below. I knelt at the lake's edge and cupped the water in my hands, lapping it up. It tasted bitter – nothing like the freshness of the mountain streams – but I cared not.

With my thirst satisfied, I sat in the shade and watched the animals. Many were converging around the shores of the lake. Like the spring in the mountains, each flock or herd knew its place, taking it in turns to drink and then moving away from the edge. There was the occasional squabble if someone didn't follow the rules, but mostly order and interdependence between these animals designed with different attributes.

Whilst the vast majority were plant eaters, it became clear that the lake also housed several predators. Sometimes jaws emerged from the water to take an unsuspecting creature. Then a whole herd might jump back and run further around the shore.

When my legs had stopped trembling, I wandered around, taking the left bank and looking for streams resembling the one I'd seen in the vision. I came upon a group of trees rich with sizeable round, brown fruit, growing in bunches high above my head. There was no way I could climb to them.

Monkeys, though, were happily swinging in those trees. When they came across a fruit, they pulled it from the bunch and threw it to the ground. Then they swung down, turned the hard shells in their hands and, on finding a crack from the impact of the fall, they put their lips to it, sucking out something inside. After that, they vigorously smashed the fruit against rocks until the outer skin broke enough to be peeled away, revealing softer skin beneath.

I waited until several fruit fell at once, then snatched one up. A chorus of protest followed me as I ran away with it, feeling a little guilty for stealing. Once I found a secluded spot, I copied the monkeys' tactics, finding inside sweet, thirst-quenching milk.

Then I broke it open to discover white flesh. After eating half, I put the rest in my pack for another meal.

I didn't find the stream I was looking for that day, but I didn't mind. I was content to dwell on the shores of the lake a bit longer. My anticipation about meeting Kayin had been rising with every movement of the sun, and I found it particularly hard to sleep that night, knowing how soon I might see him again. When I did drift off, I dreamt about the day of his rejected sacrifice. I kept seeing his face as he lit that fire over and over; then ran from our home, never to return.

The next morning, I found the stream. A flock of large birds had been encamped around it, obscuring my vision. When I approached, they took flight as one, making an incredible noise as they lifted into the air. Once cleared of birds, I immediately recognised the stream and made my way to it. By its shores, I found something else—human footprints.

They were baked into the earth on slightly higher ground where the water couldn't wash them away. I placed my foot inside one of the prints. The fact these remained, despite the presence of so many beasts and birds, convinced me that Kayin had been this way not long before. The churning in my stomach intensified.

I followed the wide stream on its northern course for the rest of that day. I kept glancing around, expecting to see Kayin somewhere, yet he didn't appear. Whenever I heard an animal, I nearly jumped out of my skin.

Into the afternoon, the landscape began to change, becoming hilly. As I ascended the hills, the stream narrowed and flowed more swiftly. These hills were still reasonably barren – nothing like the luscious green of the mountains – yet life teemed along the banks.

It occurred to me that I should expect to see cultivated crops wherever my brother lived, for he was a skilled farmer. Yet I couldn't see anything resembling cultivation from where I stood – just a few wildflowers, patches of reeds and other plants I didn't recognise.

As the sun sank in the sky, I came across a sheltered glade and, confused as to why I hadn't yet found Kayin, decided I'd better settle down for the night again. The twist in my stomach was so intense that I struggled to get comfortable. The temptation to turn about and run home was immense. I spoke to Yahweh and begged Him for strength.

Sleep largely evaded me that night. When I did doze, dreams of Kayin kept waking me. I was immediately alert each time, looking about, expecting to see him watching me. But he was not there.

CHAPTER 18

At dawn, I spent some time in song, trying to settle my stomach. I couldn't bear the thought of eating but, I had a drink of fresh water then began to walk again, higher into the hill country. This became increasingly green as I travelled further from my family.

At the highest point of the sun, I stopped to rest under the shade of a terebinth tree, glad to come across something familiar. I sat with my back to the stream looking out over a broad meadow that swept down into a valley.

I was closing my eyes against the brightness of the sunshine when a small deer – no taller than a sheep – darted into the meadow. Several short antlers were on its head with a horn in the centre. The deer was quite far in the distance but, from how it was fleeing, I knew something chased it. I braced myself for another predator.

Then I saw him. A tall, muscular man – spear in hand – bounded behind the deer, keeping up with its pace. His hair ran all the way down his back, just as I had seen in my vision, and his beard was long and unkempt. I could make out no other features from this distance, yet I knew from the slight limp that it was Kayin.

A paralysis of indecision took over. Love and hate, longing and disgust mingled in uncertainty. As I pivoted between options, the spear hit its mark. It sank into the deer's hide, sending the creature tumbling. Kayin ran to her and quickly put her out of her misery.

Then, the unexpected happened.

Another figure bolted into view from the trees. Though slighter in build, and darker skinned, the second man was dressed the same – with a bare chest and deerskin loincloth. Hurtling straight towards Kayin, he raised a spear of his own.

Kayin, busy hauling the deer onto his back, didn't see the second man. But I instantly knew his identity and intention. I cried out, but my voice flew away on the wind and neither man heard it. Fear no longer being an option, I jumped up and sprinted downhill. When I was halfway, the second spear was launched.

'No!' I screamed, as it flew towards the man I'd come all this way to see. Both heard me this time. Kayin spun towards my shout just in time. The spear pierced the flank of the deer on his back. In confusion he turned and fixed his eyes on his attacker.

Realising he had missed his chance for a quick kill, Shimon raised his sling and hurled stones from his pouch as he ran towards Kayin. Kayin dropped the deer and ducked away from most of the stones, showing remarkable agility for his size. Then, as one stone caught his thigh, he stumbled slightly. Shimon threw himself onto the larger man, thumping a rock hard upon Kayin's head.

The force dazed Kayin who fell back under Shimon's weight. But, quickly recovering, his greater size and strength soon came into play. Kayin reached around and grasped the wrist of his younger brother, twisting Shimon's arm behind his back. Shimon, sent off-balance, fell to the ground with his legs tucked beneath him.

By now I was close enough to see their faces. Determination was set into Shimon's. He swung underneath Kayin's arm then brought his free hand round to seize it. Using Kayin's arm like a branch, he pulled himself off the ground and sunk his feet into his brother's stomach. Kayin fell back, stunned. Shimon went with him, tumbling on top with a thud. Soon they were rolling around on the ground, wrestling and punching, neither one noticeably weaker.

Suddenly, Kayin's eyes met mine again and recognition hit. As Kayin hesitated, Shimon landed a blow across his face. Kayin didn't react but stared at me. Triumphantly, Shimon sent another blow to the opposite side of Kayin's head, then another and another. Blood spurted from the victim's nose. Still, he did nothing to defend himself.

I acted on instinct, desperate to stop another murder in my family. Running between them, I threw myself between Shimon's fist and Kayin's face.

The fist crunched into my back. I howled in pain and my body fell into Kayin's face. Realising he had hit the wrong person, Shimon recoiled.

'Awan, get out of the way!' he shouted. 'Let me take my revenge!'

'No!' I cried into the ground. Kayin had gone limp beneath me. Worried that I'd stopped him from breathing, or that the head blows had killed him, tears streamed from my eyes.

'Awan, what are you doing?' Shimon continued, grabbing my shoulder and trying to pull me from Kayin's body. I used all my strength to resist him, grasping Kayin's shoulder with my good arm and clinging to it.

'Why are you protecting him?' Shimon shouted. I shrieked as he yanked my braids backwards, and I got a look into his savage eyes. 'He hurt you the most – you should want him dead!' he screamed, his spittle splattering my face. I shook my head and wept, unable to bring words to my lips.

Beneath me, Kayin's chest heaved, his body stiffened, and his eyes flew open. Summoning a new source of strength, he lifted his arms and threw off both of us in one movement. I toppled into long grass as Kayin stumbled upright and backed away.

'Kayin...' I began, pulling myself to standing. His wild eyes flew to me. I saw his face fully: tortured with confusion at hearing his name, features bearing the expression of hunted prey. As I stared at him, trying to control my ragged breathing, I heard movement behind me.

Shimon had reached the deer whilst Kayin was distracted. He grabbed his spear and ran backwards, ready to throw it again.

Having no time to think or communicate, I bolted towards Kayin then turned to face the hunter, positioning my body between the two brothers. Kayin's chest heaved against my back. His laboured breaths warmed my shoulders. I had no idea if Kayin was safe; I had no idea what I would do next. I just knew I had to protect him.

'If you want to kill him, you'll have to kill me first!' I shouted at Shimon, frantically praying I was doing the right thing. Did Shimon love me enough to care, or was his hatred for Kayin so consuming that I was of little consequence?

Shimon's eyes raged like forest fire, growing angrier and angrier at my interference. 'I *should* kill you for defending him. He deserves to die!'

We paused in a silent stand-off.

'Yes.' The throaty voice came from behind me. I jumped. It was the first time Kayin had spoken. I twisted my neck, trying to look at him without moving my body away from his. The wildness his eyes had borne when defending himself had softened to deep sadness. Kayin stepped sideways and raised his hands in the air.

'I… should… die,' he stuttered, forcing the words out from a part of his body unused for many years.

'No!' I said, sidestepping in front of him, pressing my back into his chest.

'See. He admits it,' shouted Shimon as I grabbed hold of Kayin's deerskin, trying to stop him from moving again. 'Let go of him, Awan. Step away and let me kill him.'

I resolutely shook my head.

Kayin gave a deep sigh then spoke softly in my ear. 'Look.'

I twisted to consider Kayin. Though fear had left his face, it hadn't left me. I was shaking.

'I die, he dies.' Kayin pointed at himself then Shimon.

I drew my brows together.

Shimon roared in frustration. 'What is he saying? What is he talking about? Let me end him, Awan. If you refuse to move, I vow to end you too.'

I didn't look at Shimon; I could not peel my eyes from Kayin. I had expected to see something from my nightmares; I had expected to see anything but what was before me. Calm had descended between us that was in stark contrast to the rage consuming my younger brother.

Kayin was trying to communicate something. He motioned to the sky, then to his cheek. There was a scar there. It ran from just below the middle of his left eye straight down his cheek to the corner of his mouth. Two other lines branched off it, one down towards the edge of his jaw and the other up towards the outer edge of his eye.

'El-ohim...' he said, struggling to form the words, 'A-venge.' He then pointed to his chest and his eyes widened, attempting to penetrate his meaning. Somehow, understanding dawned. Trying to stay tightly pressed against Kayin, I turned my body back to face Shimon.

'He says that if you take his life, yours will be taken by Elohim.'

Shimon screeched like a wild animal. He stamped upon the ground, then strode a few paces towards me, threatening us both with the spear still raised.

'AWAN! He is trying to scare us. His blood is a just repayment for Havel's blood. Elohim would never protect him!'

I looked at Kayin again. He lifted his brows.

'Awan, think of your twin – your dead brother that Kayin killed. I don't want to end him for my own sake but because it is the right thing to do.'

His words struck me in the chest.

'Really?' I shouted back. 'What do you think Havel would say to that? Would he would want you to murder Kayin in his defence? He used to tell us not to retaliate but to let Elohim serve justice. You think you knew Havel, but you did not. I knew him – and he wouldn't want this.'

Shimon glared. 'You are blind to the truth. You've always had a soft spot for this monster. You know nothing.'

'I know Elohim has chosen to protect Kayin, and has given him a mark to prove it.' I pointed to the scar on his face.

'What does that even mean?' Shimon sneered.

'I'm not sure. But do you really want to take a chance on it? Search your heart, Shimon; search for the real motives behind your actions. You hate Kayin. That is why you want him dead, not because you wish to avenge Havel. Can't you see that by acting this way you are no different to him?'

'Don't you dare start judging me, sister.' Shimon spat on the ground and strolled a few menacing paces towards me, lowering his voice. 'You are no better than the rest of us. Why do you think I am even here? I saw you with Chayim. I was out on the hunt when I heard you two frolicking about, so I decided to watch you. I saw what you did, Awan – how you tried to seduce him. You pretend you are so righteous. You are nothing but a worthless seductress. A traitor to your own sister!'

Shame flooded my body. I started to shake again as I realised my secret was out. The pain of it sunk deeper while Shimon continued his speech.

'When I heard your exchange about coming to find Kayin, I knew this was my chance to finally avenge Havel. It's something I've dreamt about for years, while you have spent that time betraying Havel by fawning over Chayim. When I rescued you at the tannin river, and realised you didn't know where you were going, I did consider relenting and turning back – until you decided to lie to me! As if I was not worthy of your trust. Me! The brother who has never done you harm.'

His lip curled and he laughed bitterly. 'That convinced me you had truly switched loyalties; that, if you couldn't have Chayim, you would turn instead to this murderer, betraying your entire family in the process. It made me even more determined to end his unworthy life. I followed you all the way here so I could put an end to it all.'

My strength gave out. My legs began to buckle beneath me. I gasped and looked to the ground as it swam before my eyes. Kayin's hands steadied me. With all the strength I could muster, I lifted my face to him. He was no longer hunter or prey, condemned or condemner. His eyes held only concern. They gave me the courage I needed to look back at Shimon.

'You are right; I am no different to you,' I admitted with a broken sob. 'We are all fallen, brother. None of us has any right to stand before a Holy Elohim, and I am no exception. I am sorry for what happened with Chayim. I am sorry I lied to you when you gave me the chance to confess. I was wrong.'

I risked taking a few steps towards him.

'Please forgive me, Shimon. Please believe I love you. I don't wish to take anyone's side. But I cannot bear to lose another.'

He stood there stony-faced and unrelenting while my tears blurred the sight. Then Kayin walked past me. I tried to stop him, grasping his arm, but he shook his head and brushed my hand off, striding purposefully towards Shimon.

Shimon lifted his spear again. He snarled and pointed it towards Kayin's chest. Kayin continued to move forwards until the sharpened stone pushed at his beating heart. The tip pierced his skin. Blood trickled down his torso. The action forced Shimon to back away, knowing that the point on the spear could only kill if thrown from a distance.

After retreating several paces, Shimon dropped the spear in exasperation. 'Fine… I will not kill you! But only because I don't wish to be the victim of Elohim's insane form of justice.' He turned to me. 'Don't think I will ever forget this betrayal, Awan. I shall return to our home and tell everyone what you have done: how you betrayed Avigail; how you lied to me; how you abandoned your family in favour of this murderous madman.'

'Shimon, please,' I pleaded. 'It is not like that.'

'Enough, woman. Use my name no longer. You are dead to me. And do not hope to ever come home. He shall never be accepted, and I will ensure you shall not either.'

With that final pronouncement, Shimon turned and stormed off.

CHAPTER 19

The next few days felt like a strange dream. After Shimon left, the reality of what had happened sunk in quickly and, sapped of all strength, I collapsed on the meadow grass, heaving sobs of agony and loss. I had no doubt Shimon was bitter enough to act on his words. My whole family would soon hear the worst version of what I had done and there was nothing I could do about it.

Kayin sat a few paces away and watched me weep for some time before tentatively scooping me into his arms and carrying me to a cave in the hillside. He climbed steep slopes and weaved between vegetation to get there. I didn't protest. My body was too weary – both from my journey and its climax in today's confrontation.

He laid me down on a pallet in the cave. The familiar smell of Kayin's bed offered a strange kind of comfort. Even so, I spent the rest of that day and night drifting between fretful periods of sleep. Exhaustion claimed my body but my mind would not be still. I don't know where Kayin slept but it wasn't in the cave. After a while, the scent of the bed added to the weight of pain as I considered having to live with Havel's killer and never being able to return to my family and my home. I couldn't stop sobbing. I cried out for Ima and Abba, for Chayim, for Set – anyone who could comfort me. I wept again for Havel, clinging to the bed covering and pulling it to my chest as if it could somehow lessen my loss. And I moaned for Yahweh, begging Him for mercy and courage.

During the second day, a great heaviness descended. My back and my head ached; my joints were tender. I could not rise from the pallet. Kayin reappeared, bringing me food and water, which I took in my moments of wakefulness. He didn't offer any tender words or actions. On the contrary, he seemed nervous and avoided physical contact. It was just as well: if he'd touched me, I might have broken completely.

At one point, I watched through heavy lids as Kayin quietly tidied a space at the back of the cave and built himself another pallet bed. If I had expected him to ask questions about why I was here or about Shimon's words, I would have been disappointed, for he said nothing. Was it because he'd lost his speech or because   he didn't know what to do with the miserable wreck before him?

The following day was worse. I kept shifting between hot and cold shivers. Then Kayin seemed to soften and spent time sitting beside the bed, bathing my forehead when I was too hot and covering me in an old sheepskin when I was too cold. We both recoiled the first time he touched my head, before he breathed deeply and pressed the wet linen down again.

The next day was much the same; I remember little except a pounding, shivering, sweating body. Visions of my lost family flooded my mind, but I couldn't speak or move.

On the fifth day after Shimon had left, the fever finally broke, and my head began to clear. I was still too weak to stand, and I slept most of the time, but when my headache allowed, I tried to start processing what had taken place.

In one moment of lucidity, I remembered Yahweh's goodness and presence with me after I had sinned. Reassurance impressed itself deep in my soul and I knew, no matter what Shimon had said, Yahweh had forgiven me and that was what mattered. Though I dreaded my family's reaction to Shimon's revelations, their opinion was not as crucial as Yahweh's. He had called me and would give me the strength to face Kayin.

Armed with this knowledge, I tried to sit up and smile when Kayin entered the cave that afternoon. I thought I saw a slight movement of his lips, but it was hard to make anything out in the cave's gloom.

Before I could say anything, he turned around and disappeared again, returning moments later with a bowl of steaming broth. Setting it beside me, he watched intently as I lifted the bowl to my mouth and took tentative sips. Once I had finished, I passed him back the bowl.

'Better?' he asked. I nodded. He abruptly took the bowl and left. I didn't see him again until that night.

I was still fragile the following day, but I tried a few shaky steps around the cave. Again, Kayin barely made an appearance. He brought me food and water but didn't speak or linger. I realised that his distance was more challenging than his presence. All the built-up tension in expectation of finding him now felt suspended in mid-air, hovering over me with nowhere to go until I figured out where I stood and what he was like after all these years.

I had known that answers wouldn't be instant and was warned that he might be different. Yet the shock was finding him so aloof. Part of me wanted to get up and force him to speak to me, yet my legs refused to cooperate with such a request.

That night I slept well but woke to find Kayin absent, although the dawn chorus had commenced. Upon sitting, I realised my head felt normal again, and I breathed in relief. I longed to see Yemima running in to snuggle under my covers. How I yearned to sing in her ear while she twirled my hair in her fingertips. Instead, I sang quietly to Yahweh, thanking Him for my renewed health and praying for strength to face the day ahead.

I wiggled my toes and swung my legs around. When they seemed to cooperate, I pulled myself out of bed and slowly wandered outside. It was the first time I had looked at Kayin's new home, having paid no attention on the day he had carried me here. Rising sunshine greeted me, glittering through the tops of the trees that surrounded the eastern side of the glade. There was a clearing in front of the cave with a fire pit in the centre and a few boulders dotted around. One resembled a grinding stone. Another large stone sat just outside the door. It was weather-beaten with a hollowed dip in the middle, in which water was collecting. A wooden contraption was suspended above it, seemingly designed to channel water into the ring, but I lacked the strength to pull myself up for a better look.

To my left, a large oak tree sent its branches in several directions, giving an area of shade beneath where a tree stump had been placed and carved into a seat. Next to that was a large trough – carved, presumably, from the same felled tree – filled with stagnant water in which several bushels of flax were soaking. The deer Kayin had hunted was hanging upside-down from a low branch of the oak. He must have retrieved it after he had carried me back here.

I walked around to the other side of the cave entrance. Here, a small stack of firewood was arranged in a cleft in the rock and, in another crevice, various objects of clay and bone. There were also several sets of animal bones in different formations as if they'd been kept for a purpose, though I couldn't imagine what. Some flowers were growing into the grassy hillside above. The soil at their base looked freshly dug over and carefully weeded.

'Awan?' came a voice. I jumped and turned to see Kayin watching me with a bundle of firewood in his arms. He *could* say my name then. I smiled tentatively. He walked closer, dropped the wood next to the other stack, and began meticulously arranging the new wood atop the old. I stood nervously, waiting for him to complete the task.

When he eventually finished, he turned and approached me. Stopping right in front of me, his great height dwarfed mine. I looked up as my heart started to thump. He stared intensely into my eyes, as if searching for something, and stayed that way for a confusing amount of time. Just as I was about to lose my nerve, he seemed to remember something and spoke.

'You drink. From lake?'

Blood was racing inside my chest, and it took me a moment to realise he was trying to ask me a question.

'Oh, yes. I drank the lake water,' I blurted.

'Bad water,' he said. I waited. 'Make sick.'

I heaved a sigh of relief. The pause hadn't been threatening. Kayin was just trying to find words to explain my illness.

'Can you understand everything I say?' I asked.

He nodded. I smiled then, broad and wide, and Kayin's face utterly transformed as he smiled back. Then he dropped his gaze and walked to the stone that held water. He picked up a small bowl carved from wood, scooped fresh water into it, brought it back and held it out to me.

'Good water,' he said. I thanked him, took the bowl with my good arm and took a long drink. He watched me quizzically.

'What is it?' I asked.

He pointed to my shoulder.

'Oh, yes. It's out of joint; it has been for a while. I don't know how to fix it.'

He drew awkwardly close again, walking behind me and considering my stance. His face was so close to my neck that it made my hairs stand on end.

'Pain?' he said, at last, holding his fingers above my dislocated shoulder.

'No. Yahweh removed the pain.'

He grunted then tentatively touched me, feeling into the joint. 'Let me?' he asked.

I nodded, not minding his examination but not knowing what exactly he was asking either. He undid the knot binding my arm to my body and my arm flopped down. Then, pushing my head forwards, he lifted my useless arm above my head and dug his elbow into my back. Suddenly, in one quick movement, he pushed down hard on the joint with his spare hand. I gasped as my shoulder popped back into place.

It ached, but I was immediately able to control my arm again. I wiggled my fingers around and bent my elbow up and down. As abruptly as he'd touched me, Kayin withdrew and entered the cave. Perhaps that was it – his interaction for the day was done. But he returned with a tatty linen cloth a few moments later. Ripping the bottom off, he fashioned the remnant into a more suitable sling. Then he tucked my lower arm into it and tied the ends together around my opposite shoulder.

'Keep still,' he said, patting my arm. Then he ambled away and sat on the chair under the oak tree, closing his eyes. Unsatisfied with such behaviour, I followed and stood in front of him, glad to look down on him for a change.

'How did you know how to do that?' I asked. He didn't open his eyes but smirked slightly. Was he going to ignore me completely? It felt like an eternity before he spoke again, keeping his eyes closed.

'Study bones,' he said, casually. Then after another pause, 'Get bored.'

Kayin's smile didn't make another appearance, and his attitude remained frustrating for the next few days. I had expected some sort of reaction to my presence – joy at seeing me or recognition of what I had sacrificed to find him. But I got nothing. Even anger would have been better than this strange kind of silence.

Disused to idleness, I didn't know what to do with myself. I was in an unfamiliar place with unfamiliar routines. With my arm still in a sling I couldn't do much to help, and every time I tried, Kayin would remove items from my hands like he didn't want me to touch his things. If I walked away to explore the area, he left me alone and didn't offer to show me around or express a desire to come with me.

It was even more of a struggle once the sling was removed and the aching had subsided. Used to living with a busy family, I was desperate to get back to doing something meaningful. Even though I'd felt lonely without a life partner, I'd always had plenty of jobs to keep me occupied. There had usually been children playing around the huts and someone to talk to or hug. Yet Kayin only touched me if necessary. And there was no comfort in his touch, no lingering tenderness.

During my journey, I'd felt Yahweh's presence as I'd clung to Him in fear. Now that I had arrived – and Kayin seemed neither dangerous, nor responsive – it was a strange anti-climax. I spoke to Yahweh at every opportunity, trying not to lose Him. When I walked, I prayed aloud and sang, asking Him to help me understand Kayin.

Then I realised that the isolation I felt was something Kayin had experienced for decades. I tried to imagine what it must have been like to live alone for so long; how it must be peculiar to suddenly share his life. I knew Yahweh was guiding me through these revelations and felt reassurance that, with Kayin, I needed to be patient. Yet, I knew nothing of Kayin's own relationship with Yahweh and how that had been affected by his actions.

CHAPTER 20

One night, almost two weeks after I'd found Kayin in the meadow, my sleep was unsettled again. A powerful storm raged outside. The howling wind swirled into my consciousness as branches battered the cave and thunder shouted from on high.

The cave's darkness was palpable. It crawled over my skin, reminding me that my brother's killer slept a stone's throw away. As it constricted around my throat, I fixated on the tiny rays of moonlight filtering through the semi-covered mouth of the cave.

'I could do with that wall of light now,' I whispered. The wind responded with a wail.

I continued falling in and out of sleep, aware of every noise and movement. After half a night of torture, I sat up and crawled to the crevice in the rock just outside. After dragging some kindling and firewood into the cave, I started a small flame, wrapped myself up and waited for the fire to take.

I wasn't the only one who'd been sleeping fretfully. Although I could see little in the darkness, the sound of Kayin tossing and turning on his pallet had accompanied me all night. Now he was deeply in the grip of a torturous dream. He had more words in his sleep; he kept repeating nonsensical phrases that seemed essential to him in that moment.

Kayin began to settle as the fire grew warmer and, in turn, I breathed more easily. Crawling back to my pallet, I tucked myself beneath my blanket. Yet, just as I was drifting back into sleep, Kayin suddenly screeched.

'Let go! Leave me!'

He became more and more animated until I could bear it no longer.

I went to him. From the little I could see, Kayin appeared to be fighting a mirage beside him. I didn't know how to approach him without getting hit. Deciding to take a chance, I crept behind him and wrapped my arms around his chest. Then I began to murmur into his ear, as Chayim had done to me.

He grew frantic, worse than before, shoving and twisting. Throwing himself backwards, his elbow jarred me in the eye. I cried out, falling to the floor beside the pallet.

Then he turned. In a fury, he leaned over me, eyes wide and vacant, brightly reflecting the flames on the other side of the cave. I shouted his name, but he was unresponsive to sight or sound. I rolled away just as his hands crashed forward then scrambled up as he fell back onto the pallet. He grasped at it, now begging, sobbing and speaking indiscernible words.

Remembering how singing used to calm my younger siblings during bad dreams, I lifted my voice into the darkness.

Elohim, have mercy.
Yahweh, have mercy.
Ruach, breathe mercy on him.

Kayin's shadowy form twitched.

I sang the words again and watched his shoulders relax slightly. A second time, I lowered myself behind his back. When he didn't react to the touch of my hand I began stroking his hair as I sang – just as I'd done to the young children.

> *Elohim, have mercy.*
> *Yahweh, have mercy.*
> *Ruach, breathe mercy on him.*

Gradually, Kayin started to shift on the bed as if gaining consciousness. I didn't stop singing. Eventually, he turned over towards me. As he did my voice quietened and my hand slipped from his hair. He caught it and drew it towards his face. Flattening my palm against his cheek, he closed his eyes again.

'Sing,' he said.

I took a moment to collect myself before lifting my voice in a different song – one I hoped would be familiar from our years together. He sighed deeply with his eyes still closed. Then his other arm wrapped around my waist, pulling me forward until my body was flat against his. I shifted slightly, feeling embarrassed, but he held me firmly and whispered, 'Stay.'

I settled into his strange embrace and continued singing until he eventually slackened his grip and his breathing regulated. Then I allowed myself to relax, and within moments I too had drifted into peace.

At dawn, Kayin woke first. When I opened my eyes, he was looking at me. I immediately felt a flush creeping into my cheeks. He showed no embarrassment but traced his finger around my eye as his brows drew together.

'What is it?' I asked.

'Hurt,' he croaked, then coughed. 'I have hurt you.'

It was the first time I'd heard him string words into a full sentence, and it made me smile, despite the look on his face. I brought my hand up to join his above my eye.

'It's nothing. It was an accident,' I said.

Fear filled his eyes. He immediately pushed himself from me, stood and walked away. Anger boiled in my chest. I was not going to endure his awkwardness again after we'd laid in each other's arms. Mustering courage, I stood and pursued him.

'Don't do this, Kayin,' I said. 'You're not going silent on me again; not after I have endured so much to come here and to stay. You didn't hurt me on purpose; you had a nightmare. You didn't know what you were doing.'

He stared at the floor.

In exasperation I cried out, 'Look at me!'

Raising my hands to take his face, I tried to lower his gaze. He averted his eyes; he would not meet mine. Frustration welled up inside me – the same agony of confusion that had been my companion for so long. The sound of my heavy breathing split the air between us for several more moments.

Then he finally spoke. 'I knew... once.'

I stood silently, trying to understand what he was saying, before asking softly, 'What do you mean?'

He looked me decisively in the eyes. I saw the depth of his emotion and heard the confession in his one word: 'Havel.'

It struck me dumb. My hands clutched my mouth as I registered his meaning. Of course, I knew he had done it. But to hear it from his lips – to hear him confirm that he had known what he was doing; that it hadn't been an accident—

I staggered backwards and tripped over some baskets bundled on the floor behind me. I put my arm out to steady myself on the cave wall and took deep breaths, trying to control myself but utterly failing as images of my brother's lifeless face filled my mind again. I moaned, nausea now rising in waves, choking on the force of my emotion as Kayin's confession rang in my ears.

He had murdered Havel. He had known what he was doing.

Kayin stood silently watching, his face a picture of excruciating loss. Then he moved forward and picked up my old pack from where it lay tucked near the baskets. He began to fill it with food as tears formed in his own eyes, running down his cheeks and wetting his beard.

'What are you doing?' I murmured, once I had regained control of my voice. He stopped and handed me the pack.

'Awan. Go home.'

I closed my eyes and counted a long breath. My body sought to obey Kayin. Staying in his presence was like repeatedly piercing myself with a spear. The easier option was to flee and never face him again. Yet I knew I had abandoned the easy choice when I obeyed Elohim's voice. I chose to come. I would choose to stay.

'No, Kayin.'

'I hurt you.'

'Yes, you did. You still do,' I said firmly, pulling myself together. 'But don't you see? Yahweh told me to find you. I knew it would be hard. I have known what you did since it happened. I am here anyway. I am here because Elohim has not forgotten you. And I am not leaving unless He tells me to!'

I grew animated as I spoke and lifted a stubborn chin on the last phrase to let him know he wouldn't win this one.

We stared at each other for what felt like an age. I expected him to storm out angrily as he might have done in the past on losing an argument, but he didn't. Instead, he walked forward. When he reached me, he pulled me firmly into his chest. His beard wet my temple and his tears joined mine. Then he wrapped his arms tightly around me, ensuring I knew there was no point fighting his embrace.

So I didn't.

When Kayin had released me and left the cave to prepare breakfast, I took a long walk in the hills. The commitment to forgive him was one thing; I knew the reality of living with that commitment would take all my strength. Yet the knowledge that I was sinful too had undoubtedly changed me.

Of course, I'd known it in my head. But feeling it in my heart was different, and it altered my perception of Kayin. I poured it out to Yahweh again in song.

Help me remember that I'm a betrayer
when I feel betrayed.
Help me remember that I am a sinner
when I feel dismayed.
I can run straight into Your loving arms
when I am afraid.
You know all my weakness; You know all my shame;
And You love me anyway.

Help me to pray when I'm prone to stray,
not trusting my pride.
You promised me You're all that I need,
and far more besides.
I don't understand all that You have planned,
but I needn't hide.
For You made everything, Yahweh Elohim,
And You're by my side.

Elohim! You are immeasurably holy.
At Your throne is all that is glorious and mighty.
I hide my face; I'm no better than anyone else.
All I've done has been all for myself.
I kneel before You in my filthy rags.
Oh, take them and wash them,
And make them spotlessly clean.

Help me seek You when all that I view
is hard to forgive.
Speak to my fears; wipe away my tears;
teach me how to live
Safe in the place of Your loving embrace
where You freely give.
A life was laid down on the dust of the ground
So that I might live.

Elohim! You are immeasurably holy.
At your throne is all that is glorious and mighty.
I hide my face; I'm no better than anyone else.
All I've done has been all for myself.
I kneel before You in my filthy rags.
Oh, take them and wash them,
And make them spotlessly clean.

CHAPTER 21

That day things shifted between us. Kayin's fear of spending time with me abated, and he started to relax. Emboldened by my song, I did too.

After we'd eaten, Kayin surprised me by leading me up the hillside to a ridge where the view was staggering. I could see as far as the lake in one direction and the horizon in the other.

'Sea is that way,' he said, gesturing to his right.

'You've been there?' I asked, amazed.

He nodded. 'Many places. Many… wanderings.'

I had so many questions I longed to ask him. I wanted to know everything he'd been doing the last few decades; everything he'd seen; everywhere he'd been. I wanted to know what Elohim had said to him and why he had that scar. I wanted to know how Havel had died and why Kayin had never come home.

Yet now was not the time. Kayin had just begun to warm to me, and I wouldn't risk a further rift. I tried instead to focus on him.

'You must have been so lonely in those wanderings. I thought I was lonely at home, but you've been on your own this whole time,' I said.

He shrugged his shoulders and looked down. 'My fault.'

I let silence reign for a few moments before lightening the mood. 'Several days ago, you fixed my arm. I think it's time I sorted out your hair.'

Kayin let out a huge, deep laugh that echoed into the valley below. I joined him, revelling in the release of tension. When we had calmed down, he turned to me and simply said, 'I miss you.'

'I missed you too,' I said, and I meant it. Kayin looked at me intently then ran the edge of his hand down the side of my face.

'You have changed,' he smiled. 'Even more beautiful. Not me. I look bad.'

I chuckled, though tears were glistening in my eyes.

'Well, you shall look much better when I have tackled that beard.' I smirked, tugging on the strands reaching his chest. In response, he took one of my braids in his fingers and twirled it around them.

'It's like… twine.'

'Chayim's daughters did it. They are very talented at such things.'

'Daughters?' Kayin furrowed his brow as if recalling something. 'Shimon said…'

I quickly grew embarrassed and wished I'd never mentioned Chayim. Still, I couldn't leave his query unanswered.

'Chayim married Avigail. They have two daughters. What Shimon saw me do was wrong; we were wrong. We have repented.'

He considered me for a moment, then opened his mouth to say something before closing it again. Instead, he leaned back against a boulder, tucked one arm behind his head and closed his eyes. 'Tell me about home,' he murmured.

I leaned back beside him and began.

'Chayim and Avigail were married many years ago.' I related the story of their union and the birth of their daughters, telling Kayin how Yahweh had answered our prayers for Avigail. Then I described Shimon and Channah growing up and starting a life together in the hills.

I spoke of our parents and how they had delayed having another child until Set had been born, followed by my youngest siblings. I talked about Set growing in the faith, taking his place in the family and his marriage to Techiyah.

'Set is like Havel?' Kayin interrupted, not opening his eyes. A pang shot through my chest. I breathed deeply, then continued.

'No, not really. Set's actually much like Abba. He looks like Abba and has the same tendency to take everything a bit seriously. Though he doesn't carry Abba's burdens.'

Then, to distract myself, I reminisced about the triplets and how they always got up to mischief. I spoke of Liora's recent flourishing and little Yemima, whose sweet greetings and morning cuddles I missed. And lastly, the birth of Ronel just before I left home.

We spent the whole morning on the ridge. Kayin occasionally opened his eyes and looked at me but primarily relaxed, allowing me to tell stories of the family he remembered and the siblings he'd never met. Sometimes I gave my voice a rest and enjoyed the view. At other times, Kayin asked me about the crops and Chayim. It was clear he missed them both. I wondered if he would ask me more about my relationship with Chayim, but he didn't.

When I was exhausted for words, we sat in stillness, pondering what had been said and, perhaps, how things might have been different if Kayin had never left.

That afternoon, Kayin decided the deer had hung long enough and was ready to eat. Together we skinned it and stripped it of the best meat. I boiled a stew with roots and herbs, and we set some meat cuts to smoke. Then Kayin cut down the remaining carcass and slung it over his shoulders.

'Where are you taking it?' I asked.

'Cubs,' he replied. I followed him down the hill and up the next into an area of woodland studded with rocky places and more caves. Outside one of the caves, he stopped and threw the carcass to the ground. Taking my hand, he led me behind a set of rocks where we could see but not be seen. The sensation took me by surprise as my slender fingers entwined in his solid ones.

A female cat soon crept out of the cave, sniffing the scent of the deer. She was similar in appearance to the one I had seen with Chayim, though her spots had converged into stripes that ran down her back and legs and she had a longer, slightly bushier tail. After checking for danger, she called to her cubs. Four ran out of the cave and bounded to the carcass. They enjoyed their fill of the gift, not questioning where it had come from.

I studied Kayin's face as he watched the cubs. He looked like a proud father, smiling at their antics and pleased he'd supplied their food.

During the following week, Kayin seemed pleased, rather than annoyed, with my company. We walked and ate together, although we didn't speak much. Serious conversation would have been difficult at Kayin's current level of speech, but it did feel like something was hanging in the air between us.

In addition, Kayin still had nightmares most nights. Chayim had once told me about the frenzied dreams that continued long after Kayin's fever had left. Although they had often woken Chayim, knowing how much they distressed Kayin, he hadn't mentioned it to his older brother. It seemed that in all the decades past, those nightmares had never waned. Having discovered the best way to quieten Kayin, I sang whenever he woke me – sending my prayer-filled melodies across the cave until he settled.

Kayin had little linen available. There was only the tattered garment he'd ripped up for my sling and one large cloth on his pallet. I soon needed to launder my tunics but didn't know where to go. After I asked Kayin for guidance, he led me to an area downstream with a little brook and a shallow pool of water. It was sufficient for cleaning, but not deep enough to swim in.

When we arrived, he handed me a solid object that smelt like terebinth.

'What is this?' I asked.

'Mixed fat, ash and oil,' he said. 'Use it for cleaning.'

The cleaning bar was a revelation; I had never used anything but water and herbaceous oils – which helped remove smells but did nothing for stains. I wondered how and why he'd experimented with combining the materials, especially considering he hadn't even bothered cutting his beard. But then Kayin had always enjoyed experimenting.

When I arrived back at the cave, Kayin tipped some dried fruit into my palm.

'These are terebinth as well,' I said, recognising the small, soft globules. As a family, we regularly used terebinth resin for waterproofing, but Kayin had clearly been making use of the fruit too. I'd thought only the pistachio varieties edible, and this kind useless. But they must be what he had used in the cleansing bar.

'When soft, I squeeze oil. When dried, I use for food,' Kayin explained. 'Look.'

He set a batch to roast on the fire then started crushing others on the grinding stone. Those he formed into a dough and baked. The roasted ones, he pounded before adding them to boiled water.

Eventually, Kayin produced two rounds of bread and two cupfuls of hot drink. The bread was peculiar but edible, and the drink bitter but curiously invigorating. I marvelled at how he'd adapted, using whatever was at his disposal.

Towards the end of that week, I cut his hair and beard using a black stone that Kayin had sharpened.

'This stone is good,' I exclaimed. 'So much better than the ones from home.'

'Found it near sea,' he said. 'It gets very sharp. Good for flesh and hair.'

I enjoyed the fact that his words were gradually returning. Even more, I enjoyed tidying his appearance: cropping his beard short around his shapely jaw. Kayin caught my eye as I drew closer, concentrating.

'Stay still,' I complained when his mouth turned up into a grin. He forced the smile down, but his eyes still held laughter. I bit my lip to restrain mine.

I didn't cut his hair too short, for the length suited him. I just removed the ends and mats until it fell in smoother strands to his shoulder blades.

Once finished, I stood back to admire my handiwork. My breath briefly caught as I recognised the handsome man I had once loved. Even the scar dominating his left cheek didn't detract from it.

'Much better,' I said. 'Now I just need to make you a new tunic or two – unless you want to stay in those filthy, smelly skins forever?'

He grinned and shrugged then pointed me towards the flax that was now drying on a branch of the oak tree. We spent the rest of that afternoon extracting fibres from it: rubbing each stalk with sticks to remove the woody bit, then between our fingers until it grew soft.

'Where did you get the flax?' I asked, realising I still hadn't seen any cultivated fields.

'Grows wild by lake,' he replied.

'Were you there recently?'

'Yes – week before you.'

'That explains why I saw your footprints,' I smiled. 'What do you drink there if the water isn't good?'

'Coconut milk.'

'What's a coconut?'

'White flesh – gone green in your pack,' he teased.

'Oh! You mean the large, brown fruit? I remember the milk from it was good. Did I leave a piece to rot?' I grimaced. Kayin nodded with a twinkle in his eye. 'How do you get them down from the trees?' I asked.

'I climb with long stick,' he replied. With his great height and long legs, I pictured Kayin halfway up a tree, his legs wrapped around the trunk, a stick held between his teeth.

'I didn't think of trying that. I stole mine from a monkey.'

Kayin almost choked on a stalk he'd been using to pick his teeth. Then he let out an enormous laugh. 'I would like to see that.'

'The monkey wasn't as amused as you are.' I grinned back.

Kayin continued to chuckle, shaking his head as he picked up more flax.

A few days later, once all the flax had been processed, Kayin woke me during the night and led me to a place in the woods. Flies, lit up like stars, danced in the air before us. They were captivating and I couldn't take my eyes off them. Before I realised what I was doing, I threaded my fingers through Kayin's and leaned against him. At first his body tightened, but soon he relaxed. We sat together for a good part of the night, enthralled by the beauty Elohim had created, not returning to the cave until the flies had finished their dance. Once there, I fell into a peaceful slumber.

I woke to find Kayin still on his pallet. It was unusual for him not to get up at dawn, but I supposed he was just catching up on the sleep he'd missed during the night. I picked up a basket, meaning to gather some food for breakfast before he woke. I had spied some delicious-looking spring berries in the meadow a few days before. Creeping out of the cave, I placed the basket by the water stone.

Just as I was taking a drink, Kayin spoke from behind me. 'Where are you going?'

'You startled me,' I exclaimed, turning around to him. He stood stretching his arms and back. I smiled at his half-closed lids. 'I was just going to collect some berries. Then I thought I'd get to work on your tunic.'

He came forward and put his hands on my waist, causing me to shiver.

'Not today. It's Shabbat,' he murmured. 'Back to bed.'

'Is it?' I asked. I'd lost all track of the days since I'd been with Kayin. How did he know what day it was? 'In that case, you go back to bed. I'll take a walk and spend some time with Yahweh. But I shan't pick any berries.' I winked.

He groaned and tugged at my tunic. Was he going to pull me back to bed with him? Then he let me go and wobbled into the cave, throwing a smile over his shoulder.

I prayed as I climbed to the ridge and gazed over the beautiful hillsides and the plains below. It was peculiar how Kayin's hill country stood green amongst barren surroundings. Before the lake there was little grass; certainly nowhere to graze a flock. And whilst a few edible plants grew along the bank of the stream and in the meadow, I could see how it would be challenging to cultivate crops. The stream didn't have sufficient flow to fill channels.

Towards the sea the land looked similar, though the earth was a richer clay colour. Perhaps this was why Kayin wasn't farming. Though it seemed odd that he had settled here rather than trying to find somewhere more fertile.

I was alarmed that I'd forgotten several Shabbat days since my time in the mountains. Still, I'd done nothing but rest when I first arrived. Kayin's sudden observance of Shabbat was puzzling. Perhaps he had rested before without me noticing, but I hadn't seen him worshipping.

Then again, how were you meant to observe family worship on your own? Maybe he wanted to but didn't know how. I longed to learn more about Kayin's circumstances and faith. Could my mention of Yahweh calling me here have triggered something in his heart?

CHAPTER 22

When I returned to the cave, Kayin had laid out some dried fruit and meat. I sat near him and took some food, praising Yahweh for His provision and His special day of rest.

After I had finished several mouthfuls, Kayin asked, 'Will you sing?'

'Of course,' I replied, pleased that he would ask. I closed my eyes and cast my mind back to when I was at the springs in the mountains. I sang the song I'd composed then, which had come to mind several times since – of Yahweh commanding the springs to bring forth water, and guiding me through the mountain paths.

'You found pool where behemoth drink?' Kayin inquired when I'd finished.

'Yes, it's so beautiful there. I couldn't believe how warm the water was, but I wasn't able to swim,' I said, gesturing to my arm, which was now completely healed.

'Good. Big fish in that water.' he replied. 'Tastes good, though.'

'The fish with the spear-like jaws? You ate one?' I asked in amazement, considering the fish that the massive predator had feasted on in front of my eyes.

Kayin tapped his skull. 'Huge jaws. Small head. Easy to trap.'

I knew how confident Kayin was in the water, and somehow it didn't surprise me that he'd wrestled a giant fish and won.

'Is there anywhere to swim here? Preferably without giant fish.' I asked with a grin.

'Yes, I'll take you,' he smiled, then said, 'What bear?'

'Hmm?' I was still imagining Kayin wrestling the fish.

'*He sent a bear to decide my way,*' he sang back to me. I had forgotten the lilting tones of his low singing voice. It had provided richness and beauty to our family worship – when he had joined in.

'Oh! Funny story,' I said. 'Though it wasn't funny at the time. When Shimon left me at the foot of the first mountain, I didn't know how to cross the river. As I was praying, an enormous bear came out of the woods and started chasing me. I hadn't provoked her and there was no reason for the chase, yet she set her course on me and would not give up.

'I hurtled around the side of the mountain, following the riverbank, until I saw a fallen tree suspended over the water. I was able to make it across, but the bear wasn't. I realised afterwards that I might never have found that crossing of my own accord. Yahweh used that bear to guide me. Wait, how did you get across that river?'

'I swam,' Kayin replied.

'Typical. I suppose the tannin that tried to eat me took one look at you and knew he didn't stand a chance.' I rolled my eyes.

His face clouded for a moment, then he shrugged without offering an explanation. Ever mysterious Kayin.

Later that afternoon, we went for a longer walk together. We were heading to the deeper pool that we could swim in. Kayin brought the cloth from his bed to dry ourselves with. We walked for some time over familiar hillsides until we came to a steeper incline with denser tree cover. The next path was rocky, and Kayin held my hand to steady me when stones threatened to slip under my feet. Next, we ducked through shrubs and weaved around small tracks that animals had made. At last, I heard running water.

Kayin looked at me and grinned. 'Nearly there.'

I gasped when we came out from the trees, and I saw what was in front of me. It was a spring unlike any I'd seen before. Water gushed from a clifftop with such force that it turned white, then ran in torrents down a rock face, before landing in a deep, sapphire pool. This pool fed a stream below.

'Our stream begins there,' Kayin said, pointing. 'Come on!' He grinned, removing his outer skin garment. I watched him wade into the water, my mind flashing back to the past. Pulling my tunic off, but leaving my undergarment on, I followed Kayin into the water.

Once he saw me join him, he lifted his feet from the bottom of the pool and swam, gliding effortlessly over the surface. I swished my arms and legs but didn't go into the pool's centre, preferring to stay where I could touch the bottom. The water was beautiful; it was warm and so clear that I could see my body's outline below the surface.

After a short swim, I put my feet down for a rest and watched Kayin. Something was captivating about the way he transformed in the water. He looked at home – all his worries lifting with his floating body.

He swam towards the waterfall, his muscular torso taking each stride easily, even with the current against him. Then he climbed onto some rocks and stood beneath the water, allowing it to cascade over his body whilst he ran fingers through his hair. After a few moments, he shouted to me over the noise of the torrents: 'Join me.'

I was unsure about venturing into the deeper water but decided to trust him. Taking a big breath, I dipped my chin into the pool, channelling all my concentration staying afloat. It took some effort against the current, and I had to close my eyes against the splashes of the waterfall. When my stretched fingertips touched a boulder, I opened my eyes again. Kayin was there, reaching out a hand to pull me onto the rocks. I slipped as I stood up, but he held me steady and guided me until I stood beside him.

'It feels good?' he asked, still shouting above the noise. I nodded and allowed myself to smile. He had pulled us into a spot behind the main falls, where the water was not so powerful.

I looked around and wondered at the beauty in this hidden nook behind the sheet of falling water. Different colours glimmered as spray caught the sunlight and danced around us. Then I caught Kayin's eyes roaming unapologetically over my features, and my heart began beating frantically.

He lowered his lips towards me. Unease flipped my stomach. I wasn't sure I was ready to be tempted by Kayin again – particularly before we had even talked about the past.

His lips bypassed mine and drew close to my ear. I was fleetingly disappointed – then shocked by that disappointment.

'Ready?' he asked, his voice suddenly laced with mischief. He grasped my hand. Before I knew what he was doing, he took a huge leap right through the falls into the pool below – taking me with him.

As I crashed into the depths, the water swallowed me and fear seized my limbs. I flailed, losing Kayin's grip. Forgetting how to resurface, the water engulfed my mouth, nose and eyes as I sank without breathing. Something wrapped around my feet. Forcing my eyes open, I saw weeds tangled around my legs, their claws pulling me down to the depths of the earth.

Terror paralysed me. Anxiety suffocated my spirit as the water crashed around, sucking the air from my body.

I was drowning.

Kicking my feet furiously, I began to fight through my fraught panic. But I couldn't focus as my head grew light from lack of breath. *I can't breathe. I can't breathe!*

Senses blurring, I sank further; my head coming level with my feet. In a flicker of clarity, I reached towards the weed with my hand. If I could just grasp it—

Kayin was already there, ripping apart the weed's bonds. He pulled me to the surface. I gasped, then choked on the water I had consumed, spluttering as my lungs refused to take in anything other than liquid. My mind registered no safety. My arms thrashed as the unrelenting panic attack continued.

'Awan, breathe!' Kayin commanded, 'I have you.' With my fight exhausted, I went limp in his hold. I started sinking again. He pulled me up with a firm grip, then, wrapping his arms under mine, he propelled himself backwards with his legs, towing me to the shore.

When he'd hauled me onto the bank, I pushed him off and heaved, flipping onto all fours, panting uncontrollably. *Calm down.*

The solid earth beneath my fingers should have brought comfort, but the ground wouldn't stop moving. My stomach convulsed. I retched and deposited its contents onto the ground. Then I collapsed, curling tightly into a ball, as sobs overtook me and tears cascaded down my face.

Kayin's simple, stupid action had terrified me beyond belief. Now I faced unparalleled shock and rising anger.

'How could you?' Like the water gushing from the rocks above, I spewed the words at him. 'Don't ever do that again.'

'I'm so sorry,' Kayin replied, his voice shaking. He gathered the cloth and threw it over me, rubbing it against my skin. 'I forgot—' he swallowed, unable to get the words out.

Then he sat beside me, uttered a low groan and pulled my body into his lap. I pushed against him for a moment, abhorrence burning in my gut like the bile. Then, exhaustion claimed me, and I gave up the fight. Even though he deserved a beating, his warmth was the only thing offering my body comfort.

I lay there curled inside his arms for some time before my breathing returned to normal. Once Kayin sensed it, he reached for my tunic and placed it over my head, stuffing the soaked cloth into the band of his loincloth. Cradling me in his arms, he rocked me back and forth.

'Please forgive me,' he repeated over and over, regret dominating the whispered words and kisses to my forehead. I closed my eyes. I tried forcing myself to feel safe again. Part of me still wanted to push him away in indignation, but the part that craved being in his arms won. As my mind cleared, I knew he had meant no harm.

When I started shivering from cold rather than fear, Kayin shifted his legs and stood up. Navigating the narrow paths and steep rocks with my body still tucked in his arms, he carried me the entire distance to the cave.

By the time we got back it was dark. Kayin laid me on my pallet, covering me in my wool blanket and the old sheepskin. Then he lay in front of me. Curling his body around me, he rubbed my back with one hand slipped beneath the covering. Then he began to sing, stroking my forehead with his other hand.

When my body finally warmed through and stopped shaking, I recognised the song. It was the one I used to sing at the river when I was a child. Kayin had heard it the day he began teaching me to swim. I was amazed he remembered the song and surprised by how freely his words flowed when he sang.

Yahweh is my light and my salvation,
My heart shall not fear,
Though the waters roar and darkness creeps in,
Yet, I will be confident.
For He will bless those who love Him,
And protect those who draw near.
Bless the toil of my hands, my Elohim,
Clothe me in Your love,
As I clothe those dear to me.

I closed my eyes and listened to his voice, allowing the words to minister to my soul and its fears. Eventually, I drifted into sleep.

CHAPTER 23

When I awoke the following morning, I felt surprisingly untroubled. My anger from the day before had subsided as Kayin's warmth replaced it.

Kayin was still sleeping soundly, with both his arms wrapped around me. His chest was bare; he'd given my cold body every available covering and left himself without.

I tilted my head slightly, trying to look at his face without waking him. His scarred cheek was closest to me, and I couldn't resist lifting a finger to touch it.

Why had Elohim brought me here, and what did He want me to do? Every day I spent with Kayin, I was more drawn to him. He was undoubtedly different – uncouth and awkward from solitude – yet, he was slowly returning to someone I recognised. At the same time, his confidence while speaking was growing, along with his vocabulary.

In my youth, I had looked up to Kayin while also fearing the glimpses of his unpredictable anger and jealousy. Now, despite the awkwardness, he seemed to have mellowed; I hadn't detected those old characteristics in the last few weeks. I thought of the way he'd dealt with Shimon's attack, and his tenderness to the creatures around us… Still, knowing what he was capable of, could I ever trust him again?

The incident at the waterfall had frightened me, but it hadn't been malicious. Once I'd calmed down, his devotion made me long to stay in his arms. I couldn't deny that being with Kayin was beginning to feel like home. I thought less of those I'd left behind with each passing day.

Was my growing desire for intimacy wrong? Wasn't I supposed to put Elohim first and be satisfied with Him? Shimon's words still rung in my ears. Was I betraying my family by being here and dishonouring Havel's memory?

I needed to know what had happened between Kayin and Havel. I needed the truth to discern if it was something I could live with or not. I determined to speak with Kayin about it before my heart fell further into his possession.

As I was processing all this, Kayin's eyes fluttered open. 'How is Awan?' he asked, his mouth slightly upturned.

I realised my hand was still on his cheek. I began to pull it away.

'No, stay,' he said, taking my hand and covering his scar with it. Then concern flashed across his eyes. 'Does it disgust you?'

'No,' I replied, 'not at all. Although I would like to know what it means.'

'Hmmm,' he hummed, moving my hand to his lips and kissing it. The butterfly trapped in my stomach fluttered. Then he lifted our hands together and rubbed my fingers between his, like he was testing grain for ripeness.

'After breakfast,' he said suddenly. He jumped up and pulled me with him. My legs, which were not quite ready to rise, tumbled, and he had to catch me again. Laughing, he set me straight, released me and started gathering food. Once he had an armful, we walked out of the cave into the brightness of the day. I realised he was still in his loincloth and must have left his skin by the pool.

'I'll start on that tunic today,' I said, indicating his scantily clad body.

He grinned then unexpectedly asked, 'The footprints by the lake: you followed them here?'

'Oh no, I only saw a few prints in the deeper mud. Then they disappeared.'

'How did you know the way?'

'After the bear chased me, I had a vision. I saw the paths over the mountains and the plain. I saw the lake and the stream – and you beside it. As I walked there, everything was exactly as I'd been shown. Once I found the stream, I knew you were close so I followed it until I found you.'

'You had a vision? From Elohim?'

'Yes, He told me to find you and showed me the way.'

'Why?'

'I'm still trying to work that out.' I smiled.

Kayin looked puzzled. Then he said quietly. 'I was banished. From you, from Him… I don't know why He sent you here.'

It was the first time he'd spoken of the past freely. I held my tongue, not wanting to push him. He passed me some more food and caught my hand as I took it. 'But I'm glad you obeyed,' he said. 'Glad you came.'

'Oh, it took a lot of obedience,' I replied in jest, even though it was true.

'I know,' he replied, completely serious. Then he brightened. 'Come. I'll show you something.' I let out a slight groan; I'd been hoping he would continue opening up.

'Will be worth it,' he responded, misinterpreting my groan for laziness.

After quickly covering his lower half with another skin, he led me down a thin trail through the bush. I munched on my unfinished breakfast as I followed him. After a short walk, he stopped outside another cave.

'We light fire here,' he said. I had no idea what he intended – we didn't ordinarily light fires in the morning – but I gathered some wood with him and then watched as he pulled a black stone from his pouch and lit the kindling. He didn't say anything else until the fire had taken well, then he withdrew a branch from it and walked towards the cave. I did the same and followed. He took my hand and led me deep inside.

I was just starting to wonder how far into the hill this cave went when we reached a narrow ledge with an adjacent chasm.

'Careful,' Kayin said, scooting along the ledge. After twenty or so paces, he abruptly stopped and pointed at the wall.

'What is it?' I asked.

'Look,' he said, moving his torch closer. It was no ordinary stone. It was tinged bright green, like the stems of spring flowers. Some parts were reddish orange but appeared shiny, even in the cave's darkness. Using a blunt stone to hit a different sharp one, Kayin pounded at the shiny substance in the wall until a palm-sized piece came away.

Once back outside, Kayin held the object up to the light for me to see.

'What is it?' I asked.

'Not stone,' he grinned. 'Something else. I'll show you when home.'

When we arrived back at the clearing, Kayin started hitting the object with tools, like he was trying to shape it.

'I searched for a long time,' he said, 'for better things to make tools. I find this. It is beautiful but useless for tools,' he laughed.

He went to the crevice above the woodpile and produced another object. He had fashioned it into a long, wide blade and mounted it inside bone that he'd carved into a handle.

'Looks nice, but too soft,' he said, running the edge of it along the outer skin he was wearing. It didn't cut into it. 'In fire,' he continued, 'it gets harder. Then it can cut fish, but not deer. Stone is still better.'

He passed the knife he'd created to me. I ran my fingers along its hammered-smooth surface as it glimmered in the sunlight. Parts of it had started to turn the greenish colour I had seen in the cave. The rock and the blade must contain something similar. I watched Kayin as he continued to work on the new piece. I'd always found it fascinating how he'd never been content to let life pass him by; he'd always been searching out ways of doing things better.

He was unlike any of my other siblings in this respect. Perhaps discontentment with the present had been the driving force of both his successes and his failures. It had made him brilliant but also dissatisfied. I wondered if he had found satisfaction in his new life. Could he have drawn closer to Elohim when removed from the competition he had seen in our family? And yet, hadn't he said he'd been banished from Yahweh's presence? I couldn't begin to comprehend what that meant.

Thinking of his successes as a young man prompted me to ask a question I'd been wondering about for some time. 'Kayin, why don't you grow crops here?'

He looked up at me. A glint of sadness flickered in his eyes before he muttered, 'No farming. Elohim's punishment.'

Once again, we were close to a conversation about the past. I tried to restrain the desperation bubbling in my chest. Would the truth ruin our ease?

Kayin seemed to sense I was holding back. He took a deep breath. 'You really want to know?'

I edged closer. 'It's not that I want to; I feel I need to. I need to understand what happened with Havel and Yahweh.'

He nodded then put down his tool and rolled the reddish-orange object through his fingers, staring at it.

'Shimon told the truth.'

'I know that,' I responded quietly. 'Yet I don't know how – or why?'

Kayin raised one of his hands and ran it through his hair. 'I fear to tell you. Havel was your heart. I hurt you.'

'You did, Kayin. More than you can ever imagine. Nevertheless, I chose long ago to forgive you.'

He looked up. 'How?'

'I'm not sure I can explain that fully,' I replied, not wanting to change the subject. 'Ima helped me see that I needed to. Even so it took a long time. Please, tell me your story.'

He paused, then closed his eyes as if delving into the past. After a few moments, he began to speak, slowly, often lingering to search for the correct words.

'I will try. At first I loved Havel, ever since he was a baby. It wasn't until Havel went missing that there was a problem. Then things changed. Abba hated me for losing him – you saw how he was. For years it was like this. At least, I thought it was.

'After wolf attack, I grew confused. Why was I hurt? Why was Havel chosen to speak to Elohim? I didn't understand what was wrong with me. Everyone praised Havel for saving Chayim and hated me.'

'No one hated you, Kayin. Why did you think that?'

'I saved Chayim. No one knew it.'

'We did know – Chayim told us. Besides, the claw wounds on your back proved how you'd shielded him from harm. We all knew it.'

Kayin blinked and his brows drew together. 'They praised Havel.'

'Not at your expense, Kayin.'

He scratched his chin and then nodded. 'In my mind all was different. I had many nightmares: I saw you die often. I heard Abba blame it on me. I grew frightened and bitter about things not even real.'

I remembered the conversation Kayin tried to have with me, when he'd confessed to such thoughts and grabbed my arm – the first time I ever feared him. But then he'd spoken with Havel afterwards, and I thought things had improved. He'd even assured me he was at peace with Yahweh and prayed with me. Had that all been a lie?

Kayin continued. 'I tried to believe, but I blamed my pain on Abba and Elohim. They rejected me. It seemed Havel took their attention and praise away. So, I began to… resent Havel. Then, he wanted to take you too – when I loved you! It was like – like many seeds growing into thorns in my head. A blanket of thorns twisting everything I see into things pointed and sharp. Everything was about me… no, against me.

'Havel said Elohim was teaching me, but I saw punishment. After locusts came, I was sure Elohim hated me too. I did not trust Him to look after us. So I hid things: seed, food, skins.'

I recalled finding the cave with Set and the hidden supplies inside. I'd known then that Kayin had possessed secrets.

'Then I had idea to do sacrifice. To prove I could be like Havel, make Abba like me, win respect. I wanted to stop locusts coming again. But serpents attacked me at the cave. You remember?'

I nodded.

'The best grain was ruined. I told no one. I did not trust Elohim to provide enough. I wanted to keep the other grain for seed.'

Kayin paused, like the next part was too difficult to recount. He looked exhausted already from speaking so much. Tears began to fill his eyes. I tried to sift through what he had told me so far. I could see how his grievances had built slowly over time. I knew his relationship with Abba had been strained, though I'd never understood why. I knew he had been jealous of Havel but had never imagined it leading to such a consequence.

Yet now, Kayin seemed to be suggesting it was principally to do with Elohim. This was the part I'd always struggled to piece together: why had Elohim come down so hard on Kayin at that sacrifice? The things He'd said in His thundering, terrifying rebuke had shocked me. It was the first time I'd experienced Elohim's justice beyond what my parent's had told me, and my soul had been disturbed too. But why had Kayin taken his fury out on Havel?

'Elohim was right to reject my sacrifice,' Kayin continued. 'It was worthless grain. I had wrong reasons. But the shame – in front of everyone – everyone I wanted to please? And what He said – the way He knew my thoughts. He condemned me and praised Havel. I felt… what is the word? Humiliated. Furious. Again, Havel had been chosen. He was loved.

'When I ran, Yahweh tried to speak to me in the field, but I did not want to hear. I rejected Him because He had hurt me.'

'Yahweh spoke to you again after the sacrifice? Had you called on Him?' I asked in surprise.

'No. Even so, He came. He warned me not to let sin rule, but I would not listen. Then Havel found me. I told him to leave, but *he* would not listen. He kept following me. We argued. I—'

Kayin paused and sucked in a deep breath. 'I blamed him for Elohim hating me. I thought he tried to look better than me. That it was his fault. He had turned Elohim, Abba, and you against me. Everything twisted in my head. But the words of Yahweh… Those terrible words! Havel prayed for them – he told me. My rejection. I thought he wanted it.'

The thoughts, and the order, were jumbled, but the picture was clear. My chest tightened as I dreaded what Kayin would say next.

'I was so angry I struck Havel, and he fell into thorns. He was trapped. I meant to leave him, but then the serpent came and attacked…' Kayin paused, choking on his words.

'So it *was* a snake that killed him?' I asked, a sliver of hope trying to break through. Kayin opened his eyes and looked directly into mine. I could see the conflict raging within.

He lowered his head again. 'No, Awan. Havel defeated the serpent. I could not. I listened to it. I wanted to hurt Elohim. I knew Elohim loved Havel, so I put my hands around his neck, and I... I...'

Kayin's body heaved. Sobs wrung out tears that dripped into the hands cupped beneath and spilled over the object he held.

Shock stilled my heart. I hadn't expected those final words. If Kayin had believed himself unloved, why hadn't he just taken that to Yahweh? Why hadn't he asked Yahweh to help him understand instead of assuming the worst? And what did he mean by, 'I listened to it'?

That Kayin would be upset after being rejected was a given. But the way he blamed Havel for it made little sense. I had always seen Havel's relationship with Yahweh as something that benefited us all, for it had blessed me so much. I'd never considered Kayin might see it negatively; a thing to be envied and a cause of his being scorned.

To go that step further – to believe Havel would purposefully turn Yahweh against him? Unthinkable! It was not just entirely inconsistent with Havel's character but also with Yahweh's. Kayin must not understand Yahweh at all to believe such a thing possible. He had told us He loved us and wanted to bless us from the very beginning. I couldn't comprehend it.

Then I remembered. I remembered how my heart had once been bitter against my Elohim. I remembered how sorrow had consumed me after Havel died, to the point of longing for my own death. In my grief, I had doubted Yahweh's love also. Chayim helped me through once I'd been honest with him. But it seemed Kayin had never been honest until this moment; and had received no such comfort.

As Kayin's confession penetrated my heart, my eyes followed his: weeping for the depth of his corruption; weeping for Havel and the beautiful life that ended far too soon. Despite the insufficiency of Kayin's words, I could picture the fight. It completed the scene I still saw in my dreams: my brother's body in the thorns and the horror of bruises and blood.

And so, we wept, until our tears were almost spent. At some point, Kayin dropped the piece from the cave. It clanged lightly on the ground as he sank his head into his wet hands.

CHAPTER 24

Needing refreshment, I rose and staggered to the water stone. I peered into the water and prayed to Yahweh silently, 'Yahweh Elohim, please give me grace to accept what Kayin has confessed. Give me strength to forgive. I know You are boundless in goodness, faithfulness and love, even when we can't see it. He sinned against You most of all and still, You sent me here. Help me to see what You see and to understand Your goodness through this situation. Give me the words to speak Your truth into Kayin's life, and please… please open his heart to accept them.'

I took a long drink of water then refilled the bowl and walked back to Kayin. When I held out the bowl, he murmured a thank you, took it and drank. I sat down again and pondered, trying to align his words with my experience. I realised he had barely mentioned the fear I'd held onto.

'I feared it might have been about me – your fight.' I whispered.

'You?' he said, looking up slowly with eyes barely visible inside swollen eyelids. He shook his head and sighed. 'Awan, your closeness to Havel – it was hard for me; but it was just one part… one part of a much bigger picture.' He reached his hands forward to mine, then seemed to think better of it and withdrew them again. 'I was upset that you feared me. I blamed Havel for that too. And I did want to prove myself so Abba would accept me. But I thought you wanted me.'

There was both a question and an apology in his eyes. A burden lifted from my back as he spoke. A burden of guilt I'd been carrying all this time – believing my indecision had been the leading cause of Havel's death. Emboldened, I dared to ask another question. 'When we prayed together at the river, you told me you were at peace with Yahweh. I suppose that didn't last? Do you still blame Him for your misfortune?'

Kayin pondered for a few moments. 'I did not tell the truth that day. I was not at peace. I was trying to impress you. I still don't understand why the wolves attacked, why I suffered, why the locusts took the wheat, or why He chose Havel. I still struggle—'

Kayin rubbed his the scar on his cheek. 'Yet I do not blame Elohim for what I did. When He spoke during the sacrifice, I saw my guilt, but I would not change. Even after… after *it* happened, I hid in a cave, thinking I could find a way to explain. Until Elohim found me.

'He knew everything. And He sounded so… I don't know? I expected fury, but it was more like deep sorrow, or even… disappointment. This shocked me. I saw the extent of my selfishness, my pride. My evil heart laid bare.'

He looked up and met my eyes. His were wide open, desperate for me to understand that he was no longer hiding from the truth. 'Awan. I know the blame for Havel's death is mine alone.'

I don't know if he expected me to reject him. I could see how admitting his guilt was the first step, but I didn't think I could stay with him if he had not yet forgiven Yahweh or Havel for the past. And it wasn't clear to me that he'd done either of those things.

When I didn't say anything, Kayin continued.

'I thought Elohim would kill me with same fire that took the sacrifice. But He didn't. He spoke… justice. He spoke justice.' Kayin's eyes closed again.

I waited while he searched his soul.

Whilst Kayin had struggled and searched for words during his narrative, Yahweh's judgement clearly remained etched on his heart and seared into his memory. For when he recounted it aloud, his tongue flowed freely:

' "The voice of your brother's blood is crying out to me from the ground. And now you are cursed from the ground, which has opened its mouth to receive your brother's blood from your hand. When you work the ground, it shall no longer yield to you its strength. You shall be a fugitive and a wanderer on the earth." '

Kayin let out a deep sigh that stopped my breath. He hadn't been exaggerating when he said Yahweh had sounded sorrowful. *The voice of your brother's blood is crying out to me from the ground.* I could almost hear Yahweh uttering those words as He watched me cradle dear Havel's lifeless body. He had been with me then! I didn't know if He could experience the same pain that we could; I didn't know if Kayin had succeeded in separating Him from Havel, yet Yahweh had not left me alone. When I'd been wondering where He was, He had been there. He had been hearing the cry of Havel's blood.

I silently repeated a prayer of thankfulness, feeling closer to Yahweh at that moment than I ever had before.

Forcing myself back to Kayin, I considered the judgement and how it so perfectly fitted the causes of Kayin's sin. His pride had been based on his skill, which he had refused to trust to Elohim. Now, he could never work the ground. His desire had been for people to love, appreciate and respect him. Yahweh had removed him from those people. Yahweh had spared his life, knowing what would punish him more than death. His justice was impeccable. If Shimon only knew…

Kayin was watching me; waiting for me to say something.

'And this?' I asked, reaching towards his scar. Kayin flinched against my touch.

'Knowing the depths of my sin terrified me,' Kayin continued. 'I felt sure that if Elohim did not kill me, someone else would. Still concerned with myself, I pleaded, claiming His punishment was more than I could bear.

'Then the fire came, filling the cave. But still, it didn't kill me. Instead of anger, He showed mercy. And this mark? He drew it. It's a seal of His promise to take vengeance on any who might harm me. After all I had done! But afterwards, I wished I had not begged him so.'

'Why?' I asked.

'Since that day, I have desired death many times. At first, when I lived in the mountains, I defended myself against wild creatures. But I soon grew tired of it. I quickly missed the people I was banished from and longed for the company I'd scorned. I thought I'd grown tired of worship and could not bear the sight of Elohim or Havel. Yet when I had to leave – it was misery far worse than before! To live without Elohim, without hope… *That* is unbearable. The river you mentioned with the tannin? I swam there not caring if I came out alive.

'But nothing injured me. After several seasons in the mountains, my fingers itched for the soil. I moved to the plain and found the lake. I tried proving the judgment wrong; to regain purpose for my life. I dug channels from the lake, planting seeds I'd gleaned in my travels. Most of them failed. The ones that grew produced nothing edible.

'So, I moved to the hills – not these, but ones closer to the sea. I tried to train olive trees and vines, but every tree I cut or vine I pruned withered. Then I knew that Yahweh's words were steadfast. I was cursed from the ground; it would never yield to me again.

'So I gave up. For years I wandered from place to place, taking what I could find and sinking deeper into despair. I had nothing to live for, no skill I could use and nobody to share life with. What is the point of seeking joy if you cannot share it? It is meaningless.

'Then I actively sought death, walking into danger willingly, cursing the day Yahweh marked me in mercy. I swam where I knew monsters dwelt, inviting them to attack me; yet they did not. I went to the sea and threw myself in; the waves refused to claim me. Everything in me desired death, and still it refused me. If Shimon had attacked me then, I would have welcomed it.'

I was surprised at Kayin's growing eloquence as he recounted this part of the tale. In describing his anguish, his voice held a harrowing beauty and he spoke almost fluently. 'Yet, when Shimon attacked, you did defend yourself. So what changed?' I asked.

'Several years ago, the scar on my face began to burn, though it had never hurt me before. I would scratch at it, plunge it into water, bathe it in oil –

nothing subdued it. Eventually, I found myself screaming to Elohim; begging Him to take it away.

'I'd heard nothing from Him since my judgement, and I didn't expect Him to answer. I thought my sin had driven Him away forever. Yet, inconceivably, He came to me again as I cried. The holy fire surrounded the grove I slept in, and His presence scorched my cheek. I sank my face into the ground, not daring to glance at the flames, as Yahweh confronted me again, His voice booming: "I drew this mark by my own hand. Why do you despise what I have given? What right have you to reject my mercy? You begged me for your life. Now take it and live it."

'The sting of his rebuke penetrated further than the sting in my cheek. Yet, I realised He had not forgotten me! He was watching me always.'

It was incredible – that Kayin was banished and yet seen and known. 'I have felt His presence in my life very differently to you,' I said. 'Yet I am His; I have always been His. That He would watch out for you after you rejected Him?' I shook my head. 'His mercy knows no limits.'

Kayin didn't seem offended, so I continued. 'You said you thought sin had driven Him away forever. Why is that?'

'He told me I would be a fugitive. His presence is with His people, and I am alone.'

'But did Yahweh actually tell you to leave His presence forever, as part of His judgement?'

Kayin considered, face cupped in his hands.

'When I recall His words, I cannot find those. When I was begging Him, I said I would be hidden from His face, but He never affirmed that. In fact, He may have corrected me, for He said, "Not so", before He gave me the mark.'

'I believe He sees everything. I don't know that anything – or anyone – can be hidden from his face,' I murmured.

'But it did feel different when I left. The further I travelled from the family, the more the chasm grew. Perhaps His sight and His presence are not the same thing?'

'I have sometimes felt Yahweh draw away from me when I have been willingly sinful. Then He has returned when I've repented. Do you think He could dwell with you now?' I asked.

'No. He came that once, but He did not stay. His holiness was too much for me to bear – it is both awesome and terrifying! I can never be cleansed from what I have done, Awan. I know I cannot be near Elohim without perishing.

'I have repented, though. After that rebuke, I repented of my attitude and committed to living again. Though I know I deserve nothing, I have tried to find joy again in creation. I have not attempted to farm – I know that is against His will. Yet simple things like creating the cleansing bar, building water channels and growing those flowers over there – which shall never produce food but brighten up the hillside – these things I have done.'

'So, you no longer despise Yahweh?' I asked, knowing this question was the most important for my heart and Kayin's.

'I do not. I said I do not understand, and that is still true. But I feel differently now. I wonder if the fault lay not with His actions but with my ability to... comprehend them. When I consider how He's treated me since – for some reason wanting me to live – can I despise that?'

'And Havel?' I asked, with a trembling lip. 'What about him?'

Kayin took a deep breath.

'At the time, I was so jealous that Havel was chosen. I wanted to hear Yahweh's voice; I yearned to be accepted and respected. In my mind, Havel stood in the way of that. But I didn't know what I was seeking! For when Yahweh spoke, His voice was petrifying! It revealed all: the whole ugly truth of what was in my heart.

'I *had* given my mind free rein for evil. My tongue *had* framed deceit as I lied to everyone and indulged in evil thoughts and words against Havel. Yes, there had been circumstances – pain, hardships, whispers even – but that didn't excuse what I did or how I treated my brother. I was no better than Abba. I... I was worse.

'Though I felt ashamed after the sacrifice, I didn't see the truth about Havel immediately. Yet, when Elohim asked me what I had done – when he said Havel's blood was crying out – I finally did. All the lies I had built up around Havel's actions faded in that cave, in the presence of Yahweh's truth.

'I shall not lie to you, Awan. It has taken time to unpack the pain and resentment that had built up in my heart. Those lies kept coming back; my mind kept wanting to justify my actions. I had to rip them away and burn them like maggots from a festering wound.

'But I have mourned for Havel every day. I wish I could go back and see things with new eyes; see my brother again for who he truly was and love him for it. I wish – I wish I could bring him here and experience life by his side. I long to learn from him again and to listen this time. And to take away your pain, Awan – that most of all. Yet I cannot! It is too late—'

Kayin broke down again, wiping his eyes desperately with the back of his hand. 'He is gone forever. Havel is gone.'

I was struck dumb. This was an entirely different Kayin from the one I had known. Absent was the self-confidence I now realised had been a front. Finished was the anger, jealousy and deception. He had laid himself bare and confessed all, and – to my astonishment – I believed him. He had been punished. He had suffered. He had also mourned.

Kayin picked up the stony-shiny object chipped from the cave. It was still wet from tears. He placed it in my palm. 'You must despise me now. You see I am ruined and that a life with me is no life at all.'

I thought for a moment, turning the item in my fingers and observing how some areas were dark while others captured the light. I considered how Elohim had treated Kayin since the sacrifice. He had shown him the truth, then given him time to process what had happened. He had refused to let him wallow but had brought him to repentance. He had brought me here only when Kayin and I were both ready.

'Perhaps not. You see this?' I held up what he'd placed in my hand. 'How do you make it beautiful like that blade you showed me? How do you get it smooth enough to reflect the sun?'

Kayin drew his brows together as he answered, 'By repeatedly beating and hammering it; putting it in the fire and reshaping it.'

'Yes. We are imperfect and incomplete, just like this. We all have holes and ridges, black spots and green. You built your life and worth on created things rather than the Creator, despising Havel because he reflected Elohim's image and you did not. That isn't to say you *cannot*; just that – perhaps – you needed rather a lot of hammering.

'Now you have been beaten; you have been through the fire. Elohim has removed those things you should not have built your life on. Perhaps now you will allow the Creator to work, forming you into something beautiful that will reflect His glory.

'Kayin, I too remember Yahweh's words at the sacrifice. Some are stamped in my mind also. They were not solely words of condemnation. I don't believe He was just rebuking you. He was also appealing to you, desiring you to repent. I recall most clearly these: "Offer to me a sacrifice of thanksgiving. Perform your vows to the Most High and call upon me in your day of trouble. I will deliver you, and you shall glorify me."

'Perhaps, all this time, Yahweh has been waiting for you to call on Him. When you finally cried out about the burning in your cheek, He came! That may have been the first step on your road to discovering who He truly is; the first moment of your deliverance.'

Silence reigned between us before Kayin spoke, quietly. 'Havel once said something similar, and I refused to listen. I shall not make that mistake again.'

I placed the imperfect object back into his hands and, closing his fingers over it, left Kayin alone with his thoughts.

CHAPTER 25

Kayin and I did not speak in depth again for the next few weeks, but every time our eyes met, I could see thoughts working busily behind his. Spending my time on Kayin's clothing, I constructed two reasonable tunics – though they wouldn't match up to Avigail's.

Now that I knew the details of Havel's death, I regularly lay awake at night picturing the fight between my brothers. I cried often. Even so, it was good to know of Yahweh's justice; it was good to know that Havel's death had not been left unpunished as if it were nothing of consequence. And, at the same time, I ached for Kayin's great suffering since then: his cursedness; his guilt; his desire to die – all endured without the company and comfort of family or even Yahweh himself.

I could understand why Kayin would despair during the years of lonely, purposeless wandering. Yet Yahweh hadn't given up on him – that was clear. Somehow, He expected Kayin to accept His mercy, and to dwell in it.

Added to which, despite all he had done, I found I no longer despised Kayin. Even as I wept with the very cause of my agony asleep in the same cave; even when he cried out about Havel's face during his nightmares; I still desired to draw closer to him.

I was grateful to Yahweh for bringing me here. Knowledge was worth the pain that accompanied it. Seeing Yahweh's hand of goodness working, despite our failures, brought peace to my heart. Perhaps that was His purpose. Could I – should I – hope for more?

One morning Kayin announced he was going on a journey. We had been living together for some time, and it was now the warmest season of the year.

'There is a place where the grain grows wild, many days walk to the north-east,' Kayin said. 'Now is the right time to harvest it. There's not much food in these hills during the winter. If I want to eat, I must gather food to store. Do you want to come with me?'

'Yes,' I replied without hesitation. I was keen to see more of the area.

'Good.' He smiled, nervousness fading from his face. Had he thought I wouldn't?

'Isn't it late for harvesting grain?' I asked.

'Summer runs later where we are going,' he said, 'It is colder further north.'

Kayin headed towards the mouth of the cave and retrieved something from the crevice where he kept his tools.

'I have something for you,' he said. As he held it up to the light, I gasped. Kayin must have been secretly working on the material chiselled from the other cave. He'd shaped it into the form of a terebinth leaf. Gone were the uneven edges, and the black and green marks. Now it shone a stunning copper, perfectly reflecting the sunlight that streamed into the glade. There was a tiny hole bored into the top, through which he had threaded a delicate cord of twine.

'You could wear it around your neck,' he said quietly. 'It will complement your eyes.'

I stood still as he tied the cord ends together at my nape. At the slight touch of his fingers, a pleasant tremor ran down my back. Had he noticed? Holding the delicate leaf in my hand, I ran my fingertips over its surface.

'It's wonderful. Thank you.' I turned to face him, rose on my toes, and kissed his cheek. As my lips brushed over his scar, anxiety flickered into his eyes. He retreated into the cave to prepare for our journey.

We set off later that day, taking several empty sacks Kayin produced from the back of the cave. We stuffed the sacks into light packs carried on our shoulders. 'How long have you lived here?' I asked as we wandered across the top of the neighbouring hill.

'I came here a few summers past, seeking out the fruit in the meadow. I stayed awhile, experimenting with the water channels to make it more habitable. But the first winter was cold, so I walked south of the lake to an area more sheltered from the winds that come off the sea. After that, I went to the mountains and didn't return here until late spring, when the hills started producing food again.

'Over the years, I've adopted various places to stay depending on the weather and the wild crops. This hill country is roughly central, so it's a good base.'

'How long is it since you had grain?' I asked.

'I only gather as much as I can carry in one journey. It's not worth leaving supplies behind when travelling between places; animals usually find them before you return. As I stayed here this winter, I haven't tasted real bread for many moons – just the harsh loaf made from the trees.'

'Well, you now have another mouth to feed, so we will have to gather more.'

'You will stay for the winter then?'

'I have no plans to leave. Do you want me to stay?'

'Of course.'

'Good then,' I smiled and skipped down the hill.

'As long as you carry your own grain home!' he shouted after me. I turned to see him grinning broadly and laughed back.

Once we'd left the hill country, we made our way east, following the sun that rose in the morning.

Kayin indicated ahead. 'We should reach the river soon if we continue this way, then we can follow it north for the rest of our journey.'

'There's another river?'

'There are many. I haven't found the source of this one, but it flows into the sea near where I found the black stone. I suppose there must be some higher ground where it originates, for our stream flows down from the hill country into the great lake. Abba said the Tigris and Euphrates flow from the river of Eden, but they also have sources in the mountains we know – many springs converging into one place.'

'Is Eden mountainous then?'

'I believe so, though I've never seen it.'

'Abba and Channah went south last winter with the flocks,' I said. 'They said the twin rivers turned into a marshland. They couldn't walk further but perhaps if they had, they would have journeyed to the sea.'

We found the river Kayin referred to later that day. It flowed gently and had rich, red clay for its bed and bank. Lining those banks were many rushes. Wildlife flocked to it – another watery haven in a dry land.

'Two more days heading north and we'll find the fertile ground where there are grains to harvest.'

'Haven't you been tempted to settle there?' I asked. 'I know you cannot farm it, but—'

'No,' he interrupted. 'It's best that I stay away and keep moving. Besides, the hill country has much to commend it: beauty, shelter, wild fruit and nuts. It is better.'

I saw then that it would be agony for Kayin to live in the valleys without working the soil. I slipped my hand into his and squeezed it. He raised his eyebrows then drew his hand away and continued walking.

I felt his rejection in my chest. Had I offended him? Tucking my hand back into my side, I followed him, keeping my distance this time. I'd been trying to ignore it, but the truth was, Kayin had withdrawn, giving me little affection since the day he told me his story. I'd assumed he still felt something for me – but had I entirely misjudged?

CHAPTER 26

When we made camp that night, the bitter wind from the sea was blowing over the plain, and there was insufficient shelter. Even huddled under wool and next to the fire, I was cold. Kayin had barely spoken to me since I had touched his hand and he would not lie next to me. After shivering for some time, I found the courage to speak.

'Kayin, are you awake?'

He grunted.

'Will you come and lie near me? I'm cold.'

Kayin turned over. In the flicker of the firelight, I saw that his eyes were moist. He propped himself up, threw more wood onto the fire and turned away again, ignoring my request.

What had I done? I wasn't going to tolerate this treatment. I stood, picked up my blanket and the rolled-up cloth I was resting my head on, and threw them in front of him. Then I lay down and inched closer to him, almost – but not quite – touching his body.

'Awan, what are you doing?' he groaned. I knew that lying together was no small thing. Our parents had almost forced Chayim to marry me after all. And yet, no one had complained when Havel and I had huddled together for warmth when younger.

'I told you I'm cold. Don't pretend you're not,' I replied, shifting a bit closer.

'Awan, I'm trying—'

'What?' I interrupted. 'What have I done to offend you?'

'Nothing!'

'Then why won't you touch me?'

He rolled onto his back, 'Because I don't trust myself with you. If I touch you now, I might never stop!'

I let the words sink in as I watched his face. He had been crying; his cheeks were wet with it. I sat up and leaned forward but didn't touch him.

'Kayin, why are you upset? Please talk to me.'

He took a deep breath before looking my way.

'You don't understand what you are doing, Awan. You think you want to be with me now, but one day you will wake up and realise you have made a mistake. You will despise me.'

'I will never despise you.'

'Don't argue with me, Awan. Shimon was right; I hurt you more than anyone with what I did. I know you are trying to be strong, and perhaps you think you feel something for me, but it will not last.'

'It has lasted these forty years, Kayin!'

'Has it though? You have never hated me?'

I chewed my lip. 'I—I confess there have been times, yes, when I felt hatred for you. But I was hurting and confused, and affection was always mixed up in it too. That is in the past.'

'Then what about Chayim?'

I thought that would come back to bite. I composed myself and prayed silently for clear words.

'The day you left, I lost the two people I loved most in the world. I was torn apart. I grieved for Havel – his absence a hole inside my chest that would not be filled. But I was also grieving for you, and I didn't know how to manage that. Because no one would talk about you; no one would acknowledge what we thought had happened. Ima was broken and didn't speak at all. Abba just… Well, he dealt with things the way he always does: he withdrew and blamed himself.'

Kayin sniffed and rubbed his nose.

'After a while, Chayim and I began to share the second hut. I soon realised that he was the only member of our family who would acknowledge you were gone. He missed you and was willing to talk about it. He helped me to grieve and process what had happened. We would sit up at night talking through stories of the past and emotions of the present. We would laugh together and weep together. And, most importantly, Chayim pointed me to Yahweh. He reminded me to keep trusting in Him, which I was struggling with.'

'It sounds like he grew up a lot in that time,' Kayin murmured.

'He did. He took on a lot of responsibility after you left. And, although he is still the wonderful life-loving person you knew, he's had a lot of weight on his shoulders. He has borne it, for the most part, with exceptional grace.

'Anyway, after realising we had grown close, Abba and Ima tried to make us wed, but I wasn't the one Chayim wanted. I released him to go to Avigail. Yet doing so left me without my friend; without my confidante. I was lonely again.

'There was one good outcome. In my loneliness, I turned to Yahweh. I allowed Yahweh to take the place in my heart that was left empty. He had always been there, waiting to pick up the pieces of my brokenness as soon as I was ready to let Him. My journey here arose from a desire to spend time with Him when I felt myself wavering.

'However, Chayim followed me. He was also struggling in other ways, and it was nice to reconnect. Until it wasn't. Things became intense and, in my sinfulness, I almost kissed him. Yahweh protected me. He spoke to me just in time, and we stopped. It was a moment of weakness borne from loneliness and opportunity. I immediately sent Chayim home to Avigail. There is no future for Chayim and me. There never was.'

Kayin had watched me intently as I told my story. 'So, you don't love him?' he finally asked.

'Not in the way you imagine. My feelings for Chayim are probably little different from yours, for I know you loved him too.'

Kayin sighed. 'I did. I do. I would have been happy for you both if you'd married.'

'You mean that?' I asked. I was surprised, given his jealousy of Havel.

'I never expected you to come here, Awan! I always believed I would be alone forever, but I never assumed you would be. I thought you'd marry. I imagined you doing so.'

At those words, I so wanted to tuck myself into Kayin's arms, but his warning was still with me. Despite the re-stoked fire blazing nearby, my body shivered again.

Kayin stared at the stars above us. 'Do you really think Elohim can change me?'

'Hasn't He already?' I replied, softly.

'I still feel so damaged. Yet you said, just then, that He was waiting to pick up your broken pieces. Could He do that for me, even though I sinned in the worst possible way?'

'I, too, have sinned.'

'Oh, that is not the same! You had one moment of temptation, Awan, in a lifetime of goodness. I told Havel I hated Elohim – and it was true! I despised Him; I set my whole heart against Him. How can He possibly forgive that?'

'Yet something in you desired Him, or you would never have made that sacrifice. I am not saying what you did was not horrific. Nevertheless, I believe that, whatever we do, Yahweh's goodness is always far greater than we can imagine; His mercy reaches deeper than we can ever fall.'

There was a moment of silence while Kayin blinked as if holding back further tears. 'I hope you're right. He just feels so out of reach. I used to consider Elohim unreasonable and unjust. I thought He didn't listen to me or answer my prayers. I was envious of His relationship with others. Since you arrived, I feel like my blinded eyes have been peeled open. I now remember experiencing His presence when I was younger; I remember times when He did answer my prayers. Like when Havel was lost: He revealed Havel's location when I prayed, and He helped me cross that river. I never thanked Him for that.

'Perhaps everything started going wrong at that point not because of Havel or Abba, but because I let pride into my life. I see now that Elohim has always been there; I was just too blind to see Him.'

I nodded. It was tragic that sin like Kayin's could happen so easily, yet no longer surprising. 'Sometimes Yahweh does feel distant, intangible even,' I said. 'Although I know He is with me, it doesn't always feel that way.'

'Yes. Whereas, by contrast, the serpent is so real.'

'The serpent? What do you mean?'

'The serpent has followed me. Several times. Perhaps it was not the same one as in the Garden – it may only have been a physical creature – yet it seemed to have intentions. Every time I started slipping into sin, it was there to encourage me.'

'Did it have a voice?' I muttered.

'A voice?'

'I heard a voice encouraging me to kiss Chayim that day. Telling me it would do no harm.'

'Sometimes the serpent spoke in my nightmares, but it was confusing. I believed it was Havel's voice. In Havel's final moments, I heard a hissing whisper in my ear, spurring on my worst thoughts.'

'It was the Deceiver then,' I concluded.

'Yes, I think. The same Deceiver that tempted our mother. Awan, I'm beginning to think there is a battle going on that is far bigger than we realise.'

'It would seem so.' I shuddered.

'I now recognise Elohim's righteousness and how often I scorned Him in favour of the Evil One,' Kayin said. 'But how can I ever earn His favour after what I have done?'

I paused to consider, taking a moment to join Kayin in gazing at the stars, and I prayed for an answer. It came from a well of wisdom I hadn't known I possessed.

'You cannot earn His favour, Kayin. None of us can. We can only accept it. In the Garden, our parents already had Yahweh's favour and blessing, but the serpent convinced them it wasn't enough – that they should seek to be like Yahweh himself. In eating the forbidden fruit, they took control – trying to earn greatness by their own action – rather than accepting everything the Creator had given them. I don't believe that's what He wants for us. He doesn't want us attempting to work our way up to Him.'

'But didn't the banishment change everything, replacing the blessings with curses? Didn't it mean we could no longer please Elohim?' Kayin asked.

'Certainly it changed things. No longer could our parents walk with Yahweh Elohim in innocence; no longer could they eat from the tree of life. Yet, it was not the end of Yahweh's kindness. Previously you mentioned everything shifting the day Havel went missing. It did not only change for you; it changed for Havel also,' I said.

Kayin's eyebrows drew together. 'What do you mean?'

'I remember Havel telling me about it. He was stuck on that cliff for so long – cold and terrified. He thought he might die and began considering his life and actions. Even though he was only young, he realised he had been living sinfully. As the darkness crept in, he cried out to Yahweh to forgive him for how he had been – selfish, possessive and often violent. He realised and accepted his place before his Elohim.

'That day, Havel experienced Yahweh's grace: His undeserved favour. His hunger for a relationship with his Elohim began, and he never looked back. When he told you to cry out, he wasn't talking in some abstract way. He was speaking from his own experience. He longed for you to receive the same gift he had.

'Havel knew he had not earned favour. The only thing he'd done was call out and confess. He was loved and blessed despite his sin. And so, he loved in return. He valued Yahweh above all else and would have sacrificed everything for Him.

'Yahweh won his heart, Kayin. Who will win your heart? Who will own it? Will it be you? Will it be me? Or will it be Yahweh?'

Shock crossed Kayin's face. Then he placed his hands over his eyes.

'What is it?' I asked, daring to touch his arm.

'Havel tried to tell me this before he died,' he gasped. 'He told me that Elohim desired my heart before my sacrifice. At the time, it just made me angrier. If only I had listened.'

'We cannot change the past,' I said softly. 'You have repented of what you did. You've repented of your selfishness and your attempts at self-destruction. You have humbled yourself and accepted Yahweh's judgement. Now it's time to accept Yahweh's forgiveness and grace, Kayin. It is time to leave the darkness and walk into the light.'

'But I shall always be in debt to Him!'

'Yes! But are we not already? All things have their breath in Him, through Him and by Him. We have nothing without our Creator. Ima once said we all have something we need to lay down before our Elohim. I think Ima didn't go far enough. It's not one thing we must lay down, but everything. We have to admit that, by ourselves, we can never be good enough. We owe everything to Yahweh Elohim.'

Kayin sighed, gazing up into the vast, sparkling sky. Then he turned his head towards me and offered a small smile. 'Will you sing a prayer for me?'

I lay down next to him but did not move closer. Then I lifted my voice to the Creator of the stars. I sang a song that had been my companion for many years, amending the words into a prayer for Kayin:

I sang of despair, eyes flowing without ceasing;
Yahweh from heaven looked down and saw.
So call on His name from the depths of your sorrow;
He'll hear your plea and take up your cause.

Redeemer of life, all-sufficient one,
Help him grasp the heights of Your love for him.
Quieten his thoughts, fill him anew
With songs of your goodness, faithfulness, truth.

Your soul continues to remember its pain.
It will stay bowed down 'til it calls to mind
That the steadfast love of Yahweh never ceases;
His mercies are new every moment of time.

May Yahweh be your portion and your rock;
Put all your trust and hope in Him.
For He does good to those who wait;
Perfect salvation He will demonstrate.

Despair turns into hope.
Food for the soul; food for the soul.
Despair turns into hope.
Yahweh make him whole; make him whole…

I sang until I heard Kayin's breathing regulate and his body relaxed. Only then did I pull my wool blanket over me and snuggle in close to his warmth.

When a cold wind hit me during the night, I woke to find Kayin absent. I looked about and saw him kneeling a short way off with his head bowed on the ground. I didn't move, not wanting to disturb him, but I could hear his mutterings carried on the wind:

> Out of the depths, I cry to you –
>> From the bleakest place, I plea –
>> Tune your ears to my anguished prayer;
>> Oh hear my cry for mercy!
> If you, O Eternal One, marked my sins,
>> I could surely never stand.
>> So, I kneel and humbly beg
>> That you hear my cry for mercy.
> My sole hope is in you alone,
>> For with you is steadfast love.
>> Heal my broken spirit – forgive!
>> Oh! Hear my cry for mercy.
> I will wait now, Elohim;
>> On your goodness I will depend.
>> Cleanse my heart, Yahweh, my Elohim,
>> Until light beckons and darkness ends.

I woke twice more during that night, the chilly wind still biting. Each time I opened my eyes, Kayin was in the same place. He did not return to me; he stayed in the dust before Yahweh until dawn.

CHAPTER 27

It was morning when I woke again, and Kayin was still kneeling on the ground. I propped myself up on my elbow and watched him. This time he was not praying but was searching through his pack, presumably for food.

He was wearing his new tunic which, as it was sleeveless, allowed me to appreciate his muscular arms and the legs he crouched on. His long hair was loose and blowing in the breeze. Only the dark hollows under his eyes hinted at his sleepless night. I yawned loudly when he didn't acknowledge me and stretched my arms out.

'Good morning,' he chuckled.

'Is it? I feel terribly cold.' I grinned.

'You are asking for trouble, woman,' he laughed, crawling to me and prodding my shoulder.

'So, you are still determined to ignore me?'

'I am determined to preserve you.'

'I trust you, Kayin. Will you not accept that?'

'That is… completely irrelevant.'

I laughed back at him and tugged his arm, trying to draw him closer.

'Awan, do you really want to stay? To be my wife, body and soul?' he asked, suddenly becoming quite serious.

I wanted to answer in the affirmative; everything in my body desired his. Yet I knew he was right, and I had to consider my soul before my body. I had heard his cry to Yahweh the night before; I hoped that meant he was trusting Him again, but I knew it might still be some time before all the past pain had been resolved. I decided not to answer his question but to stall with one of my own.

'Do you love me, Kayin?' I asked.

He drew back and pursed his lips. After a short pause, he tucked into a cross-legged position and took my hand in his.

'You know that I do. My love has not wavered at all in our time apart, and, in the last few weeks, it has ignited into something I am struggling to contain. I want every part of you to be mine to explore and know. I want to be with you always and share with you everything that brings me joy. The problem is, ever since you defended me from Shimon, I have not stopped wondering how you could possibly be here and what I could ever do to deserve you.'

I blinked. I hadn't been expecting such a speech.

'Then I suppose you understand something of love…' I murmured, thinking how to draw it round to what I wanted to say. 'Our parents say that the love they share is but a reflection of Yahweh's love for His people. He also wants us to be His. He wants to be with us, show us everything that brings Him joy and share it with us. Yet He cannot share love with us if we refuse to accept it. Accepting His love is part of our walk with Him.'

Kayin squeezed my fingers but said nothing.

'I saw you praying last night,' I confessed. 'Have you surrendered your heart?'

'I have. At least, I have tried.'

'Then accept not just Yahweh's justice, not just His forgiveness, but also His love. Allow Him to show you how much He loves you! Although I do want you, Kayin, I should not be your wife unless we can share His love together.'

'How will I know I'm doing it for His sake and not yours?'

'What do you mean?'

'You said last night that I must allow Him to own my heart. So, I must ensure I do things in the right order. If I am to place Him first and try loving Him above all else – and allowing Him to love me – then you must be second. Consequently, if I am still unsure where my heart lies then you, my love, will have to wait.'

He dropped his seriousness and grinned as if the thought of me having to wait was highly amusing. Then he stood and threw me a fig out of his pack before walking away towards some shrubland nearby.

I groaned and took a bite of the fig. He was right: it was my turn to be patient. I needed to stop goading him for affection.

When we reached the area where wheat grew beside the river, Kayin walked ahead of me into the midst of the crops. After running his fingers through them and pulling the odd stalk, he tested the grain between his teeth. I watched him and considered how at home he looked and how he must feel having to stay away.

When Kayin walked back towards me his face was neutral. 'We've arrived at just the right time. The wheat is ready, but there's not a lot of it. Come here and I'll show you what to do.' I followed him to the edge of the field. 'These are tares. It will be hard not to pull them up with the wheat, but as you gather what I cut, try to keep them separate. Later, we shall burn them. The more we burn, the less will come back next year. These taller, thicker stalks are rye; we can harvest them with the wheat.'

'Your fields didn't look like this,' I commented.

'No, there are a great number of weeds here – more weeds than grain. Now you see why I spent such a long time pulling them up around the young plants. Once they get tall, removing them without damaging the crop is impossible. You can only do it when you harvest. I fear this won't be enough to feed us both. However, I know of an area further north where some wild emmer grows. When we've finished here we should go there.'

'It will take us a while to tackle this.'

'I expect to be here for almost a week, and then we shall have to wait for it to dry. We may as well thresh it here so we just carry back the grain.'

'Ok, let's get started then.'

Kayin was right. It took six days to harvest and separate the good wheat. He was mostly on his hands and knees, cutting with his black stone and throwing the stalks behind him. I gathered them and separated the tares and thistles from the wheat, piling them up at the outer edge of the field and tying the wheat stalks into bushels so they could stand up to dry in the sun. We burnt the weeds at night, using them as fuel for our fire.

It was exhausting work, and we also had to find food to eat each evening. Fortunately, the river was easily accessible and full of fish, so spearing them wasn't an issue. Kayin usually waded in to do this while I gathered from nearby shrubs and trees. We were so exhausted by the time we'd eaten that we went straight to sleep each night, meaning conversation was sparse.

We stopped for Shabbat – which this time I remembered and greatly appreciated. Even on the rest day, Kayin didn't say much about his relationship with Elohim, seeming content to listen to me singing.

When we had reaped the whole field, I couldn't believe how little yield there was compared to how much we would have harvested at home in the same area and time frame.

'I suggest we leave the stalks here drying while we seek out the emmer I mentioned, which grows close to the shore. How would you like to see the sea?' Kayin asked.

I hesitated. I longed to see where the land ended, yet even considering such a great expanse of water made my stomach knot.

'Do you promise not to throw me in?' I asked.

He laughed with a slightly nervous lilt. 'I promise. I think I have learnt my lesson.'

I agreed, and we set off immediately.

At one point on our walk, Kayin motioned towards the distance, in the east. 'There is another small lake in that direction. Various crops grow around it; some I hadn't come across before. We could go there on the way back and see what there is to gather. There is also an olive grove on that hillside, but the olives won't be ready for some time.'

'Are those the olives you tried once to tend?'

'Yes. All the trees that I pruned withered. Even so, the ones left produce fruit without assistance, so long as we get to them before the animals do.'

I wanted to put my arms around him, to comfort and reassure him that I understood his pain, but I kept them tucked into my sides and stayed silent.

Partway into the afternoon, we began climbing to higher ground. Then, just as the sun was setting and throwing the most glorious colours across the sky, we reached a mound where we could see the vast expanse of the sea in the distance below us.

'We haven't taken the most direct route,' Kayin said, sitting down, 'but I couldn't resist showing you this view. It's the best in all of Nod.'

'What's Nod?' I asked, joining him.

'The name I've given to all the land of the East. Nod: my land of wandering.'

The view was staggeringly beautiful. The water before us, which stretched to the horizon, reflected every colour of the sky above. Waves caressed the shore below in maroon, orange and yellow ripples. An expanse of yellow sand met the water's edge. It was dotted with stones and boulders and contained small pools of water that also reflected the light from the setting sun. Behind the yellow expanse rose blueish-white cliff tops to meet the land above.

Kayin was watching my face as I took it all in. I turned to him and saw the joy in his eyes. 'Better shared?' I asked.

'Better shared.' He put his arm around my shoulders, and I leaned into him, revelling in his renewed touch as he supported the weight of my relaxing body. He rested his head on top of mine, and we sat in silence as the sun slowly lowered in the west before finally dipping below the surface of the earth.

Then the moon was able to show its glory. Now whites glistened over the water, and creatures of the night began to dip under the surface, creating further ripples.

After a few moments of moonlit stillness, the creation threw us another surprise: the Great Serpent appeared. Abba had told us about Leviathan – the master of the seas – created with the giant whales, yet able to rise out of the water and breathe fire upon the land.

As one creature flew down from above, the jaws of Leviathan came up from beneath, astonishingly wide, with rows of giant teeth set upon their prey. His body followed, covered in scales that glinted in the light of the moon which highlighted every impenetrable shield running the length of his neck.

Reaching a sufficient height, Leviathan's jaws snapped shut, trapping the body of his prey. Just the tip of one wing remained outside those jaws as he dragged his catch back into the depths. Head down, his tail flicked upwards: a tremendous spear-tipped whip whose length looked like it could reach the moon.

Shivers ran down my spine at the shock of Leviathan's appearance. I snuggled closer to Kayin.

'Magnificent, isn't he?' Kayin said, wrapping his second arm around my front. Then, when I continued shaking, he drew a blanket from his pack and wrapped it around me.

'Are we safe here?' I asked. It felt like the giant had been so close.

'Oh yes. Leviathan won't trouble himself with what's on land when he has his pick of the sea and the sky.'

Despite the wool covering, I shivered again.

'You're still cold, though,' he said. 'Let's find some shelter, away from the wind blowing off the water.'

We shuffled back into the tree cover just behind the mound, Kayin keeping his arm around me. When we had found a sheltered spot with space for a small fire, I curled up on the ground as Kayin built one up and lit it. Soon the flames were warming me through, and sleep beckoned.

Kayin sat beside me and stared into the blaze. Then he opened his heart, as his voice created a tuneful verse that danced with the flames:

O Yahweh Elohim,
Your wonders know no measure.
Throwing on a cloak of light
as a garment for Your pleasure.
The beams of Your brilliance
rest on ripples now before us;
Moving on wings of the wind,
You show Yourself so glorious.

You made the moon to mark the days;
The sun knows when to set.
But make Your face to shine on us,
And we shall be blessed.

You set the earth in place,
spreading water as a covering.
At Your voice mountains rose
and left the valleys trembling.
You formed creatures by Your wisdom;
seas vast with countless wonders;
And Leviathan plays there
as the sky above him thunders.

May every being praise You –
Pledge honour to Your name.
Glorifying Elohim
For the bounty He has made.

All look to You for food
in the seasons You've appointed;
You open your hand wide:
blessings fall on your anointed.
Yet if You hide Your face,
then terror will abound;
If You take away our breath,
we return unto the ground.

So send out Your ruach
And cause our flourishing.
Renew the entire earth;
Set the curse to vanishing.

Oh, Yahweh Elohim,
my feet are always wandering.
May foulness leave my heart
and every thought be pleasing.
May evil fade away,
and Your people bear Your likeness.
Alone, we can do nothing,
yet grace shines forth brightness.

May Your majesty endure –
Rejoice in what You've made!

I'll praise Yahweh forever,
For faithful He has stayed.

Deep, contented peace reigned as I drifted into sleep. Kayin had found his joy in Yahweh at last.

CHAPTER 28

We spent several days by the sea. For the first three, we decided not to bother seeking the emmer. Instead, we climbed down to the shoreline and paddled in the water. Keeping his promise, Kayin didn't push me in. We moulded the soft sand with our hands, competing to create the most elaborate pictures. Kayin's skill far exceeded mine; everything I made looked the same, but he could fashion an eagle and even Leviathan from it.

I collected shells and spent time staring into the rock pools, fascinated with the creatures that scurried and swam in the clear water. At one point, Kayin wrapped his arms around me as I stared into a pool, then kissed my shoulder, sending ripples through my body. Just as quickly, he withdrew and left me to watch the creatures alone.

At night, we climbed to a cave in the shore's cliff. Kayin told me how he had spent time dwelling in this cave. Sitting beside the fire, we told stories and boiled seaweed to eat. The fireside banter made me yearn for the rest of my family; yet I knew that I now longed for Kayin more, and the two were not compatible.

On the fourth day, Kayin led the way across the cliff tops until we reached an area slightly west of the beach, where wild wheat was growing down the hillside.

'We don't need to cut these stalks,' he explained. 'Emmer throws its seed onto the ground when it's ready. There's only a small amount of seed per pod, but, once ground thoroughly, it's good.'

Kayin pulled the old cloth out of his pack and ripped strips off it, handing me four. 'Wrap these around your hands and knees, or they shall bleed.'

I was very grateful for his wisdom. The kernels had sharp tips and, since gathering them required crawling around in the field and scooping them into a sack, I would have bled profusely if not for the linen. As it was, only the tips of my fingers and a few scuffs on my legs bled.

The insect bites were another matter. Numerous bugs dwelt in the field and, apparently, they thought I was tastier than the plants. By the end of the day, I was covered in bites and stings. When Kayin surveyed me, he looked devastated. 'Awan, you must be so uncomfortable. Why didn't you stop ages ago?'

'I couldn't stop when you were still working. We need the food,' I responded.

'The insects don't like me much; I have barely a bite. But you've been eaten alive. Come, we must return to the water and bathe your skin.'

He tipped the contents of my sack into his own, then stuffed my empty sack in the top. Throwing that and our other belongings over his shoulder, he started walking back the way we'd come that morning.

I trotted along behind him. 'Won't you let me carry anything?' I asked.

'Not a chance,' Kayin replied. He didn't say another word until we got to the cave, where he dropped off the food and packs. Then he started climbing down the cliff to the beach. I followed him in silence. When we reached the bottom, I stopped.

'Are you going to speak to me?' I asked.

'Come and sit by the water,' he instructed. I obeyed. Then Kayin sat beside me and began gently unwrapping the strips of cloth from my hands and legs. Discarding them on the sand, he took my hand and pulled me towards the sea. 'You must bathe your wounds. The bitter water helps.'

I was unwilling to go in deeper than my knees, but Kayin's face told me that refusal wasn't an option. So, I pulled my tunic off and trudged to where he stood in the shallows. Every bite and cut stung as I entered the water.

I drew in my breath. 'Are you sure it helps? It stings!'

'Trust me,' he said, putting a steadying arm around my waist as we waded further into the depths. Soon just my head and shoulders were above the surface.

'I won't let you go,' he whispered, as the water lapped at my neck. I closed my eyes, trying to assuage the fear bubbling in my chest.

'What if Leviathan comes?' I thought aloud.

'He hunts at night, and we're too close to the shore,' Kayin responded in dulcet tones. His words couldn't calm my fear. Unwittingly, my breathing became shallow and panicked. Kayin put both arms around me and held me tightly. He was so much taller than me that his chest was still out of the waves, so I leaned against it and focused on the steady drum of his heartbeat.

After some time allowing the bitter water to minister to my wounds, Kayin mumbled, 'I think I finally understand what Abba was talking about that day.'

'Hmmm?' I said, incapable of opening my eyes or mouth but wanting to know.

'Abba told me that seeing me suffer in the fields, with bandaged hands from the thorns, filled him with so much guilt he couldn't bear to work with me. That was why he'd avoided me. He acknowledged he'd been wrong and tried to beg for my forgiveness, but I withheld it.'

I forced my eyes open, bypassing the waves and centring on Kayin's face. He looked distraught – as if the pain he had felt all those years ago was as present now as it had been then.

'Abba was wrong to treat you the way he did.'

'And yet, I understand now. Seeing you suffer today because of me... I see how it could have made him feel that way.'

'What do you mean, I suffered today because of you?' I asked, lifting my head from his chest and drawing back slightly.

'It's my fault you are here having to live in the wild, gathering grains on your hands and knees. You could be at home with Ima in comfort—'

'What are you talking about? How is my being here *your* fault? You didn't ask me to come! Now *you* are acting like Abba: taking on a burden that's not yours to bear.'

Kayin sighed and drew me back into his chest. 'I wish I had forgiven him.'

We remained there until we both grew cold. Then Kayin permitted me to escape from his clutches. The bites and stings did feel better afterwards, and I was glad he'd insisted I wade in.

On our way back to the original wheat field, we took a detour to the eastern hills which Kayin had spoken of. Finding many small vines scattered over the ground, we lingered there. Broad, bright green leaves were interspersed with white flowers bearing a black mark and green pods containing large beans.

We worked our way up a gently sloping rock face, where more elegant vines poked out between boulders, sending smaller pods cascading down the rocks, inside which were round, yellow beans. At the top of that slope were edible leaves and roots to forage, but, as Kayin predicted, the olives weren't yet ready. When it grew dark, we settled behind a thicket to sleep.

Early the following day, with one sack full of beans, peas, leaves and roots; one sack of emmer; and our travelling packs, we trundled back to the wheat we'd left drying, arriving as the sun was at its height.

It took us an additional two days to thresh and winnow that grain. Finally, after three weeks away from the cave, we had almost four full sacks of food – plenty enough to carry home on our backs. It was the sixth day since our rest at the beach.

As I woke on the morning of Shabbat, I saw Kayin had risen early and was standing a little way off, surveying our harvest. Walking to his side, I rested a hand on the small of his back. He turned, and my hand fell away.

'I would like to offer some of this produce to Elohim,' he said nervously. 'But I don't know what to do. Do you think He'll find it acceptable?'

My chest tightened as I considered burning the food we had worked so hard to gather. I'd never had to give anything in sacrifice as my brothers had. Even the birds Chayim and I had burnt were a gift of the wild, with no effort needed on my part.

I realised Kayin was waiting for my answer – for affirmation that Elohim wouldn't reject him again. Although I had felt confident up to this point, I didn't know whether I could offer that.

'Why do you think Elohim rejected it before?' I asked.

'There was evil in my heart. I was trying to bend His will to mine rather than letting Him be Elohim. Besides this, I didn't even give Him my best grain. Yet, He said that if I offer Him a sacrifice of thanksgiving, He will be glorified; if I order my way rightly, He will show His salvation.'

'He did say that,' I affirmed.

'These few sacks of food are all I have. I want to give Him some in thanksgiving. I want to start afresh; begin living right.'

I believed Kayin was sincere and hoped this sacrifice was the right thing to do – that Yahweh would accept it. Even so, something wasn't right. Like a stopper in a jar, preventing oil from pouring, it wouldn't release. Were we missing something that might lead to rejection again? Knowing how far that would set Kayin back, I couldn't encourage his desire.

'Perhaps we should carry this food home and pray more before we try to burn anything,' I said.

Pain radiated in Kayin's eyes, and I felt terrible for not encouraging him. Nevertheless, he consented to my idea.

After we had eaten, he asked me to sing. As we sang and talked of Yahweh, he softened again. Indeed, he grew animated, saying he was learning something new every time we spoke, even though I was just repeating things he must have heard many times before. The old teaching was coming alive.

That night, Kayin kept his distance from me again. The strain on our relationship was like the ache in my shoulder before it's healing. The brief few days of intimacy by the sea had ended. The joy when he looked at me had withered.

CHAPTER 29

With our heavy load, it took us a while to make the journey back. Kayin insisted on carrying most of the produce as he was still concerned about my injuries from the emmer field, even though the bites had calmed and I was perfectly fine.

When we finally approached our hill country it felt like returning home. Excitement bubbled in my chest as we crossed the meadows where the wildflowers were growing in abundance and displaying the glory of Yahweh. Finding a new lease of energy, in haste we ascended the familiar hill into which our cave nestled.

Yet when we reached the plateau and ducked through the bushes encircling it, we could immediately see something was wrong. Kayin was naturally very tidy; everything had its proper place. Now, the cave's contents were scattered all over the glade in what appeared to have been a deliberate destruction of our home. Pots and baskets were upturned and emptied; a straw brush was lying broken by the disturbed ashes of the fire. The deerskin over the entrance had been pulled down and ripped into several pieces.

Putting his hand out to stall me, Kayin dropped his sacks to the ground, cautiously moving forward to investigate. Only his travelling pack remained strapped to his shoulders. His bulky frame moved surprisingly lightly. Loosening his pouch, he retrieved a sling and stone. Nothing moved. Picking up a spear discarded on the ground, he tiptoed towards the cave.

I lowered myself to the ground, dropping my sack and holding my breath – as if I could make myself invisible by doing so. Anticipation grew as Kayin neared the entrance to the cave. Would a wild creature emerge, or something worse? Could Shimon have come again?

Nothing happened.

Kayin ventured inside, disappearing into the darkness. Just as I started breathing again, I heard a scuffle in the bush behind me.

I twisted my neck but, before I could identify it, a creature sprang upon my lowered back. Its claws and teeth dug into my shoulders, slitting my tunic like a knife on pomegranate. The assault was ferocious.

With my body sent off-balance, I cried out and toppled forwards. The creature didn't loosen its hold. On the contrary, its claws sank further into my skin. Warm, rancid breath stroked my neck; its teeth were a hair's breadth from my throat.

I rolled on the ground, trying to throw it off. Caught beneath my turning body, it howled and loosed its grip. I rolled in the other direction, sending it flying off to one side. Trying to focus through the searing pain, I pushed up onto my arms, but not before it was upon me again. My ripped tunic offered little protection as claws tore at my flesh. Blood splattered across my vision, but I still couldn't determine what was attacking me. I could see only blood.

Dizzy with pain, I crashed face-first into the dirt.

Then Kayin was near, trying to draw the creature's attention away. Snarling at him, it held fast to my back. I knew if Kayin pulled it off, my flesh would follow. I coiled my body, squeezing my eyes tight against the pain.

Kayin provoked the beast with his spear. Withdrawing its claws, it launched itself towards Kayin. He was ready for it. As it leapt up, the creature impaled itself on the spear's merciless tip.

It landed with a thump at my side. I opened one eye to see the beast's glistening orb glared emptily at me, convicting me of its slaughter.

'Awan,' Kayin cried, kneeling beside me.

I groaned and slowly unwound my body from its cocoon. Kayin heaved a sigh of relief then immediately scooped me up, hoisting me into his arms.

I shrieked as he chafed my wounds.

He muttered numerous apologies, sat on a boulder and adjusted his grip. Then I slumped into the safety of his embrace. His heart was beating even faster than mine. Nestling into his chest, I wished I could calm it with my touch.

Blood was soaking my tunic. Kayin went wide-eyed, then shuffled his body, allowing his pack to fall from his shoulders. Retrieving a strip of linen with one hand, he scrunched it and pushed it into an exposed wound. I winced as the pain increased.

'I'm sorry, I must stop the bleeding,' he whispered.

'What was it?' I murmured thickly, through waves of nausea.

'Some kind of badger,' he replied, 'but larger and bolder than ones I've seen before.'

'Why would it attack me unprovoked?'

'There are young cubs inside the cave. It's been nesting here while we were gone. It thought we were the intruders.'

'So, you've just killed a mother?'

'I'm afraid so.'

I glanced at the lifeless heap on the ground. She wasn't tall – perhaps up to my knee if standing on four paws – but she had a long body, a broad chest and stocky legs. Her ears were short and round, her fur thick and dark brown with a white stripe down her face. Below those accusing eyes, a set of meat-tearing teeth surrounded a lolling tongue. Pity overwhelmed me, despite the pain she'd caused. She'd been defending her young. Wouldn't I have done the same in her position?

I began to cry – the shock of the attack superseded by sadness.

Kayin repeatedly apologised, stroking my hair and kissing the top of my head, as if the guilt lay with him. He held me tightly, caressing what remained unhurt. Then, slowly, his kisses moved down my face. I lifted my eyes and saw the burning intensity in his.

Kayin's lips suddenly and furiously met my own.

I had never tasted anything like it. New, tingling sensations coursed through my body as all the years of longing and confusion culminated in this answering moment. As he enveloped my lips with contrasting softness and ferocity, the affliction of sadness and pain dissolved, replaced by a different kind of agony – an exquisite ache – as all that had slept suddenly awoke in delectable anguish.

I tried to breathe. His hand held the back of my head, refusing to let me come up for air; refusing to let me go.

When Kayin finally released me, his head tilted downwards. Our noses brushed as we both gasped for air. I opened my eyes and what I found shocked me. His eyebrows were drawn together, the crease deep and evident. He looked... tormented. The smile tugging at my lips fell away. That kiss had felt like the most wonderful moment of my life, yet something was very wrong.

'Awan, I can't do this,' Kayin said.

I took another steadying breath but my voice trembled nonetheless. 'What do you mean?'

'I shouldn't have... I'm sorry. I couldn't help myself. It was wrong.'

He stood up, placed me gently on the boulder, and stumbled away. Determined to face him, I also stood, though the lacerations in my shoulders screamed, compounded by the lesion in my heart.

'Why was it wrong?' I asked, my voice rising. 'I have told you I want to be your wife, Kayin.'

'You cannot mean it,' he shouted with his back to me.

'Yes. Yes, I can. What is the matter with you? Did you feel nothing just then? Kayin, I love you.' Striding to where he stood, I tugged on his arm, trying to pull him around. 'I have forgiven you. I want you. Kayin – please.'

He stared at the ground, as unable to move as the corpse behind us.

'Of course I felt it,' he said slowly. 'I feel every movement of your body. I am conscious of every breath you take as if it were my own. But that doesn't change the fact we should not be together.'

'Why would you say that?' I asked, moving around to face him. 'Elohim brought us together! When will you stop punishing yourself and accept His blessings?'

'I cannot! That is to say – I will try to accept everything He has given me, apart from you, Awan. I cannot accept you precisely *because* I love you!' He covered his eyes with a hand, rubbing at the bridge of his nose. 'I am not good for you. I will drag you down. Your fate will be my curse – a curse you do not deserve. I have been trying to convince myself it's not true, but seeing you hurt in the emmer field and seeing you attacked just now – I can pretend no longer!'

Kayin began to pace. Then he looked at me and, almost coldly, uttered, 'I must insist you go home.'

'How is home any different from here?' I replied, anger rising in my chest. 'You were attacked by wolves there, remember? Your back still bears the scars of their claws, just as mine shall bear the scars of that creature.' The linen strip dropped from my shoulder. 'Speaking of which, I would be grateful if you could stop pacing and find my poultice.'

At my glare, Kayin spun and went into the cave. I heard clattering and clanging as he searched in the darkness for the poultice I had made from the tree in the mountains. While he was gone, I brushed my cheeks dry and set my face against my shaking exasperation. Eventually, he came out with the correct clay jar in his hands.

'Will you apply it for me?' I asked, my voice calmer.

His expression said it would be the most excruciating thing in the world. Even so, he did it. We sat down and he lifted my torn tunic, which had begun sticking to my back as the blood dried. Gently easing it over my head, he left it dangling down my front as he started to apply the poultice with his fingertips.

'The blood is already clotting,' he said quietly. 'That's good; the wounds can't be too deep.'

They felt deep. I turned my head to get a look. He was right; these scratches were far shallower than the ones Kayin bore after the wolf attack. But they still stung at each tender touch. I grimly considered how much pain he must have been in with his much deeper wounds.

After a little while, Kayin's fingertips softened further, along with the rest of him. 'In the past, I almost enjoyed getting injured, knowing the result would be your ministrations,' he said gently into my ear. The caress of his breath was almost enough to push me back over the edge. My stomach clenched.

'Why are you pushing me away then?' I retorted through gritted teeth.

He paused a while before speaking again. With his fingers still on my wounds he said, 'Awan, I need you to tell me something.'

'Yes?'

'When exactly did Yahweh tell you to find me?'

I sighed and thought back. 'Not before I left home. I intended to go away for a few weeks; I didn't know I would end up here. He told me it was time to find you when I was on the way.'

'When?'

'What do you mean?'

'Exactly when did He tell you?'

I realised what he was getting at, and I sighed again. 'After I sent Chayim away.'

'After you tried to kiss him?'

'Yes,' I replied. Kayin's touch was entirely gentle, yet I could suddenly feel the scratches more sharply, like the claws were sinking in again.

'And before that, had He ever told you to find me?' Kayin asked.

'No.'

'What had Yahweh said?'

I took a deep breath. 'He had said… He'd said He was sufficient for me.'

Kayin slowly put the lid on the jar and placed it down. Easing my tunic back over my head, he let it fall down my back. Then he walked to the water stone and washed the poultice from his fingers. A single tear ran from my eye. Kayin came back, knelt in front of me and took my hands.

'So you see. I was a concession, Awan. Yahweh told you to find me to prevent you taking Chayim from Avigail. I am incredibly grateful to Him for bringing you here and allowing you to speak the truth into my life. I am grateful for His forgiveness and healing. And I shall love you until my dying day. But this is not what is best for you. I am not what is best for you. He is. And His presence is back with our family in the land between the rivers.'

'But you said that He met you here! And I have spoken to Him here!' I cried.

'I cannot help you serve Yahweh better, Awan. Havel would have done. He would have helped you grow in faith, but I will only pull you down. You know I speak the truth. For your own sake, you must leave.'

His words struck me in the face. Tears flowed unrestrained as he vocalised my previous fear. Yet, recently, he had changed so much. I had been almost sure…

Kayin stood and went back into the cave. He emerged moments later with a large linen bundle in his arms.

'Where are you going?' I asked in broken tones, terrified he was leaving me.

'There is a family of similar creatures nearby. I'm taking the cubs there on the chance they will accept and care for them.'

I stood and approached him, then eased back the covering to see six tiny cubs squirming in their nest. They must have been merely a few days old.

'Don't put your scent on them,' he whispered. Then he covered them back up and left me, making his way down the hillside towards the stream.

A new, throbbing emptiness opened up – a cruel companion to my pain. To combat it, I rubbed the tears from my face and began tidying, pushing past the shards in my shoulders. Carefully collecting all the items thrown out of the cave by the nesting mother, I put each back in place.

CHAPTER 30

Kayin was gone for some time. Either the family of badgers were further away than he had made out, or he wanted to be alone. Having tidied everything up, I tried to move the sacks of grain into the cave, but my wounds screamed at the effort. Suddenly overcome with exhaustion, I tried lying down on my pallet, but I couldn't get comfortable. Eventually, even though my legs were aching, I decided to go for a walk.

As I meandered down the hillside, Kayin's words weighed on my soul like a boulder. I was so conflicted; I did not know how to reconcile anything inside my mind. When I arrived at the meadow where I had first seen Kayin, I leant against the same tree and pondered the last few months.

In this place, I had thrown myself between my two brothers, instinctively protecting one from the other. Kayin had been silent, awkward and fragmented, but he had transformed before my eyes since then. That couldn't have been down to me. Elohim had healed him; I had no doubt of that.

How could I go back to my family now? How could I forget the life I had begun here – forget Kayin? What if Shimon had made good on his promise and told everyone of my betrayal? Could Avigail ever forgive me? As I had been living here, yearning for the repair of Kayin's heart, had my own sister's heart been broken?

'Oh Yahweh!' I whimpered. 'What should I do? I think I desire You above all else, but what if I am wrong? What if Kayin is a distraction who will stop me from truly following You? Please help me; please show me what's best.'

Through tears and song, I cried out my desire for my Elohim.

May You alone be my strength;
You alone be my guide;
May You alone be my desire
In the weeping of the night.

May you alone be my shelter;
You alone be my song;
May You alone be the one
That I praise all day long.

I sank my face into my hands. My head told me that Kayin's reasoning was sound; my heart protested that I could not go back. I couldn't leave him. I thought I'd loved Kayin once when I was young and he made my heart quicken. Then, he had betrayed me and been lost to me. Now – beyond all hope – life with Kayin was a possibility again. I could see the man Yahweh was transforming him into, and I knew the potential for loving him was endless. If I left now, I would never forget these days. Nor how it felt to be with him.

'Awan?'

A voice shouted my name, interrupting my thoughts. It came across the meadow. A voice that sounded familiar yet didn't belong here.

'Awan!'

I lifted my head, tear-filled eyes too blurry to see. After rubbing them with my sleeve, I saw two figures approaching. As I stood, the shorter of the two began running up the hill, her arms open wide, dishevelled dark curls flying behind her. I struggled to reconcile the sight, but she beamed as she reached me, throwing her arms around me.

'Ima!' I cried as her arms skimmed my wounds. She was so thrilled to see me that she overlooked my intake of breath.

'Awan. My darling girl! How I have missed you,' my mother said, raining kisses on my face.

'And I you, Ima.' I sobbed into her warm embrace.

'But you have been weeping already; your eyes are red. What is wrong?'

Becoming aware of my awkward situation, I stuttered, 'Praise Yahweh that you are here, Ima. But... but how? Why? Didn't Shimon tell you—'

'That's why we are here,' she exclaimed, drawing back and placing her hands firmly on my shoulders. I winced.

'What is it?' She turned me around and saw my ripped, bloodied tunic. 'Awan! What happened?'

'I was attacked by an animal just before you came, but all is well. Kayin, he—'

'Where is Kayin? Is he with you?' Abba had reached the top of the hill and heard our exchange.

'Abba,' I said, warmly. I moved to kiss him on his weather-worn cheek and found myself looking at my youngest brother, who was tied to his front. 'Ronel. Look at you! You have grown so much. But how did you manage to get here carrying Ronel? The journey is perilous.'

'It was challenging,' Abba affirmed as I noticed the state of my parents' clothing and the fatigue lining their features.

'Now, why have you been crying?' Ima pressed. 'Where is Kayin?'

I couldn't process their presence here: how they had taken the same journey as me, and what obstacles and dangers they must have faced. I stuttered a response. 'He is about somewhere; he just went to re-home some cubs… I couldn't be more glad to see you both. You have come at just the right time. But why are you here? How did you find us?'

'Shimon told us everything,' Abba replied. Fear must have flashed across my eyes. 'When we heard his report, we knew at once that we must come to find you both. Not to condemn you – before you fear the worst – but to reassure you. However, we had new lambs, and then harvest… I'm afraid this is the earliest we could get away.'

'Perhaps that is as well…' I trailed off. 'Kayin should be back by now. Do you need to rest? Or shall I show you to our home? It is a short walk uphill.'

Ima raised an eyebrow at me, and I realised I had used the word *our*.

'We haven't walked far today. I think we'll manage,' Abba replied.

Then it occurred to me that they must be as apprehensive about meeting Kayin as I'd been the first time I sat in this meadow.

'Are you prepared for meeting him?' I asked, looking specifically at Abba as I led the way.

He sighed. 'We have been preparing our hearts over our long journey. Though, as I'm sure you found yourself, that is not an easy task with his condition unknown. Shimon described him as a wild man who could barely utter a word.'

'The truth is, Awan, it's no surprise to us that you came here,' said Ima. 'Even before you commenced your journey, I foresaw your destination.'

'How?' I asked, astonished.

'It was something in that vision before Set's naming day. I didn't tell you at the time, but you were with Havel in that vision. And you left with him. Of course, I didn't know what that meant. But, as I pondered it over the years, I came to believe you would one day leave us – perhaps to find Kayin. I think Yahweh was preparing my heart for it. It's why I pushed you so hard to let go of your bitterness. Then, when you announced your intention to go on a journey, I finally confided in your father about my suspicions.'

'That's why you held me so firmly when I left,' I said. 'It seemed odd at the time.'

'We thought we might never see you again,' Abba confirmed.

'But that vision was over twenty years ago! How could Elohim have known?'

'He knows everything, for all time. He is the Eternal One,' my father said.

'But that means He *knew* what Kayin would do. He knew you would take the fruit in the Garden—'

'Yes.'

'I cannot even begin to comprehend that,' I confessed.

'Nor I.' Ima smiled. 'Yet it is comforting to know He holds all of time in His hands, and we can never surprise Him.'

'And so, here I am, and here you are,' I pondered. 'And my question remains: can you cope with seeing

Kayin? I have tamed the wild man a little, but the reason he left remains the same.'

'Have you learnt the truth about that, Awan?' Abba asked.

'I have.'

'And you're still prepared to live with him?'

'I am.'

'Then we too desire to be reconciled,' Abba said. 'Yahweh is a just and merciful Elohim. If He has chosen to spare Kayin's life, and if you have been able to forgive him, then who are we to withhold the same?'

'He did do it, Abba. You must know that,' I said, looking my father squarely in the eyes. 'Yet, he has changed. And I know he would desire reconciliation also.'

'If he has changed, then why are you sitting in the meadow so upset?' my mother asked, narrowing her eyes. 'I don't believe those tears are related only to the wounds on your shoulders.'

'Perhaps we can explain that to you together,' I said, not knowing where to start.

I led them further up the hillside until I reached the bushes where Kayin had made an opening. Then we hiked up and around the well-worn path until we arrived at the glade I had called home. I walked out in front, intending to give Kayin some warning of our visitors.

He was sitting in front of a fire, upon which he'd set a flat stone to heat. Balls of dough from freshly-ground grain were on a platter beside him, and he was stretching a piece, ready to throw onto the hot stone. He didn't look up as I approached. I knelt in front of him.

'We'll need that bread to go a little further,' I said gently, placing a hand on his. 'We have visitors.'

Kayin looked at me then. 'You've been weeping.'

'So have you.'

'Awan, I'm so sorry...'

'Shhh.' I put a finger to his lips. 'Did you hear what I said? Abba and Ima are here.'

Shock hit as realisation dawned. His hand went rigid and his eyes widened. Then he gripped my fingers.

'Don't be afraid. They've come in peace.'

'Why are they here?'

'I don't know. Something about Shimon. They want to see you. May I invite them to come and sit?'

Kayin nodded, shrinking into himself like a child afraid of being scolded.

I rose and went back to those waiting behind the bush.

'Come,' I said, entwining my arms in theirs and leading them forward. Then I stopped.

'Actually – first pass me Ronel.'

Abba unwrapped the infant from his sling and handed him to me. I went ahead to where Kayin was, jiggling Ronel on my hip.

Kayin had stood up nervously, expecting to see his parents. When I approached with the baby, he softened his stance.

'Meet your youngest brother, Ronel,' I said, holding him out to Kayin. He peered at me apprehensively. 'Go on, take him.'

Kayin reached out his hands and took the babe, then settled him into an arm and gazed down at his face. Ronel immediately giggled, threw a hand up and grasped Kayin's beard. He gave it a good tug, and Kayin laughed then tickled the little one's belly. Seeing him warm to Ronel, I beckoned my parents to come out from the bush.

Ima spoke first. 'Hello, Kayin.'

Her eldest son looked up and beheld the mother he hadn't laid eyes on for half a lifetime. She walked towards him and reached her hand up to his scar. A tear rolled from Kayin's eye over her fingers.

'Ima...' He choked.

Extracting Ronel from Kayin's arms, I watched as mother and son embraced, shedding a thousand tears to cleanse an age of separation, hurt, betrayal, sorrow and sin.

Then, becoming aware that my Abba had held back and remained in the shadows, I turned. I couldn't read his face, so I approached him, putting my hand on his arm.

'Can you do it now that you see him?' I whispered.

Abba clenched my hand and closed his eyes, touching his forehead to mine. I could feel his trembling.

'Yahweh Elohim,' he whispered, 'give me the strength to forgive my son. And give him the ability to forgive me.'

I repeated the prayer over him and then opened my eyes. Kayin and Ima had separated, and Kayin was regarding his father expectantly. Ima held out her hand.

'Come, Adam,' she said. He walked forwards and grasped his wife's outstretched palm. Then he put his other hand on the shoulder of his son.

'My father, I committed unspeakable sin against Havel and against you, but mostly against our Elohim. I deserve nothing from you except condemnation,' Kayin muttered, hanging his head.

'Your sin would never have taken place if it weren't for my own. Please forgive me, son.'

Kayin looked up in disbelief. 'You mean it?' he said.

Our father nodded.

'Abba, I forgive you a hundred times over! Your sin is nothing compared to mine. I dare not ask for your forgiveness, but—'

'You have it,' Abba finished. 'You have it.'

Then Kayin threw his arms around his abba. If it were possible for the Tigris to flow from Kayin's eyes, I wouldn't have been surprised to see it.

I smiled and carried Ronel to the boulder Kayin had vacated. Ima came and sat beside me, instinctively picking up the dough that Kayin had been stretching and throwing it onto the cooking stone. Despite the solemnity of the moment, I chuckled.

'Make yourself at home,' I said, squeezing my mother's arm.

'Well, what shall I do with my time if I have no mouths to feed?' she smiled. 'You all grow up far too quickly.' I leaned forward and kissed her cheek, then squealed as Ronel tugged one of my braids and chewed the end of it.

Despite our common exhaustion, we spent a pleasant evening together. As well as the fresh bread, Kayin brought out summer fruits he'd picked that afternoon and some smoked meat. I provided water for my parents to refresh themselves with and watched over Ronel, who was the only one with energy left.

As we ate, Abba told Kayin all about the harvest and what he and Set had been doing in the vineyard. He lifted a skin from his pack and handed it to us.

'I think you'll find this better than the last time,' he said as Kayin sipped at the wine in the skin.

'Yes, that's fairly pleasant.'

'Be careful with it. Drink too much and it addles the brain. I tend to mix it with boiled water now. It works well for a journey, not tasting off after a day as water alone tends to.'

Remembering my sickness on arrival, I asked if they had drunk from the lake.

'Oh, no. It's never a good idea to drink from a lake. We made sure we filled enough water-skins before venturing onto the plain.'

Of course, my parents had far more experience of journeying than I had, having spent years doing so before they settled between the rivers. Even so, we had all journeyed that day, experiencing a range of landscapes and emotions. It wasn't long before we all felt that little Ronel, who was now sound asleep in his mother's arms, had the right idea. Kayin began making a bed for our parents near the cave's entrance, using a combination of straw from our pallets and linen from their packs.

'Don't worry much about us,' Ima said to him. 'We're so exhausted, we'll sleep anywhere.' She proved the point by lying down on the half-made bed and promptly falling asleep with Ronel tucked in the crook of her arm. Abba grinned at us, then lay beside her and did the same.

Kayin and I were left standing outside alone. I started clearing things away, but he took my hand and led me gently aside.

'Thank you,' he whispered.

'For what?'

'Just for being you. I know I upset you today, yet you came back and acted wonderfully with Ronel, Ima and Abba. I never thought this day would come. You have made it possible, Awan.'

I reached up and stroked his cheek. Then, lifting onto my toes, I touched my other hand to the back of his head, curling his hair into my fingers.

'I love you, Kayin.'

Kayin closed his eyes and let his head tilt downwards until our noses touched. He breathed in deeply, savouring every moment of closeness, then pulled himself away.

'To bed,' he said, walking away. Deflated, I watched him disappear into the cave without looking back.

CHAPTER 31

The following morning, I rose at daybreak. Kayin and my parents were still asleep. Tiptoeing out into the dawning light, I set about making some more dough. Then, removing some wood from Kayin's neat stack, I lit a fire and wiped down the stone, ready for the first batch. Kayin must have returned shortly after I'd left the day before, as he'd carried the sacks of supplies into the cave and already sorted them neatly into baskets.

I rinsed the clay dishes and set them to dry in the sunlight dappling through the trees. Hearing a slight whimper from inside, I turned to see Ima emerging with Ronel in her arms. 'He's an early riser, like his sister,' she whispered at me, yawning widely. She settled on a boulder and put the babe to her breast. I filled a bowl with water and sat beside her.

'You have a nice home here, Awan.'

I sighed. 'I don't know how long I can remain.'

'What do you mean?'

'Kayin thinks I should go. And, in any case, I don't know how long he will dwell here before he moves somewhere else.'

'Why would he want you to leave? Is that what you were crying about?'

'Yes, we had the conversation yesterday just before you arrived. He's mentioned it before, but yesterday was different; he was adamant—' I paused to pass her the bowl after I'd had a sip.

Ronel spluttered and beat his mother's breast. She lifted him onto her shoulder and tapped his backside. He let out a tremendous belch. We both chuckled while Ima latched him back on to feed, then she took the bowl from me.

'Kayin seems to think Elohim only brought me here because I couldn't control myself,' I said. 'He's worried I shall not flourish under his care, and he doesn't want me to bear his curse. Every time something happens to me, he panics and – I don't know – sees it as a sign I shouldn't be here.'

'And you disagree?'

'Honestly, I don't know what I think. Ima, how much did Shimon tell you?'

She sat back a little and surveyed me a moment before speaking. 'Shimon trudged into our Shabbat gathering one day, riling and ranting. It was clear he'd come straight from the mountains for he hadn't washed, and Channah was surprised to see him. She rose to greet him, but he was determined to speak and pushed her away.

'He began shouting about how you had found Kayin, abandoning us all by going after a murderer. He described his efforts at taking vengeance for Havel's life, saying Kayin concocted a story about Elohim giving him a mark of protection, and you had believed it. He began to rage, asking the other men to join him on a crusade to take Kayin down; saying that Elohim wouldn't dare strike them all if they killed him together.'

Ronel spluttered again. Ima winded him then moved him to the other side.

'Channah tried to take him aside, but he struck her. I have never been so shocked, Awan! To see my sweet girl struck by her husband. Rising and restraining Shimon, your father and Chayim dragged him inside the hut. There they spoke to him alone while I attended to Channah, who was weeping and had a nasty bruise forming around her eye. Then I realised what the desire for vengeance felt like. I wanted nothing more than to go inside and give Shimon a black eye of his own.'

I stifled a smile.

Ima noticed and gave me a wide grin. 'Don't worry, I got over it. Kayin always said Shimon needed more discipline. I used to think he was being grumpy, but perhaps he was right after all.

'Anyway, later Chayim exited the hut looking incredibly pale. Shimon followed, stalking back to his cave alone. I asked your father what had been said. He told me how Shimon had accused Chayim of having an affair with you, saying he had seen the two of you together in the hills.

'Chayim confessed that you had almost kissed but said you had stopped short, repenting to Elohim and offering a sacrifice together. He said that, afterwards, you had insisted he return home to Avigail whilst you went to find Kayin. We were surprised he hadn't confessed these things earlier; we have never known Chayim to be deceitful. He asked for time alone with Avigail to tell her himself, and we agreed and prayed together for them.'

By this point in Ima's story, tears were welling in my eyes once more. Avigail certainly knew of my betrayal now, which made it so much worse. My heart stung for Chayim and the difficulty I had caused my sweet brother.

'They are well, Awan,' Ima said, reaching out a hand to me as she noticed my tears. 'I think it gave them the push they needed to improve their relationship. Things have not been right between them for some time, but they love each other and will work it out with Yahweh's help.'

I nodded and choked back a sob. My mother lifted Ronel onto her opposite shoulder and put her spare arm around me. I winced as she touched a wound.

'I'm sorry, I forgot,' she said, removing her hand.

'It's alright, Ima; they are less tender this morning. That poultice does wonders.'

'Awan, Elohim will heal your brother and sister, just as He will heal your wounds. Sometimes things must come out in the open to get dealt with.'

'That doesn't make right what I did.'

'No, it doesn't. And yet you have been forgiven, and what you have been forgiven must be left in the past. Now – tell me more about why you are here and why Kayin wants you to leave.'

I took a deep breath to gather myself. 'I hadn't considered finding Kayin before my journey. Of course, I had wondered about him, and – interspersed with anger – I had missed him. But Yahweh had told me to trust in Him and, at the time of setting off, it was Yahweh I longed for more than anyone else. I took my trip to the mountains to spend time with my Elohim. But then, after I sent Chayim away, Yahweh told me to find Kayin.'

'And Kayin knows of this?'

'Yes. Kayin says he was a concession: that Yahweh allowed me to come here to get me away from Chayim, but it's not what is best for me. He is trying to be selfless, Ima. He is trying to protect me and wants to put Yahweh first. Yet, it feels like he is tearing my heart in two all over again.'

'You love him, then. Do you want to be his wife?'

'Yes! And I know it doesn't make sense after what he did, but my feelings remain. He is different now, Ima. And, despite what he thinks, I *have* grown in faith since I have been here and seen Yahweh's work in his life. I am not dismayed by his curse; I don't fear wandering or gathering or even being attacked by wild animals. I just want to be with him!'

I sank my head into my hands. My mother gingerly held me, taking care to avoid the wounds.

'What exactly was Kayin's judgement from Yahweh?' she asked softly.

'He is to be a fugitive: he can never return to our family; and a wanderer: he cannot farm or settle in one place for too long. He can only glean the produce of the wild. He seems to think this means he must be alone forever.'

My mother pursed her lips. 'Let me speak to your Abba about it,' she said after a time. 'We will consult Yahweh, and then perhaps we can advise you both.'

'Thank you, Ima,' I whispered, sinking further into her comforting embrace.

When the men had risen from their beds and we had all eaten, Ima asked if Kayin and I would watch Ronel while she and Abba had some time alone. I readily agreed, knowing her intention.

With the little one to distract us, the atmosphere was less intense between Kayin and me.

'I think I've forgotten what to do,' Kayin grimaced as Ronel grew restless in his arms.

'Nonsense, you were always a natural with children,' I said, taking the baby from him.

Ronel blew a raspberry.

'I agree, bubba! Naughty Kayin is being grumpy with you, isn't he?' I rubbed my head into Ronel's tummy, making him giggle. Then I realised why he was squirming. 'Ah. He needs a change of linens! Would you like naughty Kayin to do it for you? Would you, little brother?'

I tickled Ronel's tummy again and caught Kayin's facial expression. 'Don't worry, I'm joking; I'll do it,' I laughed.

I hunted around in Ima's pack, retrieving some rolled linens and old cloths.

'Perhaps Ronel would enjoy a stroll to the brook?' Kayin suggested. 'We can wash the soiled linens there.'

Ronel perched happily on Kayin's shoulder as we walked, chewing on a chunk of his brother's hair and looking around at the wildlife. I carried a basket of laundry with an empty one beneath to collect any food we might see on the way. When we passed some berries, Ronel held his hand out and squealed.

'Is he allowed to eat those?' Kayin asked.

'They're quite soft. It should be alright if we squish them in our fingers first,' I replied.

Kayin picked the berries and soon had juice all over his new tunic as Ronel put them one by one into his mouth and then dribbled them all over Kayin's shoulder.

'Thank goodness you invented that cleansing bar,' I smiled. I instinctively took Kayin's spare hand and kissed it. He looked at me awkwardly for a moment but did not pull away. Then he smiled and squeezed my fingers.

By the time we reached the brook, Kayin had relaxed. He threw off his tunic, leaving his chest bare. It reminded me of the first day I'd seen him hunting. Yet he was so different now, kneeling on the ground and playing with the baby, picking flowers and twirling them over Ronel's head. Ronel kept trying to grab the flowers, but Kayin kept them safely out of reach and made a game of it, lifting them up and down and from side to side.

When I had finished washing all the laundry, I swapped places with Kayin and he wrung the water out of it while I rocked Ronel to sleep. Kayin had always done this job for me at the river when we were younger. He could squeeze out far more water than I could.

'Ready to go?' I asked as he finished the last item. Walking up behind me, Kayin watched the baby perched on my shoulder. Ronel had taken his thumb into his mouth and was contentedly suckling on it in his sleep.

'You haven't lost your touch,' he smiled, leaning down and placing a gentle kiss on Ronel's head. A few of my braids had fallen over Ronel's face. With his thumb, Kayin gently lifted and tucked them behind my ear, then he turned and picked up the baskets.

CHAPTER 32

When we returned to the cave, I tucked a sleeping Ronel into bed as Kayin hung the laundry over branches of the oak tree. My parents appeared as he finished the last item.

Helping themselves to a drink from the water stone, Abba asked Kayin about his contraption suspended above it.

'It diverts water from a source higher up the hillside, channelling it here so I needn't collect it and I know it's fresh. I simply lift this lever to let the water into the stone bowl,' Kayin replied, demonstrating. Once they had fully discussed the cleverness of the design, Ima grew impatient and coughed into her hand. My father looked over at her then obediently sat down.

'So, we have been discussing your predicament,' Abba began. Kayin glanced at me, surprised.

'I told Ima this morning,' I confessed. He nodded and looked back at my father. I was relieved to see he didn't look annoyed.

'We brought it before Yahweh. He has reminded us of several things He said in the Garden many years ago.

'When Elohim first blessed us, we were told to multiply and fill the earth. These things we have taught you. And yet, we haven't done it. As it stands, our family is living in one area – except for you, Kayin. You are the only one who has left, and not by your own volition.

'Yet Elohim has covered the ground with all manner of creatures, and they have multiplied rapidly, adapting to their environment. Our responsibility as His image-bearers is to care for and bring order to the creation, which we can only do if we expand with them.

'We were also given another special responsibility. What can you remember about our purpose as image-bearers?'

'Havel said we should display the character of Yahweh to His creation. Yahweh is love, goodness, kindness, joy, peace and patience; complete in justice and mercy; always faithful and true. This is what we must endeavour to reflect,' I said.

'Yes, Awan. So, as we expand, we must also reflect His attributes. The question for you two is this: are you bearing Yahweh's image as you live here in this land? None of us can do this perfectly – not since the banishment. And yet, if we are honest with Yahweh, confessing our sins and giving Him the praise due to His name, He will display His mercy in our lives. He has shown that He forgives us and helps us.'

'Kayin, do you see the work of Yahweh in Awan?' my mother asked.

'Of course. She has shown me nothing but love and mercy. She speaks His truth into my life.'

'And Awan, do you see the work of Yahweh in Kayin?' my father asked.

'I do. Kayin cares for the creation. He has proven that he is willing to put my needs above his own.

Lately, he has accepted justice and mercy. And, he has found joy in Yahweh.'

'And so,' Abba continued, 'we have established that separately you are following Yahweh. Now we must consider whether you are better together or apart. It is essential to realise, Kayin, that no walk with Yahweh is smooth. We all have times when we feel closer and further away from Him. I can testify to that better than anyone: I have always struggled, even though I was once closer to Him than even Havel was.

'Despite this, I know He is always faithful, even when I am not. As long as I lean on Him, He will be there. Awan too will face times of closeness and times of struggle. That will happen regardless of whether she is with you or not.'

I knew this was true from my years without Kayin, but I wasn't sure Kayin would be convinced.

'I am scared,' Kayin admitted. 'Living with Yahweh's justice taught me to appreciate His holiness and my rightful place before Him. I know I deserve nothing. Yet, in His mercy, He sought me out. Awan has helped me see Yahweh's goodness once more. She has helped me realise that Havel was right: Yahweh never punished me undeservedly but was training me to rely on Him.

'And yet, I've spent a lifetime refusing to surrender. What if I fail again? What if the next time I suffer, I sink straight back into my old ways and drag Awan down with me?'

'Kayin, do you know why I took the fruit in the Garden?' my mother said, reaching forward to stroke Kayin's hand.

'When I was a boy, you used to tell me this story,' Kayin replied. 'You said the serpent promised you more wisdom and something better than Yahweh had provided – even though that was impossible. It was a lie that convinced you Yahweh Elohim was not good, and not to be trusted. A lie I was too quick to believe myself.'

'Yes, son. In short, I sought equality with Elohim. I stripped Him of his rightful place and refused to trust His goodness. You finally know your place, Kayin. You acknowledge your own wretchedness. Do not forget it! Remember that no matter who or what we love in this world, the Creator is always superior to the creation. He is always better than we can imagine. And still, He loves us and values us!

'You doubted His goodness once,' she continued. 'The tempter will lie to you again. The lies are always the same. They will always cause you to doubt Yahweh's love for you; they will always be false. Blessing is found in trusting that Yahweh is who He claims to be.'

As my experience matched what my mother was saying, I spoke then. 'Kayin, I haven't always seen the truth. When Havel died, every circumstance pointed away from Elohim's goodness, and I could not see it. Yet I chose to believe in it despite my feelings. I chose to praise Him regardless, even when my words felt empty. And, somehow, the difficulties grew smaller over time, while my Elohim grew bigger.'

Although I spoke to him, Kayin didn't look my way but stared downwards, still deep in thought. 'But if we stay together, don't we run the risk of reducing Yahweh to less than our first love?'

Ima smiled. 'The fact you have asked this question tells me the state of your heart. You are right: loving people always carries risk. We are fickle creatures, inclined to put anything and everything before Yahweh, who rightly deserves to be supreme.

'Nevertheless, we are called to love one another. Consider it this way: I don't have a finite amount of love that must be split between my husband and children. Each time I have another child, my capacity for love increases. And, as I have held each babe in my arms, I have also loved the Creator more for blessing me with them.'

Then Kayin looked at me – with an intense stare that tore my insides. I still had no idea if he was softening with all that had been said.

'We have spoken of many things. Let us try and bring this conversation back around,' Abba said at last. 'When we ate the fruit in the Garden, we sought our own glory. Yet why do you think Yahweh created the earth? Was it for the glory of His name or the glory of man?'

'Surely the glory of His name,' I exclaimed.

'He fashioned the skies with his words. He ordered everything into its place that He might be shown glorious, and we might have life to the full,' Kayin murmured.

'Indeed.' My father smiled, recognising Ima's words from our childhood. 'And tell me again why Elohim made man in His image?'

'So we might honour His name,' Kayin answered.

'Yes. Children, this is His desire for humanity. Wherever we go – wherever we wander – we should praise His name! I believe He wants us to spread over the earth so that, in all places, there may be people who bear His image faithfully: caring for His creation and, most importantly, lifting high the name of Yahweh. And He is not limited: wherever those people are, His presence will be.

'As regards marriage, perhaps there will be some for whom marriage is not the right thing. Perhaps there will be others – like Avigail and Channah – who do not easily bear children. Yahweh knows this, and He may have a different purpose for their lives. Yet, as long as you are both walking with Him, I say this: seek to fulfil His command together! Raise another generation of image-bearers in the land where you dwell. After all, Kayin cannot fill this land on his own.' Abba winked at me.

'But why would Yahweh say He is sufficient for Awan if she is meant to stay with me?' Kayin asked, his voice rising slightly.

'What makes you think His sufficiency will decrease if Awan becomes your wife?' Ima asked. 'Yahweh Elohim should be sufficient for all of us. We should all have Him at the centre of our lives. Yet He still said it wasn't good for us to be alone. Your solitude may have been necessary for a time, but that doesn't mean it's the permanent state required of you. Awan's taught her to rely on Yahweh, which may have been the very footing she needed for this next stage in her life.

'As our family has grown, it's not just my love that has grown but also my dependency on Elohim. He is no less sufficient for me now than in the Garden. On the contrary, I need Him more than ever.'

'But He didn't tell me to find Kayin until I sinned,' I said. 'Doesn't that show it wasn't His original intention?'

'Perhaps, but I suspect it's something else. Tell me, Awan. Do you think you could have accepted Kayin's story before becoming aware of your own sinfulness?'

I paused to consider. I hadn't accepted Dorit's words until I'd tried to take Chayim for myself. And I'd grown closer to Yahweh when I realised the extent of His mercy towards me. Awareness of that mercy enabled me to accept and help Kayin.

'No,' I conceded, 'I don't think I would have understood Kayin before. I'm not certain I would have obeyed and come here either.'

'Yet now you know the condition of your own heart – that you too are capable of evil – you can understand and truly forgive him, as Elohim has forgiven you. Only once we recognise our own fallenness can we reconcile with those who have wronged us. So, you see, Yahweh can turn even bad things to good in the end.' She smiled.

I turned to consider Kayin again. Although we'd both spoken, I'd not dared glance at him since that last stare. He seemed deep in thought, but then his eyes lifted to mine and he held them once more.

'Why don't we leave you two alone to talk it through?' my father said. I scarcely registered as our parents rose and did just that.

CHAPTER 33

Kayin held my gaze after our parents left. It felt like he was piercing my heart, considering the very state of my soul.

'What do you think?' I eventually asked, unable to bear it any longer.

He didn't immediately reply, but continued staring.

I nervously tapped my fingers on the boulder beneath me. Kayin's gaze shifted from my face to my hands. I wondered if he found my fidgeting annoying, but he didn't comment.

'I need to pray,' he finally said. He rose and strode away, heading up the side of the cave towards the plateau. Of all the things he might have said or done, I hadn't expected that. And yet, as his body disappeared behind a bush, I found myself smiling. The old Kayin wouldn't have 'needed to pray'.

'Thank You, Yahweh,' I said. 'Thank You for everything. For forgiveness, for love. For bringing Abba and Ima to us at the perfect time. Thank You for Your wisdom and goodness. Whatever happens, thank You for this time of reconciliation and joy.'

Then I prayed for the rest of my family. I prayed for Shimon and Channah, for Chayim and Avigail. I prayed for Set and Techiyah and especially Dorit. I asked Yahweh to mould them into His image and show them His perfect, loving kindness. I prayed that, as our family grew and expanded over the land, we would all glorify Yahweh's name.

My parents returned before Kayin. When I told them we hadn't talked yet, Abba set off up the hill to find him, whilst Ima stayed behind and helped me prepare the evening meal.

'How are you feeling?' she asked as we set beans and roots to boil and toasted pistachios to crumble on top.

'At peace,' I said. 'I feel my questions have been answered. I know Yahweh will work it out for good.'

We sang together as we stretched out dough to throw on the heated stone. It was lovely to have Ima with me, my companion of many seasons and many songs.

'How long can you stay?' I asked.

'There's no great rush and I'm not in a hurry to journey again. Avigail has Yemima with her. Channah is living in our hut. She combined the flocks and agreed to keep an eye on the triplets.'

'I've missed you all. What do you think will happen with Shimon?'

'Last time he spoke to us, he attempted persuading Channah to go home. But he was still riling against you and Kayin even whilst trying to apologise. I refused to let Channah go. I hate to create a rift between them, but I shall not risk her being misused. I hope he has stayed away while we've been gone.'

'Poor Channah.'

'She is strong. Perhaps she needed this time to find her way back to Yahweh. She loves her Elohim and her husband; it's hard to be torn between them.'

'I can imagine,' I said, thinking back to earlier times when I had felt similarly torn with Kayin. Once again, despite the circumstances that brought us here, I was grateful that Yahweh hadn't left us where we were.

Abba appeared, with Kayin behind him, just as the food was ready. Kayin looked different – like another burden had lifted. As we reclined to eat, I caught his eye. His lip twitched upward but he said nothing.

After our meal, Ima went inside to lie down with Ronel, and Abba made himself scarce, saying he would collect firewood. Kayin and I were alone.

'You look well,' I mumbled.

Kayin stood, walked to me, took my hand and pulled me up. 'I am well,' he replied, dipping his chin so his words caressed my shoulders. Then his hands stroked the small of my back, sending shivers up my spine. 'Abba and I spoke at length. We talked through everything that happened in the past, and I know all is truly forgiven. At long last, I feel like he is my abba again.'

'And I?' I asked. 'Am I to be your Awan?'

His lips brushed my neck. 'Are you still willing to have me?'

'Well, that depends,' I replied.

Kayin drew back and raised an eyebrow. The low rays of the sun highlighted the auburn streaks in his hair and the glimmer of his skin. I stood on my toes and touched my lips to his nose. 'That depends on whether you can kiss me satisfactorily again.'

A wide grin spread across Kayin's face and his eyes sparkled. 'Is that a challenge?'

I began to laugh, but he caught me around the waist and pulled me closer. Then he kissed me again – a long, deep kiss, more tender than before. This kiss carried the taste of goodness, allowing our movements to combine and my heart to soar. When he drew away, we watched each other breathlessly for a moment before he sank his head into my neck again.

'Marry me?' he asked with a moan. Then, before I could respond, he chuckled, 'before you change your mind.'

I was so surprised by his finding the prospect amusing that I took a moment to answer. 'Who are you, and what have you done with my Kayin? He would never joke about such things!'

'I am yours,' he replied, kissing me gently. 'But firstly, I am Yahweh's.'

The following morning, I woke with longing in my bones. I had dreamt of all things Kayin, no longer with any resentment but with resounding love. Even though we had retired to separate beds, my whole being had not stopped seeking him. I was so nervously conscious of his form on the other side of the cave it had taken ages to fall asleep. Now, as I reached out, I found he wasn't beside me, and hadn't been all night.

I sat up and glanced over at his pallet. He wasn't there either.

Then Ima's singing came from outside the cave. I rose and pulled my bed covering around my shoulders. There was a chill in the air, or perhaps it was just me.

'Good morning, love,' Ima said as I ventured outside. 'Breakfast?'

The remains of a morning meal were scattered on the cooking stone: I had risen much later than everyone else. I sat down and helped myself to the leftovers.

'Where are the men?' I asked.

'Missing him already?' Ima smirked. I caught her eye and she laughed. 'It doesn't get any better, I'm afraid.'

'What do you mean?'

'I still long for your father, dream about him, and hate waking up to find he's not beside me. Still, it's better,' she said, coming to sit next to me, 'always better than the alternative. In the past, when I've stayed away from him, it's affected every part of our relationship. With each other and with Yahweh. I never want to go to that place again.' She stared winsomely into the distance, like her mind was journeying back there.

'Did Kayin tell you what we decided last night?' I asked.

'Yes.' She smiled. 'I will miss you, of course, but I am glad.'

'We want you to be here with us, but we are conscious you need to get home.'

'So, you wish to be married immediately?' she asked.

I shrugged.

'That's good. I'm not sure Kayin will last much longer now he's made his mind up,' she chuckled.

My cheeks warmed.

'Don't be embarrassed. Marriage is good, and intimacy in the proper context is beautiful. My advice to you, daughter, is this: embrace it. Embrace the longing, enjoy it and keep it. Whilst your soul rightly longs for Yahweh and finds satisfaction in Him, let Kayin fulfil your every bodily desire.

'You shall soon find out what it means to be a wife. Don't be afraid. Be vulnerable, honest, steadfast and loving, but do not be afraid. Give yourself to Kayin. I have confidence he will look after you.'

My mother then explained what I could expect of my body and Kayin's when we joined as one flesh. When she had finished talking, we sat in silence for a while. I was glad she'd told me, but my nervousness prevailed. It was strange, given that I knew Kayin was mine. I hadn't felt this way when I'd been goading him a few weeks ago.

I asked again, 'Where *are* the men?'

She chuckled. 'Oh yes, I never answered that did I? They went for a walk, saying they had something to attend to. That's all I know.'

It wasn't long before they returned, though I heard their approach before seeing it. Bleating preceded Kayin's appearance with a small goat wrapped around his shoulders.

'Where did you find that?' I asked. 'I haven't seen any goats since I was in the mountains.'

Abba began explaining how they'd found a small flock in the meadow, but Kayin placed the goat down, walked straight to me and kissed me full on the lips. I squirmed slightly, feeling conscious of my parents' presence.

'I missed you,' Kayin said, drawing me into a firm embrace and kissing me again longingly.

'Don't mind us,' Ima chuckled.

Smiling at Kayin, I allowed him to kiss me once more before I pinched my nose. 'You smell of goat!' I gasped as I noticed the crimson splatters on his neck and tunic. 'Whose blood is this?'

'Another goat's. When Abba and I spoke last night, I asked him about giving an offering to Yahweh. He said for my thanksgiving offering to be acceptable, I should first conduct a blood sacrifice to atone for my sin. Because we were made in Elohim's image, human life is of great value, so Havel's blood requires a reckoning. It reminded me of Yahweh's words, that Havel's blood was crying to Him from the ground. Yet Abba believed if I were true of heart, Yahweh would look on the blood of a sacrifice and see it as a substitute for my own.'

'That's what Havel said when he offered his first lamb,' I recalled. 'He said her blood was spilt to pay for our sin.'

'Yes. The problem was, I had no lambs. How could I offer a blood sacrifice? So, Abba and I set out early this morning to seek Yahweh. In faith, we built an altar of stones in the meadow. Just as we finished, a flock of goats casually walked out from the woods. I've never seen goats in these parts either; it was a miracle!

'Abba and I herded them together like we did with the sheep when I was a child. Once we'd brought them into a group, we noticed this one was injured, so we took it aside ready to bring it back for nursing. Then we carefully selected a young one with no blemishes for the sacrifice. I placed my hands on it as Abba drained its lifeblood, which splattered over me. Then we offered the goat to Yahweh on the altar.

'The most incredible release accompanied that burning fire, Awan. Even greater than being reconciled to Abba last night.'

Holding Kayin tightly, I revelled in Yahweh's mercy. I realised this must have been the reason for my hesitation in the wheat field. Somewhere, in the back of my mind, I knew this blood sacrifice was needed for Kayin to start afresh.

I nuzzled into his chest. 'I love you. Even if you absolutely stink.'

Kayin laughed. Then, refusing to let me pull back, planted kisses all over my neck and rubbed his hands over my arms. His stench marred the pleasant feeling and I protested.

'I'll go wash in the stream,' he said at last. 'Though you'd better join me, now that you smell too.' He grinned. I fisted him on the arm, realising what he'd been up to.

'Take a fresh tunic, Awan. I'll repair yours,' Ima said as we grabbed some supplies. We strolled together to the stream.

Whilst washing, Kayin broached a new subject. 'Awan, I know you've just begun settling here, but Abba thinks we should move on soon. He says Shimon hasn't calmed down and fears it won't be long before he returns.'

His words saddened me. I had indeed begun to consider this my home, and the thought of leaving created a fresh pit in my stomach. Nevertheless, I knew this was the life I was committing to if I chose to be Kayin's wife. My home would be with him, but that would be an impermanent home – a life of wandering, never settling for long in one place.

I considered him, took his hand and entwined his fingers with mine. 'I will follow you wherever you lead – if possible, not too far away from Abba and Ima so I can see them sometimes. But I accept whatever comes with being your wife.'

He drew me into his chest again. I breathed in deeply, relishing his warmth and fresh terebinth scent, all traces of goat having been washed away.

Kayin and I were married the following day. Alongside our parents, we walked to the meadow and took vows of faithfulness in front of the altar. Abba joined our hands together as he blessed our union:

> *Blessed are those who walk in Yahweh's light,*
> *who rejoice in His name, committing their sight.*
> *Yahweh Elohim, bless Your children here;*
> *May they follow You, love You and stay ever near.*
> *As creatures who walk humbly before you.*
> *Be their strength, and guide all that they do.*
>
> *Wherever their wanderings take them*
> *Bless them with love for each other.*
> *Yet, more than this, may they find their bliss*
> *In obedience to Your will.*

Then Abba strode to the terebinth tree. Lifting a stone from near its base, he scooped something into his hand, brought it over and held his palm out to Kayin. Kayin placed his palm next to Abba's and a beetle scurried from one hand to the other.

'May the earth display the grace of Elohim and bring forth new life, even where we destroyed it,' Abba said.

Kayin choked in remembrance of those words from his childhood – from a time before doubts had crept in, squeezing out his faith and hope – when he and Abba discovered a colony of beetles making their home in the corpse of a fallen tree.

Then Kayin lifted his voice:

> I will speak of Yahweh's steadfast love forever.

With my mouth, I will proclaim His faithfulness
    to all generations.
With my lips, I shall praise Him
    for my wife, my life and my salvation.

In my prosperity, I thought I could endure
    And I praised the work of my hands.
Yet only by Your favour, O Yahweh,
    did my mountain stand firm.
When You hid your face, I was dismayed.
When I turned from You, I lost everything.

Yet, Yahweh, You did not leave me in darkness;
You restored my life from the pit.
When I cried out for mercy, You healed me,
And turned lament into praise.

O Yahweh, my Elohim, I give thanks to You,
For Your anger lasts a moment,
    but Your favour lasts a lifetime.
Weeping may consume the night,
    but joy comes in the morning.

After this, Kayin and I retrieved the best of the food
we had gathered on our recent journey and offered it
as thanksgiving to our Elohim.

And the fire burned steadily, consuming all
presented on it.

EPILOGUE

Chanoch exhaled a deep sigh as his mother concluded her tale. Of course, he'd already known much of the story; that's why he'd asked his parents to come. But he hadn't heard it recounted in such detail before, or chronologically. She'd answered questions he'd never thought to ask.

Being less sturdy on her feet, Awan had varied her position during her narrative. Presently she sat on a chair, her cane resting against her leg. Kayin peeled himself off the stool where he'd remained determinedly by her side. The sun, having reached its highest point, shone on his face, highlighting signs of age and weariness. Yet, there was a sparkle in his eyes. He stepped forward, brushing a hand over his wife's back as he passed. It appeared he was ready to speak again.

Chanoch considered the state of the onlookers. During the tale some had listened in respectful silence. Others had talked amongst themselves, or – made drowsy by a generous breakfast – nodded off into a deep sleep. Still others, longing for the comfort of their own beds, had slipped away once they'd had their fill of Lamech's hospitality. His young companion had remained, but moved part way though to sit with someone else. Chanoch had noted each response and stored it in his mind for later recollection.

As Kayin raised his voice once more, those whose attention remained leaned forward to hear the meaning of the night's interruption.

'Over seven hundred summers have passed since the events we have relayed,' Kayin announced. 'Our first son we named Chanoch, dedicating him to Yahweh. Once Chanoch was mature, Awan took him to the land between the rivers to find a wife. He fell in love with one of Set's daughters. Shiphrah was a good woman, like her Aunt Awan, and was willing to leave her home to join us in Nod.

'Whilst staying with our parents, Awan discovered that several of our siblings had already made their way to other parts of the earth, taking their children and grandchildren with them. They'd followed the Pishon and Gihon rivers that flow from Eden to distant lands in the west. And so, Yahweh's presence on earth extended with His people.

'Here in the east, Chanoch's family soon grew too large to sustain themselves in the caves. So we built this city on the river, naming it after our son and dedicating it also to Yahweh, and the continuing glory of His name. I taught my children everything I knew about farming, although I didn't touch the land myself so I might not curse it.

'You know Chanoch as the elder of this city, for I have never resided here. We helped build several other cities as our family grew, and our children settled in groups on these plains. Yet Awan and I have always lived in the wilderness, continuing to move from place to place, entering the cities only to visit loved ones or get supplies.

'Each generation has built on my knowledge and become competent farmers, craftsmen and even metal workers. You, people of Chanoch, have produced incredible things, and the best crops, even though the toil has been hard at times. You have built numerous homes in this city, so it has grown mighty and prosperous. This grand hall and gathering is a testament to the fact.

'Yet, people of Chanoch, I lay this charge against you: you have forsaken Yahweh to whom this city was dedicated. As you have prospered, so has deception, greed and evil intent. You have forgotten to rely on Elohim for your strength. Even as Awan and I have wandered, we have heard many tales of your exploits here. And so the name *Chanoch* has become a byword amongst my kin, for you are known far and wide for evil. I declare today that Yahweh shall surely not stand this violation!

'Furthermore, my son came to me last night and told me of the particular wickedness of your host.' Here, Kayin broke from his position facing the crowd and turned towards the man in question, his face stern, though not unkind.

'Lamech. You have celebrated taking the life of two innocent men. You have taken a declaration of Yahweh's specific mercy upon my life and turned it into a curse as protection for your evil. Do you expect to be spared – nay, avenged – by Elohim Himself?

'The same error I committed is yours: you seek to bend Yahweh's will to your own purposes. Well, He shall not be bent! He shall not be moved. He is Yahweh Elohim, and He does as He pleases! I warn you, Lamech, you shall not be spared. The spilling of lifeblood requires a reckoning. Invoking my name will achieve nothing when this city faces Yahweh's justice for its evil.'

Sweeping his gaze across the entire gathered room, Kayin continued. 'I declare tonight, in the presence of many witnesses, that if you do not repent of wickedness, then before the next generation has entirely passed away, all that dwell here shall be wiped from the face of the earth!'

Chanoch felt Yahweh's burning presence as his abba's voice rose in a crescendo with his verdict. *Wiped away… Everyone?*

As Kayin paused, catching his breath, his stance softened a little. 'Even so, our Elohim is merciful. He is full of loving kindness to those who turn and call on His name. Yet, He is also holy, and the evil that I committed – that you, Lamech, have committed – will not be tolerated.'

Kayin fixed his eyes back on the crowd then stretched out both arms, beckoning. 'Turn back to Yahweh, Oh people of Chanoch! Repent in the dust of the ground. Remove what is sinful from your midst or face the righteous judgement of your Creator – who shall not avenge Lamech, but shall surely avenge the glory of His own name!'

Silence.

A goblet clattered to the floor and the noise it made reverberated about the walls. In front of Chanoch, people shifted nervously. Kayin lowered the arms he had raised. His brows drew together, then he turned and took two steps towards Lamech, who was semi-reclined on his couch, eyes wide and cup half-hanging.

Chanoch saw his father soften again, as he always did after a reproach. He knew well that if Lamech would surrender and repent, Kayin would embrace him with open arms. But Lamech didn't know this, and he had just been humiliated in front of his guests. Chanoch held his breath.

'What say you, my boy?' Kayin said gently to his host. 'Will you listen to the words of an old man and turn back to Yahweh, or will you remain in your stubbornness? These people look to you.'

Lamech glanced around, considering the assembly. Chanoch did the same. Some were indeed watching, waiting to see how their host would respond. Others rubbed their eyes, having woken from slumber when his father's commanding voice took over from the soft lilt of his mother's. Places previously occupied were empty, and several bodies remained slumped in drunken stupor. The remainder of the boar lay coldly abandoned on one side of the room, and the musicians and dancers had merged into the crowd. Lamech's reputation as a good host had been threatened, and his reputation was always his priority.

Suddenly Lamech laughed, a booming roar designed to conceal nervousness. 'Why should I change when my people are clearly content?' He stumbled to standing. 'You tell a good tale, O Great Wanderer, but what do you have to show for it? One wife and a pauper's cave? Why should I believe I will fare better by heeding your warning? I have all I could desire here. I have worked hard to build my home. I have wives and servants, sons and daughters. My children are known far and wide for their skill, and they shall leave behind a firm legacy in my name. So I say to my kin: eat, drink and be merry. Who cares if tomorrow we die? At least we shall have enjoyed ourselves while we lived!'

Lamech laughed again, but his laugh echoed. Few joined in, and they soon trailed off in embarrassment. It was a far cry from the rapturous response to his announcement the previous night. Even so, the absence of so many, and Lamech's obstinance, didn't fare well for the city's repentance. Chanoch shook his head, mirroring the gesture his father made on the platform.

'Then you have heard nothing,' Kayin muttered.

Any optimism Chanoch might have felt sank as his father took his mother's arm and helped her rise. They descended the steps and walked across the room, bodies parting before them. When they reached Chanoch, a slightly unsteady hand reached for his shoulder.

'We will pray for you, son, though I fear there is little hope. Perhaps among those who stayed awake, there may be some who pass the message on; some who take note and return to Yahweh. May He have mercy on you,' Kayin said.

His mother placed a kiss on his cheek. 'Visit us again soon.'

'Thank you for trying,' Chanoch replied. 'I'll walk you out, then you may take my mount home.'

They shared a smile, before entering the shadows of the corridor and making their way through the compound.

As they neared the outermost court, a voice whispered, 'Great-Abba.'

Turning, they saw Adah stealing almost silently towards them, only the rustle of her tunic revealing her haste.

'I would hear you again on this matter,' Adah continued as she reached them and pressed fresh figs into their palms.

A second voice revealed she wasn't alone. 'Yet, they must not return here.'

Stepping out from the shadow of a colonnade was the young man who had breakfasted with Chanoch, and, obediently at his heels, the wolf-like creature.

'This is my son, Yaval,' Adah said, motioning to the one whose scar caught the sunlight as he neared them.

'The musician?' Awan asked.

'No, that is my brother, Juval,' the young man replied.

'Yaval and Juval?'

Adah rolled her eyes. 'It was Lamech's crazy idea.'

'Forgive my intrusion, Great-Abba, Great-Ima,' Yaval said, nodding his head in respect towards his elders. 'I too would like to hear more of your story and learn more of Yahweh. Yet I fear my father. He endured your disruption last night because he was caught off guard. He shall not let that happen twice. Indeed, I've just witnessed him ordering his man not to allow you into the compound again.'

'With whom did he speak?" Chanoch asked, scanning the courtyard.

'Azurak.'

A shiver ran through his bones, contrasting the heat of the day. Adah, too, looked alarmed.

'Yaval is right; you must not return,' Chanoch said to his parents. 'I suggest you do not even enter the city.'

'I wonder, is it possible for us to visit you? It might be safer,' Yaval asked Kayin.

'Indeed, though we move often. Chanoch will know where to find us, if you have gained his trust.'

Chanoch studied the young man who had been his breakfast companion. Yaval had shown some promise in the past, and their conversation that morning had confirmed that not all Lamech's children were alike. He nodded his head in affirmation.

'Then come; come soon,' Awan confirmed. 'We shall be glad to speak with you both again.' She held out her walking cane. 'My son, would you return this to the woman I sat beside last night? She noticed me struggling to rise and passed it to me. An act of kindness I won't soon forget.'

'That is Sarai's cane,' Adah said. 'I shall return it.'

Awan reached forward and placed a hand each on Adah and Yaval's shoulders. 'May Yahweh bless you and keep you until we meet again.'

An efficient attendant had brought out Chanoch's animals and was waiting by the mounting stone. Chanoch led his parent's there as Adah and Yaval retreated to the colonnade. Kayin swung himself onto the first creature's back, his bones creaking as he did so. Chanoch supplied his mother a steadying hand until she'd done the same and settled behind her husband. She wrapped her arms around Kayin's broad chest and snuggled into him.

Then Chanoch mounted the second creature and encouraged the animals into a walk. Together they trundled through the entryway and down the winding passageways. At the city entrance, a dozing gatekeeper was momentarily roused by their approach. Muttering something under his breath, he opened the gate to let them out. Chanoch called out a final goodbye as the gate shut firmly behind The Wanderer and his wife. And so, they returned to the wilderness, taking a piece of his heart with them.

As he rode the short distance to his home, Chanoch felt the presence of eyes upon him. It wasn't until he dismounted that he spied Azurak observing him from the shadows.

TO BE CONTINUED

AFTERWORD

Dear Reader,

Thank you for giving me your precious time and journeying with me through this tale.

When I started writing this series, it was with Kayin's narrative in mind. I didn't envisage Chanoch's story or Awan's. Yet, before long, I found I couldn't resist the idea of a redemption narrative. Having only a few Scripture verses to go on (Genesis 4:14–17 & 25), I took considerable artistic license with *The Wanderer Reborn*. Perhaps you were shocked that I redeemed Kayin?

I believe the scripture that 'Jesus is the same yesterday, today and forever.' He is the perfect embodiment of God's will and love for humanity (Hebrews 13:8). I wanted to show God's heart for His people – a heart we may struggle to see when we consider certain biblical stories. That Yahweh would seek out the worst of sinners is entirely consistent with the character of our Lord Jesus as revealed in the gospels. If we miss that when we read the Old Testament, may I gently suggest that is not a fault with Him – or indeed with Scripture – but with our understanding.

If you've read this book and don't yet know Jesus for yourself, may I encourage you to consider a relationship with Him? In the story, blood sacrifice was necessary to atone for Kayin's sin. Though perhaps an unfamiliar concept in the modern West, it is needed to atone for all our wrongdoing – whether or not we've murdered someone. We have all fallen short of the glory of our Creator (Romans 3:22-24).

But God loves us! He loves us so much that He sent His only Son to save us. 'For God so loved the world that he gave his only Son, that whoever believes in [Jesus Christ] should not perish but have eternal life.' (John 3:16).

My book doesn't include the name of Jesus because it's set before He was humanly born. But you can be sure that God had Jesus' sacrifice **for you** in mind from the very beginning. The blood sacrifice needed to pay for your wrongs was paid by Jesus Christ at Calvary's cross. You can find the story in any Bible by turning to the end of Matthew, Mark, Luke or John. If this story has touched your heart and you want to reach out, do contact me.

Before leaving you, I must thank my Beta readers, Richard Fairbairn and Sophia Anyanwu, and my editor, Hannah Morrell, without whom this novel would certainly be poorer. To all at the ACW who have supported my journey, I appreciate each one of you. Thank you to my husband, Ben, and my children, who have graciously allowed me countless hours away from them for the sake of this manuscript. Especial gratitude to Joy Vee at Broad Place Publishing and my Kingdom Story Writers family for inspiring this second edition. Your prayers and love are invaluable.

Finally, none of this would have been possible without my Elohim. He loved me, sacrificed Jesus for me and provided every inspiration and provision for this project. Thank you, my Father, Saviour and wonderful friend.

N.W.

APPENDIX

KAYIN

Before we turn to anything else, let's address the possible elephant in the room! Did Kayin repent? In short, we don't know. Nobody else seems to think he did. The New Testament scriptures I review in the Appendix to The Wanderer Scorned discuss Cain's sin but do not say categorically that he never repented. The closest we get is 1 John 3:12: 'We should not be like Cain, who was of the evil one and murdered his brother.' This is still referring to the murder and being 'of the evil one' is no different from the state of all who have not repented (Ephesians 2:2). This is something I take pains to present through Awan's story of sin and redemption.

Additionally, whilst Jewish commentary often asserts Cain was responsible for the establishment of evil people and hostile lands, it's also true that by the time of Noah, all peoples on earth were considered evil (Genesis 6:5). Cain's offspring were no different to anyone else by this point.

So, what gave me the idea that Cain could have repented? Well, this whole story is based on just one verse, Genesis 4:17: 'Cain knew his wife, and she conceived and bore Enoch. When he built a city, he called the name of the city after the name of his son,

Enoch.' Whilst researching the Hebrew names, I discovered that Enoch (Chanoch in Hebrew) means 'dedicated'. Whilst there is no condition in the name, it is possible it was intended as 'dedicated to Yahweh'. I asked myself, *What if Cain gave this name to both his son and the first city because he was seeking a relationship with God?* From here, I began to envisage a story about not just the power of sin but also the power of redemption and forgiveness. The God that judged Cain is the same God that sent his Son all the way to the cross for his enemies.

In short, although perhaps improbable from the biblical account, it is at least possible that God sought out Cain in the end. I decided that was good enough for me! The reading of Gen. 4:14–16 remains slightly tricky if Cain repented, which is something I explore in this story in chapter 24.

Kayin certainly believed in God. Yet scripture is clear that believing in God is not enough (even the demons do that). We must allow Yahweh to change our hearts. We must ask Him to forgive us and surrender to Him.

NAMES

I discuss my choice and use of names (including God's name) extensively in the Appendix to *The Wanderer Scorned*, so I shall not repeat that here.

Perhaps the one that warrants a look is the rendering of name translated as Seth (Gen 4:25). There is no 'th' in Hebrew, and the 's' at the start of this name is שׁ which is best rendered as 'sh'. So, Seth should be Shet. However, this feels a bit uncomfortable in English, so I settled for Set, which is similar to the ancient Egyptian name Seti. Here's my updated list:

Character	English	Meaning	Biblical?	Pronounced
Adam	Adam	(Red) Earth/Soil	Yes	Ah-dom
Chavah	Eve	Life (fem)	Yes	cHa-vah
Kayin	Cain	Acquired	Yes	Kay-in
Havel	Abel	Breath	Yes	Ha-vel
Awan	N/A	Vice	Apoc.	Ah-wan
Chayim	N/A	Life (masc)	No	cHigh-yim
Avigail	Abigail	My Father is joyful	No	Ah-vi-ga-yil
Shimon	Simon	He has heard	No	Shim-on
Channah	Hannah	Favour/grace	No	cHan-nah
Dorit	Doris	New generation/gift	No	Dor-it
Set	Seth	Appointed/Substitute	Yes	Shet
Techiyah	N/A	Revival	No	Te-cHee-yah
Liora	N/A	My light	No	Lee-or-a
Nadav	N/A	Generous	No	Nah-dav
Raham	N/A	Mercy	No	Rah-ham
Shalom	N/A	Peace	No	Shah-lom
Yemima	Jemima	Dove	No	Ye-mee-ma
Ronel	N/A	Song of El (God)	No	Ron-el
Chanoch	Enoch	Dedicated	Yes	cHa-no-cH
Lamech	Lamech	Possibly 'Robust'	Yes	La-me-cH
Tzillah	Zillah	Shade	Yes	Tz-il-lah
Adah	Adah	Adornment	Yes	Ah-dah

HISTORY & MEAT

For me, reimagining Genesis 4 was an opportunity to explore theology through storytelling, not a historical investigation. Nevertheless, I have tried to make it realistic and inclusive of people's differing opinions as far as possible.

I discuss the historicity of the account, the geography, the inclusion of giant beasts (and their co-habitation with humans) in the Appendix to *The*

Wanderer Scorned. I also discuss my reasons behind including some meat-eating in the book. If any of these matters concern you, I would encourage you to look there.

Here, it is enough to say that I interpret the Hebrew word tannin (pl. tanninim) to include large reptiles, of which behemoth (plant-eating land creature, see Job 40) and leviathan (meat-eating sea creature, see Job 41) may have been a part. I have also included in this story some large mammals and other carnivorous dinosaurs alike to Sarcosuchus (the river tannin) and Spinosaurus (predator at the pool). Evidence of these have been found in the Middle East/ North Africa.

SONGS & SCRIPTURES

As discussed in the previous Appendix, I believe that, just as our modern-day songs and hymns draw on biblical verse, so biblical verse would have drawn on an ancient pattern of Yahweh worship, featuring phrases, picture language and theology that had been handed down through generations of worshippers since the beginning of time.

Accordingly, many songs in this book are paraphrases of Scripture, or contain hints of it. Some I wrote with a psalm in front of me, others were composed from scratch. Several of them have tunes! If you would like to hear them, head to my website https://natashawoodcraft.com or search for my YouTube channel @natashawoodcraft

These are the references:
- Ch 2: 'Lament' – Lamentations 3:16–20
- Ch 2: 'Satisfy Me' – Psalm 90:14–17.
- Ch 4: 'Redeemer of Life' – Lam 3:16–25.

- Ch 5: 'Wedding Song' – Psalm 128.
- Ch 8: 'Deliver Us' – Psalm 143.
- Ch 10: 'Set's Song' – Psalm 1.
- Ch 14: 'I Need You' – Psalm 43.
- Ch 16: 'Song at the Springs' – Hints of Luke 1:46–47 and Psalm 104.
- Ch 20: 'Help Me Remember' – Imagery from Isaiah 6.
- Ch 22: 'Yahweh is My Light' – Hints of Psalm 27.
- Ch 26: 'Kayin's Confession' – Psalm 130.
- Ch 27: 'In Wonder at Leviathan' – Psalm 104.
- Ch 33: 'Kayin's Prayer' – Psalm 30.

THE USE OF OTHER SOURCES

Finally, the questions these chapters of scripture raise are not new. Who was Kayin's wife? Why was he afraid of being killed if no one else existed? Among others. Indeed, the myriad forms of the story in Jewish and Christian tradition (as well as others) show that they were questions not unconsidered by our forefathers. I have answered them in my own way. Several sources claim that Kayin and Havel were both twins and married their own twin sisters. I decided not to go down this route for several reasons:

1) None of these sources are canonical nor as ancient as the Genesis account, which does not mention Havel having a wife. Indeed, if Havel had a wife he would likely have had offspring, which he presumably didn't, as it fell to Set to bear out his line.

2) I thought it challenging enough for a modern audience to accept Kayin marrying a sister, let alone his twin. It is generally accepted that early humans would have interbred with less

consequence than we would expect to find today, for the gene pool was different. The law against marrying within one's family does not appear in scripture until the time of Moses (though certain relations were individually condemned before that) and familial marriage was commonplace in societies such as ancient Egypt. I have tried to make the idea less peculiar for the reader, without, of course, suggesting it's an acceptable practice today.

3) It fitted my story to have Kayin as an only child for a reasonable amount of time, and Awan (whose name I did borrow – it features in *Jubilees* and the *Midrash*) as Havel's twin, to weave in the story of forgiveness and redemption. Her ability to forgive Kayin is made more powerful by her closeness to Havel.

THE MARK OF KAYIN

Again, 'the mark' was a source of fierce speculation in ancient literature. I chose to side with those Jewish Rabbis who saw it as a mark of mercy on the face or hand, rather than the more outlandish ideas of some literature (like a giant horn).

What did I choose to use? The symbol ⟨ is the first letter in the most ancient written Canaanite script: Paleo-Hebrew. It is the precursor to the letter *'aleph* in later Hebrew script (א). *'Aleph* begins the three words that make up God's mystical name in Exodus: *'Ehyeh: I AM*. I nod to this name in Chapter 4.

There was no particular reason for choosing this symbol except that I thought it a likely letter to represent something about Yahweh's possession and, therefore, of expressing Yahweh's protection over Kayin's life (saying that it belonged to Him).

Obviously, this script wouldn't be invented until several centuries later – just as the jar of oil Havel passes on to Set in the vision was probably not symbolic for a long time afterwards – but it was fun to imagine.

QUESTIONS TO CONSIDER

1. Sometimes God doesn't respond to our prayers in the way we expect, but He always answers. If you read *The Wanderer Scorned*, how do you see Havel's prayer at the end of Chapter 12 answered in *The Wanderer Reborn*?

2. After Havel's death, the characters go through various stages of grief. They all deal with it in different ways. Who do you most relate to? Have times of grief drawn you towards God or deepened your understanding of Him? Or have they pulled you away?

3. Adam continues to hold onto shame long after he has been forgiven. It has a massive impact on his family. Are you holding on to any shame regarding past sins? Perhaps it is time you claimed the promise of Isaiah 61:7: 'Instead of your shame you will receive a double portion, and instead of disgrace you will rejoice in your inheritance.' Jesus Christ endured the shame of the cross to remove yours. Please don't take it up again.

4. Did you anticipate the progression of sin in Awan's life? Are there any 'subtle' sins you fall prey to that might not be evident to anyone else? Perhaps you could ask the Holy Spirit to help reveal these subtle sins so they can be dealt with.

5. When he rescues her, Awan considers whether it's right to lie to Shimon about her journey. Do you think it is ever acceptable to lie? Is concealing the truth the same as lying? What if you were trying to protect others (such as those who hid Jews during the Holocaust or those in the persecuted church?) Do you think the consequences of her decision change its morality?

6. How do you feel about Awan marrying Kayin? Is it something that you wanted to happen, or not? Do you think you could have accepted someone like Kayin after what he did? Is there anyone in your life who you are struggling to forgive?

7. The Epilogue draws us back to the sad reality that the majority of people do not, and will not, accept Yahweh. Perhaps you could take this moment to plead on behalf of some of your loved ones who are rejecting him, knowing that our God desires that none should perish (2 Peter 3:9).

Can you help?

If you enjoyed this book, please consider leaving an online review. You can do this at Amazon (even if you didn't purchase from there) at Goodreads and at other online bookshops. It will help others find us and help us publish more books.

Further Artwork, Reviews and Teasers available at natashawoodcraft.com

Keep up to date by signing up to the author's newsletter, and receive an exclusive ebook, *The Wanderer's Sister*. natashawoodcraft.com/subscribe

Follow the Author on Social Media:
Facebook: Natasha Woodcraft, Writes, Wrongs & Songs
Instagram: @natasha.woodcraft
TikTok: @natasha.woodcraft

Watch songs from the series on YouTube:
youtube.com/@natashawoodcraft

SERIES DETAILS

BOOK 1: The Wanderer Scorned

ISBN: 978-1-915034-81-6

Wholesale Distributor:

Ingram Spark UK (Paperback)

eBook ASIN: B0B6D6179R

"Sin is crouching at the door, ready to pounce. You must master it before it masters you."

Kayin is The Wanderer: a legend shrouded in a curse. A man untouchable, unable to farm or settle.

Centuries after the horrendous act that defines his life, Kayin recounts his soul-stirring chronicle, exposing the far-reaching fallout of his parents' expulsion from Eden and revisiting the moments that shattered his youthful faith. Then came forbidden love and rejection, driving a wedge irrevocably between Kayin and his brother, with tragic consequences.

Why did God scorn Kayin's sacrifice? What transpired during that final, fateful encounter in the field?

BOOK 2: The Wanderer Reborn

BOOK 3: The Wanderer's Legacy. Coming Soon.

NOVELETTE: The Wanderer's Sister. *Exclusive to newsletter subscribers.*

ALSO BY

BROAD PLACE
publishing

www.broadplacepublishing.co.uk

A tea tin. Owned by one girl, found by another over half a century later. What mysteries does it hide?

Vera dreams of rising thorough the Kirov Ballet and maybe becoming a People's Artist. Fay is a pastor's kid, disillusioned with her parents' faith, who attends a theatre summer programme in the hope of improving her skills. The girls' plans do not work out as they'd hoped, and their lives become entwined when Fay accidentally finds an old tea tin.

An intriguing split time-line story, alternating between Leningrad in 1960's and modern day England.

Amy-Hope keeps a diary. Anna writes letters. Can this unlikely friendship give one a voice and help the other escape the past?

When Amy-Hope's parents separate, she and her dad move to a new house. Next door lives a shy, reclusive lady, who Amy-Hope wants to befriend. Their shared love of dogs and dance leads to a friendship which will give both of them more than they ever imagined.

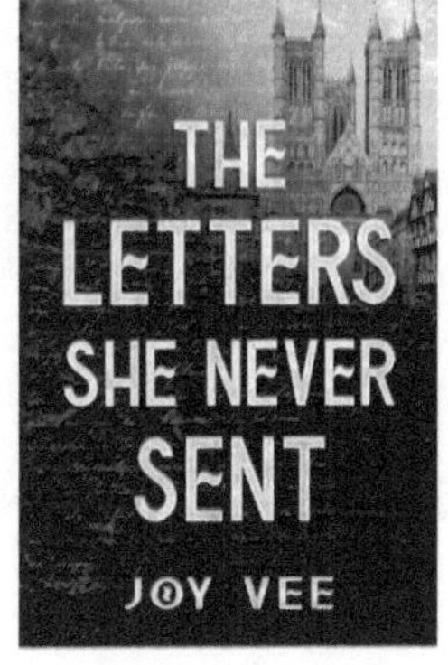